*The Ugly American* is the frightening novel of what really goes on behind the secret, red-tape curtain of American diplomacy.

Authentic, infuriating and explosively candid, this daring best seller unmasks the blundering hypocrisy of some of our top-level diplomats. It exposes the opportunism, incompetence and cynical deceit that have become imbedded in the fabric of our public relations, not only in Asia but all over the world.

Even those who have but a casual understanding of politics and foreign affairs will find *The Ugly American* a compelling and memorable reading experience. The authors are master story tellers and their novel is a suspenseful and deeply human story that cannot but touch the heart and excite the pride and fury of every intelligent American.

## devastating

### damning indictment

"The book lines up a parade of characters, Americans abroad, most of whom testify to the outright refusal of many of our salaried personnel—whether diplomats, aid merchants or information agents—to come to an understanding of the country and conditions in which they find themselves."
—SAN FRANCISCO CHRONICLE

"It is to be hoped that THE UGLY AMERICAN will have a lot of readers. There is a further hope that a lot of readers will want to do something about the problem it presents."
—MAURICE DOLBIER
N. Y. HERALD TRIBUNE

### far more than fiction

"It should be must reading for all who contribute, through taxes or otherwise, for American overseas aid . . . A powerful, searching book."
—LOS ANGELES TIMES

William J. Lederer

and

Eugene Burdick

---

# THE
# UGLY
# AMERICAN

FAWCETT CREST • NEW YORK

*THE UGLY AMERICAN*

THIS BOOK CONTAINS THE COMPLETE TEXT OF
THE ORIGINAL HARDCOVER EDITION.

Published by Fawcett Crest Books, a unit of CBS Publications,
the Consumer Publishing Division of CBS Inc., by arrangement with W. W. Norton & Company, Inc.

ISBN: 0-449-24201-3

Printed in the United States of America

41   40   39   38   37   36   35   34   33

# Contents

# A NOTE FROM THE AUTHORS

THIS BOOK is written as fiction; but it is based on fact. The things we write about have, in essence, happened. They have happened not only in Asia, where the story takes place, but throughout the world—in the fifty-nine countries where over two million Americans are stationed.

At the end of the book we have added a documentary epilogue which we hope will convince the reader that what we have written is not just an angry dream, but rather the rendering of fact into fiction. The names, the places, the events, are our inventions; our aim is not to embarrass individuals, but to stimulate thought—and, we hope, action.

BILL LEDERER
EUGENE BURDICK

Pearl City, Oahu
Territory of Hawaii
1958

# 1

# Lucky, Lucky Lou #1

The Honorable Louis Sears, American Ambassador to Sarkhan, was angry. Even though the aireonditioner kept his office cool, he felt hot and irritable. He smoothed out the editorial page of the *Sarkhan Eastern Star*, the most widely distributed paper in Haidho, and studied the cartoon carefully.

I don't give a damn what the Prime Minister and all those little advisers of his say, Ambassador Sears said to himself, that damned *Eastern Star* is a Red paper, and that cartoon looks too much like me to be an accident.

He jerked his head away from the paper, with a tic of anger, and turned toward the window. The lawn of the Embassy swept down to the main road of Haidho in a long, pure green, carefully trimmed wave. On each side it broke into a froth of color . . . the red and purple of bougainvillea, the softer colors of hibiscus, the myriad orchids hanging in elegant parasitic grace from banyan trees, the crisp straight lines of bamboo trees. At the end of the lawn the pickets of a wrought-iron fence separated Embassy grounds from the confusion and noise of the road.

From the countryside an unbroken line of women were moving into Haidho, as they did every morning, carrying on their backs faggots of wood, or baskets of vegetables—radishes, spring onions, and beans laid out in simple perfection on moist leaves. Occasionally a woman went by with a basket of fish on her head, the tiny silvery bodies catching the early morning sun. Whenever a man passed he was on a bicycle, making his way along the chattering lines of women.

Strange little monkeys, Ambassador Sears thought, forgetting for a moment his pique at the cartoon. Women do all the work, men have all the fun.

The only motorized vehicles he could see were trucks which had been given to the Sarkhanese government by the American military advisory group. They went down the road at a fast clip, their horns blaring steadily as if they had been turned on when the engine was started. They carried military supplies toward the north; neat boxes of hand grenades, bundles of barbed wire, barrels of gasoline and oil, big rectangular boxes which contained disassembled 50-calibre machine guns.

And all of it made in America, Ambassador Sears thought. At once his anger returned and he looked down again at the *Eastern Star*. The cartoon was obvious. Although he could not read Sarkhanese beyond a few words forced upon him by constant repetition, the point was clear. The cartoon showed a short, fat American, his face perspiring, and his mouth open like a braying mule's, leading a thin, gracefully-built Sarkhanese man by a tether around his neck toward a sign bearing two of the few Sarkhanese words the ambassador could recognize—"Coca Cola." Underneath the short fat man was a single English word: "Lucky."

Ambassador Sears wished to hell some American in the Embassy could read Sarkhanese. He hated to interrogate the native translators attached to USIS about the meaning of cartoons. He suspected that the damned little monkeys always lied. But they couldn't soft soap him on this one, not when the fat character was called "Lucky."

Lucky, Lucky Louis had been Ambassador Sears' nickname when he was in politics in the United States. For eighteen years he had been a popular and successful senator; but it was said about him that he always won his elections by a lucky fluke. When Sears, a Democrat, first won, Drew Pearson had said that he had been elected because he was lucky enough to be a Democrat in a Democratic year. In his second race his Republican opponent had dropped dead ten days before the election, which even Sears had recognized as luck. His opponent's wife had got involved in a scandal during his third campaign. But, as Sears had noticed wryly, no one had thought it was bad luck when he lost the fourth time up.

Actually Sears had not been too much worried when he lost this last election. He had been in politics long enough to know that the party owed him something. Two days after the election, with his voting record under his arm, he called on the National Committee.

The political strategists were ready for him.

"What kind of a job would you like, Lucky?" they asked.

"A Federal judgeship with a nice long tenure," he answered promptly.

"Okay, but there won't be an opening for two years. In the meantime, Lucky, how would you like to be an ambassador?"

"Me, an ambassador?" said Sears, immediately picturing himself appearing in a morning coat and striped trousers before the court of St. James, or running the big handsome embassy building in Paris. Sears was a shrewd enough politician to keep any look of expectation from crossing his face. "Now look, boys, an ambassador has to spend a lot more than he makes. That's all right, if you've got a philanthropist who might stand the gaff for me; but you know my personal situation. After eighteen years, everything I've gotten has gone into the party."

The strategists nodded without comment. It was a remark they heard often, but it never failed to touch them.

"There's an ambassadorship open in Sarkhan," the strategists said. "It pays $17,500 and you ought to be able to save money on that. There's an entertainment allowance of $15,000, and you can buy liquor tax free. There's also an ambassador's mansion which you get rent free."

"Where the hell is Sarkhan?"

"It's a small country out toward Burma and Thailand."

"Now, you know I'm not prejudiced, but I just don't work well with blacks."

"They're not black, they're brown. Well, if you don't want it, we can fix you up as legal assistant to . . ."

"I'll take it."

At first Ambassador Sears had liked his assignment. It was true about the cheap liquor, and the ambassador's mansion was the most spacious and beautifully furnished house he had ever occupied. Mrs. Sears was in ecstasy over it. However, soon after his arrival, the cartoons had started and Ambassador Sears had been profoundly hurt by them. In America he had never minded being kidded about his stoutness and his red face. In fact, at Rotary meetings he always started out his speeches by saying, "Now, for a fat man I think I'm doing all right by you boys in Washington." It had always gotten a laugh. But Ambassador Sears felt that it was a bit uppity and quite another thing for natives to joke about his physique.

He was still looking at the cartoon when the door opened. It was Margaret Johnson, the embassy's press attaché. She was flushed with excitement, and began talking without even saying good morning.

"Ambassador, a mob of people beat up John Colvin—that powdered milk man—and dumped his body on the embassy steps some time last night," she said in a rush. "We called the doctor and he thinks the man will live, but we'd better prepare a statement for the papers."

"Oh, for Pete's sake," Ambassador Sears said angrily. "Why does this kind of thing always have to happen so early in the morning? Why did they beat him up?"

"We're not sure," Margaret said. "There was a note pinned to his body which said something about his molesting Sarkhanese girls."

Ambassador Sears sat back in his chair and laughed.

"Well, I'll be damned," he said with pleasure. "I always thought that guy Colvin was a little too serious. I tell you,

Maggie, it's always those quiet kind that when they can't get a piece of tail they resort to a little force."

Margaret's face showed her distaste for the Ambassador's words, but her voice was calm when she spoke.

"This might turn out to be a pretty serious thing, Mister Ambassador," she said. "You never can be sure when one of the political parties might pick up something like this and blow it up all out of proportion."

"Aw, come off it, Maggie," Ambassador Sears said. "Since when is a boy meets girl affair something that involves big politics? If you want something to worry about, worry about this cartoon. Get me that Prince Ngong, or whatever the hell his name is, the one reponsible for protocol. When we get this newspaper business cleared up, then I suppose I'll have to go to the hospital and see that fool Colvin."

Miss Johnson nodded politely and left the office.

In the midst of vague and unremarkable dreams, John Colvin became aware of his bandages. He came back to reality slowly. The hospital room emerged, sunny and quiet. The washstand in the corner took its place firmly, and his bed appeared before him. Finally, he realized that he was part of the scene himself. He was in the bed, swathed in gauze, and aware of pain behind a soft barrier of drugs.

The memory of the events which put him in the hospital returned to his consciousness until finally the events were in order and established as fact. He even remembered his disbelief of them while they were happening, and his thinking that it was impossible that Deong, a man who had been his friend, who had saved his life ten years ago, who had shared terrors with him, was now holding a gun in his back. He had met Deong shortly after he had parachuted into Sarkhan in 1943. It had been a meeting which had saved his life.

Colvin had been dropped into Sarkhan with two other Americans. They had been carefully selected. They all knew the Sarkhanese language perfectly, and they all had approximately the size and stature of the average Sarkhanese man. Their faces had been dyed the light brown native Sarkhanese. They were OSS agents, and all three were tough enough and competent enough to think they would live forever. Two weeks later Colvin was the only one still alive—and he had had four narrow escapes from Japanese patrols. Only his friendship with Deong made it possible for him to survive.

Colvin was running down a jungle path in what he knew was a futile effort to escape the fourth Japanese patrol which had encircled him, when he had come out into a small clearing where Deong was watering the family water buffalo. They had stared at one another for a long moment, and Colvin had instantly decided to trust Deong.

"I am an American intelligence agent here to fight the Japanese," Colvin had said rapidly in Sarkhanese. "I am surrounded by a Japanese patrol and if I cannot find a hiding place in a few moments they will capture me. Can you help me?"

Deong, from his seat on the water buffalo's shoulders, looked down at Colvin for a moment. Then he slid off the water buffalo and walked over to Colvin.

"I will help you," Deong said, his eyes shining with excitement.

Colvin nodded and at once Deong took his arm and started to run with him toward a broad shallow ditch. With one hand he snatched three hollow reeds from the edge of the ditch, and with the other hand he pushed John into the water.

"Breathe through the reeds, do not move your head even the least bit, and do not come out of the water until I pull the reeds from your mouth," Deong said.

He pushed Colvin into the water and put a large stone on Colvin's chest to hold him under. The ditch was two feet deep and held enough water so that John was covered by six inches. For a few seconds he felt real panic. Then he relaxed and discovered to his enormous relief that he could breathe through the reeds.

Five minutes later, three of the soldiers from the Japanese patrol came into the clearing. John could dimly hear them talking, and was able to tell when they had left. He stayed where he was for ten more minutes; and then he felt a gentle tug on the reeds. He sat up, muddy water dripping from his face and body. Deong was grinning at him.

In the next eight months the two men roamed over most of Sarkhan. In that time they blew up twelve Japanese munitions trains, demolished six military bridges, and put time bombs on the hulls of eight armed Japanese river patrol boats.

During that time, as if the chance of death made every impression more penetrating, Colvin came to know Deong and also to know the people of Sarkhan. Once the two of them had to hide from a Japanese patrol in the mournful and exquisitely beautiful Plain of the Tombs where generations of Sarkhanese lay buried under intricately carved pieces of rock. Ringing the plain was a magnificent fringe of cypress trees. For eight hours they had crawled among the tombstones, always keeping a row or two of the stones between them and the Japanese patrol, until, at dusk, the Japanese patrol broke off the search.

On another day they hid in a Sarkhanese temple on the shores of the beautiful Orange River, this time from no ordinary platoon of Japanese troops, but from a special detail of antiespionage troops that had been flown in from Indonesia for the specific purpose of running Colvin to ground. Colvin didn't want to hide in the temple; its back was on the river, which closed off a possible avenue of escape. Deong didn't argue; he insisted, with complete confidence, that the temple was the safest place for them.

The temple was presided over by two monks in saffron-colored robes. They were kept company by an enormous number of sacred monkeys who swarmed in and out of the magnificent, decaying stone of the temple. The two priests were in the midst of a long morning prayer when Deong and Colvin came trotting into the temple. They did not look up when Deong and Colvin climbed high up into the temple and hid themselves among the heavy stone rafters where normally only monkeys dwelt, and they did not look up when the Japanese patrol arrived. The two priests, their shaven heads gleaming in the sun, continued to bend over their folded hands, and their chant continued on above the harsh questions of the Japanese lieutenant. Even when the lieutenant, his face contorted with anger, placed a pistol against the head of one of the priests, their voices did not cease. When the lieutenant pulled the trigger and the brains and bloody fragments of bone shot in a savage gout across the steps of the temple, the other priest did not stop praying. In the presence of such single-mindedness, the Japanese lieutenant was helpless. He led his detail away from the temple after a fruitless and perfunctory search.

They remained among the stone rafters long after the Japanese had left, talking softly. Deong patiently explained the beauty and grandeur of death in the land of Sarkhan; but he also explained, with equal patience, why he did not wish to die that day. Deong was a country boy and he came from a simple family, but he wanted to live in a city and to find out about bigger and more exciting things.

In his eight months in Sarkhan Colvin came to love the people of this strange country. They were small, delicate people, their skins a lovely shade of brown, all of their motions graceful and restrained. Even people of the meanest caste had a dignity and charm which impressed Colvin enormously. They were all very generous. They had given him food, and information, and help. They had run great risks on his behalf, and the only request they made was that he discuss philosophy with them. The word *philosophy* in Sarkhanese, Colvin learned, covered questions of life and death, cruelty and generosity, good manners, the rearing of children, the delights of strong wine, and the possibility of a life after death.

Just before the liberation, John taught Deong about ipecac. They received instructions via radio to meet a submarine in an isolated cove. The submarine arrived on schedule and the captain told them that the United States Marines would land in Sarkhan in five days. He gave them a 25-pound tin of ipecac, and told them to make every effort to introduce the powder into the food at the Japanese army camp the morning of the landing.

John explained why to Deong. Ipecac was the most powerful emetic known to medicine. Until it was eliminated from a person's body he had energy for only one thing: vomiting. If he were given enough of it, a person could actually die from the spasms.

With the aid of the Sarkhanese cooks in the Japanese army camp, they were successful. The next day they waited in a clump of bushes outside the camp. At 7:30 a.m. the Japanese ate breakfast. At 8:00 a.m. the Marines landed. At 8:10 a.m. the Japanese came staggering out of the camp.

For a few moments it had been funny—a road full of soldiers who stopped running to vomit. But the exertion compounded the effects of the ipecac, and men began to stagger and fall. Their bodies heaved and racked and twisted as they vomited with nothing left in their stomachs. An hour later, when the first Marine patrols approached the camp, the road and the grass beside it were covered with bloody and exhausted men too weak to lift their heads.

It was the last thing Deong and Colvin did together. Three weeks later Colvin was flown back to the United States. A year later he had resigned from the O.S.S. and was running his family's business in Wisconsin, buying bulk milk, drying it into powder, and packaging the powder. It was a good business and a sound one, and Colvin ran it well.

About 1952, the newspapers reported that the country of Sarkhan was having internal difficulties and was leaning toward Communism. Colvin could not believe it. He wrote long letters to his Congressman explaining the elaborate fabric of Sarkhanese culture, and suggesting how the Sarkhanese should be handled. He got back polite letters informing him that his suggestions had been forwarded to the State Department. But the policy of the United States did not change. When the border difficulty with the Communist country to the north of Sarkhan began, Colvin could not restrain his impatience.

He was convinced that the Sarkhanese situation was being handled badly. He was also convinced that he had a personal responsibility in the situation. He came up with an ingenious plan.

The rainy hillsides of Sarkhan were covered with a tough, low growing, and very thick grass. This grass was so rugged and its root structure so detailed that it was often impractical to clear it from otherwise usable land. Colvin sent for samples of the grass and discovered that it was edible by a short-legged, agile, and fast-growing breed of cattle that had been developed in Texas. If the people of Sarkhan could be taught to use milk and its by-products, there was no reason why the cattle would not prosper on land that was otherwise useless. Also, there were good markets in Asia for the by-products. The butter could be reduced to *ghee* and sold to India, the leather could be tanned and made into finished goods by the artisans of Sarkhan, the entrails could be used in the native medicines preferred by non-Christians.

But first the Sarkhanese had to be exposed to milk. Colvin did this part himself. He was in Sarkhan to sell milk made from powder. When the Texas cows began arriving a year later, the switch would be made to fresh milk. Once the business was established and running, Colvin intended to sell out his shares and leave.

Colvin knew that the thing was risky; the first thing he did when he got back to Sarkhan was to try to locate Deong. Deong had vanished. So Colvin, without Deong's help, set up the first milk-distribution center outside of the city of Haidho. He had been operating it only two weeks, and it was a success despite the embassy's saying the project was impracticable. In fact, Louis Sears, the American Ambassador, had, after several conferences, washed his hands of the whole thing.

Then suddenly, Deong appeared from nowhere, and pulled a gun on Colvin. Lying in the sun and quiet of the hospital room, Colvin remembered how he had felt the muzzle of the gun pressing cold against his skin, and how unreal it had seemed in the normal routine around him. The soft jungle breeze moved through the open warehouse, and outside the long queue of Sarkhanese women waited patiently for their milk, their voices a low and undeniably real murmur beyond the door. Next to Colvin stood the huge Atlas Automatic Milk-Mixer ready for the 100-pound tin of powdered milk. But in the midst of these ordinary sounds and sights were unrealities—the package of ipecac on the floor behind the mixer, and Deong, his old companion, behind him with a gun held against Colvin's ribs.

"Come on, John. Start your machine and put in the milk and ipecac."

"Deong, you're crazy," Colvin said. "Put away the gun."

"Perhaps whenever a man is about to die he always thinks his executioner is crazy," Deong answered softly. "But you're wrong. There's a reasonable time for everyone to die, and this may be your time."

"What's reasonable about it?" Colvin asked. "I'm not in politics, I'm just trying to organize a milk-distribution center for your country. Your people need it."

"John, powdered milk and cattle are part of politics, and therefore part of history," Deong said. "Hurry up. Put the powdered milk and the ipecac in the machine. I don't have much time."

"No," Colvin said. "I won't put ipecac in the milk, you know what it does."

"Of course I know," Deong said. "You taught me."

"Deong, those people might die from the ipecac," Colvin pleaded. "They're your people."

"You can't make an omelette without breaking eggs," Deong said. "Come on, John. Don't stall. Start the mix going. If I knew how to work it, I'd do it myself. But if you don't do it by the time the doors are opened in about three more minutes, I'll shoot you and tell everybody that *you* were planning to mix the ipecac in the milk."

"But what good will it do? Who will it help?"

"Look, John, I told you milk is part of history. If you get this crazy milk and cattle scheme of yours going, it could in time change the economic balance in Sarkhan."

"What's wrong with that? That's what I want to do."

"Nothing. It's a good idea. Out in the bush we've talked it over a lot. But you're the wrong person to be permitted to do it. If it succeeded, the Sarkhanese would believe that America was their savior."

Colvin understood.

"Deong, you're a Communist," Colvin said.

"As if there were a choice," Deong replied softly. "Look, John, you took me off the back of a water buffalo and taught me about the big outside world. And I learned that the side with the most brains and power wins. And, John, that's not your side anymore. Once it was, but not now. America had its chance and it missed. And now the Communists are going to win."

"Look, Deong, you trusted me once," Colvin said quickly. "I can tell you that our side is going to win. We've still got the power and the will."

"No, you haven't got the power or the will or anything," Deong said, and his voice was rock hard with assurance. "You've done nothing but lose since the end of the war. And for a simple little reason: you don't know the power of an idea. The clerks you send over here try to buy us like cattle. You people are like the fable of the rich man who was an idiot."

Colvin knew then that there was no chance of persuading Deong. He realized sickly that he could now only save himself.

"Hand me the ipecac," Colvin said bitterly.

"Pick it up yourself and put it in the mixer," Deong said.

For the first time Colvin felt the muzzle of the gun removed completely from his back. With a quick whirling motion Colvin spun his body and hacked his hand through the air, aiming for the base of Deong's neck just where it joined the shoulders. If he hit in exactly the right place, Deong's gun-hand would be paralyzed. But although the blow lit with a terrific force, it was slightly off the mark. Colvin came to his feet in a half-crouch—but the gun was still in Deong's hand and now it was aimed at Colvin's chest. There was a look of excruciating pain on Deong's face, and he appeared to be trying desperately to keep himself from fainting. Colvin dove for a stack of powdered milk drums and at the same moment Deong fired. In that split instant, as he was falling to the floor, Colvin was aware of two things. First, that the bullet had hit him in the right forearm and had probably broken the bone. Second, that Deong was about to drop the gun because of the accumulated pain of his blow.

The moment that he hit the floor Colvin scrambled again to his feet. He darted down the row of barrels and came around them without any attempt at deception. Either Deong would drop the gun or he would be able to stalk Colvin in the narrow warehouse, so there was no point in hiding. Deong was staring at his hand, his face contorted as the reaction to the blow registered. Deong's hand opened convulsively, the .38 revolver hung for a moment on his trigger finger, and then it crashed to the floor.

Colvin lunged toward Deong, his right arm hanging helpless at his side, and crashed into him with his left shoulder. The shock of the contact erased the effect of the earlier blow, and instantly Deong was struggling furiously beneath Colvin. Colvin had to keep Deong away from the gun without using his arms. He wrapped his legs around Deong's middle and tightened them in a powerful scissors grip. For a moment there was almost a dead silence in the emptiness of the warehouse. Colvin heard the breath being forced from Deong's lungs. Deong, however, had seen Colvin's damaged right arm, and he hammered it twice with his fist. The pain came roaring up out of Colvin's arm in a white-hot bolt, and Colvin's legs relaxed. Deong took several sharp breaths. Then Colvin twisted his legs so that Deong could not reach his injured arm, and the pain, like some sort of mist that had gathered inside his head and obscured his view, slowly lifted.

Colvin saw, with a sense of dull surprise, that the line of Sarkhanese women had moved up to the door of the warehouse and were peering curiously in at Deong and Colvin. In the front of the line was a deeply wrinkled, sharp-eyed woman of perhaps seventy years. Like all the rest she was staring in confusion, but it was also apparent that she was a leader.

"I shot him because he was about to put *cocol* in the milk," Deong shouted shrilly. "Help me get away from him, and we'll turn him over to the police."

For a moment Colvin's numb mind did not comprehend fully what Deong had said. Then the levers of memory shifted and he felt an enormous outrage. *Cocol* was a native drug derived from coca beans; it was supposed to be a powerful aphrodisiac. There were numberless folk stories in Haidho about virtuous girls who had lost their maidenhood through *cocol*, and other tales about its use as the fatal technique by which virgins were persuaded to become prostitutes. The Sarkhanese believed in its swift and complete action, and consequently feared it greatly.

"He's lying!" Colvin screamed. He was dizzy now, and underneath his rage he felt something like humor welling up. It was as if he were in the midst of a dreadful comedy. "This man was trying to persuade me to put ipecac in the milk."

For several seconds the men remained locked in the same position, both of them studying the face of the old woman. Then Deong gasped out the same accusation.

Colvin tried to shout his denial; but with a sense of utter futility he realized that his voice was so weak that the women were not hearing him correctly. He also saw that the women had been deeply shocked by the mere mention of *cocol*.

Colvin had only five more minutes of consciousness, and they were minutes of a wild and violent nightmare. The tiny, delicate women of Haidho, the women whom Colvin had regarded as friends, fell upon him like a group of outraged hawks. Small hands tore at his legs and sent tiny stabs of pain through his body. Fingers scratched through the material of his shirt and drew bright red lines across his chest. Hands, suddenly violent with anger, slapped his face and added to his confusion.

"I am a friend," Colvin said, in a voice so weak and small that he was the only person who heard it. With an awful clarity he was aware of the inadequacy of his words and of the helplessness of his body.

The blows of the women fell upon him with increasing viciousness and violence. One of the women was standing directly on his shattered forearm and had turned it into a huge single throb of pain. The white mist of pain and shock was not only behind his eyes and inside his head, but was rising slowly like a vapor through the warehouse. Colvin dimly perceived the disorganized mass of women screaming and shouting above him. At some point he stopped feeling the pain, even the pain that came from having his head gripped by both ears and banged savagely against the concrete floor. The noise was shrill and harsh and indescribable.

The fingernails, the tiny scratching angry nails, came at him from all sides. Each little wound by itself was bearable, but so multiplied they set his body afire. He felt as if he were being scratched to death by strange chicken-like claws. But even in the midst of the pain, he felt something worse—the loss of the vision he had had of himself and the people of Sarkhan, and their friendship.

At last relief came. His eyesight faded, his hearing grew

dim, and a dull release slipped over him. He felt his tongue start to bulge from his mouth. Blood flowed from his nose and ears, and Deong escaped from the grip of his legs. Colvin embraced the unconsciousness which seemed to be nothing more than a thickening of the mist of pain and terror.

Two hours later Colvin's unconscious body was deposited on the steps of the American Embassy in Haidho. He was entirely naked and his body was covered with hundreds of tiny scratches which had hardened into ridges of dry purple blood. He was breathing, but just barely. Attached to his left breast, by a large pin which had been driven twice through the flesh, was a note in English. The message said, "Here is an American rapist. You can have him back. The same thing will happen to other Americans who attempt to seduce our daughters."

Prince Ngong was in Ambassador Sears' office. He had been through these interviews before.

"A few more cartoons like this and I'm going to have to report to Washington that your people are not very sympathetic to American representatives," Ambassador Sears was saying. "It doesn't mean anything to me personally, but cartoons like this are damned disrespectful, and hurt relations between our countries."

Prince Ngong was one of Sarkhan's most distinguished poets and drama critics; but like all Sarkhanese intellectuals, he was expected to serve his country where his talents were needed most. Right now, he was needed as a protocol officer.

"Mr. Ambassador, I will not try to deceive you," Prince Ngong said. "I think that the *Eastern Star* has, perhaps, become somewhat critical of our foreign policy. In particular it is reluctant to have us grant air bases in this country in exchange for foreign aid. But as the representative of a democratic country, you can surely understand our reluctance to interfere with a free press."

They talked for a few more minutes, during which time Prince Ngong told Ambassador Sears that he understood the ambassador's irritation, and admired his forthrightness. When he left, Prince Ngong estimated the situation correctly—Ambassador Sears was offended.

That afternoon the special advisory committee of the Sarkhanese Cabinet met in executive session. Prince Ngong spoke first.

"Gentlemen, I think we've never deceived ourselves about our relations with the United States and the Soviet Union," he said. "We don't want to be in the camp of either of these nations. What we desire is Sarkhan's independence and development. This means that we'll take aid and assistance from anyone who will help us, but not at any price. And not at the price of the loss of our independence."

"So the Communists accuse us of being 'lackeys of the colonialists' and the Americans say we are 'neutralists,'" the Prime Minister put in.

"We'd like to be helped but without any strings; but this, apparently, is almost impossible," Prince Ngong went on. "As a result we do what any small nation surrounded by powerful nations must do: we bargain. I think we're agreed that there are only two types of men with whom one can bargain with profit: with the wise man who can see one's problem clearly and is without vanity or pride; or with the stupid man. The Americans, for reasons which are not clear to me, have chosen to send us stupid men as ambassadors."

"Tell them of your conversation with Ambassador Sears this morning," the Prime Minister said.

"Lucky Louis is not in a happy frame of mind," Prince Ngong said without smiling. "Do not underestimate this man. He is more stupid than most, but he is quite capable when it comes to protecting himself. He was deeply offended by the cartoon this morning in the *Eastern Star*. There was no way to joke him out of it. I think that the twenty-million-dollar loan we're trying to negotiate with the United States will be in serious jeopardy if Ambassador Sears' feathers aren't smoothed."

No one in the room said anything. The Prime Minister

made a signal and full cups of hot tea were served. Still no one spoke.

"Gentlemen?" the Prime Minister asked. Everyone sensed what had to be done, but it would have been impolite for the Prime Minister to have asked directly for action.

"I suppose that we could ask the publisher of the *Eastern Star* to run a flattering cartoon and editorial on Ambassador Sears," U Nang said reluctantly. Nang's brother-in-law was the publisher of the *Eastern Star*.

"I should think that would be a very excellent solution of the problem," the Prime Minister said. Then, to save U Nang's feelings, he went quickly on to the next order of business.

Late that afternoon Ambassador Sears went to the hospital to see John Colvin. He was in an excellent mood. The publisher of the *Eastern Star* had called only a half-hour ago and read to him over the phone the substance of a flattering editorial that paper was going to run on him the next day. Ambassador Sears had thanked the publisher, and had promptly instructed his secretary to send him a case of whiskey.

Sears paused as he came into Colvin's hospital room. Colvin's eyes were open; his face was covered with a multitude of tiny scratches. The Ambassador walked over, and leaned forward in a confidential manner.

"Well son, you must have picked yourself a real hell-cat," he said cheerfully. "You look as though you tangled with a buzzsaw."

Colvin closed his eyes.

"Do you know what happened to me yesterday?" he asked.

"Why, sure, my press attaché tells me you tangled with the wrong girl. Now, son, remember I warned you about free-wheeling here in the hills. This kind of stuff puts America in a bad light. I'm going to arrange for you to go back to the States as soon as you can be moved."

Colvin did not open his eyes again. The ambassador waited a few minutes, then turned to go. When he was halfway across the room Colvin spoke with such intensity that it stopped the ambassador short. "Sears," he said, "I won't go."

## 2

# Lucky, Lucky Lou # 2

Louis Krupitzyn was born in Ivanovo, Russia, in 1917, the son of a farmer. One day when he was still a boy he saw both of his parents shot. It happened almost casually. Louis stood in the window of the sod hut and listened to his parents argue with a lieutenant in charge of a group of soldiers. His father shook his head and turned away. The lieutenant took his short ugly revolver from a leather holster and shot Louis' father in the back of the skull. Wheeling, he then shot the mother.

It happened too quickly for Louis to feel anger or loss. All he felt was fear. He recognized what perfect safety would be: holding the short ugly pistol, or a substitute for it.

He was sent to the Orphans' Educational Center at Murmansk, where his peasant body grew tall on the coarse food. Louis found he had a good mind. By the time he was sixteen he had also found a foster parent: the state. He learned that his parents had been killed because they were guilty of "willful obstructionism of state agricultural policy." They were "kulaks," a group whom Louis had already come to hate.

In 1934 his essay "The Dynamics of Soviet Dialectics" won the Lenin Prize for Komsomol Literary Achievement. Everyone knew that young Louis Krupitzyn was a comer. Some of his colleagues began to call him "Lucky," but not to his face.

In 1935 his diplomatic career began: he was assigned to the Soviet Trade Commission in New York as chauffeur. All diplomatic servants—chauffeurs, valets, charwomen, and scullerymen—were chosen from the Foreign Service Apprentice Corps. They worked half-time as servants, and spent the rest of their time at assigned studies. This way the Russians avoided having aliens in their embassies or commissions, and at the same time were able to train their young foreign service officers.

While he was stationed in New York, chauffeur Krupitzyn studied the organization of American unions. At night he took Professor Alexander Willard's course in "The Psychology of the American Elite" at Columbia University.

In 1937 he went to Prague, again as chauffeur. In 1938 the Foreign Office sent him to Pekin as the clerk for a cultural commission.

In 1939 he was recalled to Moscow and spent the next two years in the Foreign Institute Academy. At night he worked as a decoding officer.

There is no record of what Krupitzyn did between 1941 and 1945, although it is definitely known that he was not in military service.

In 1945, now 28 years old, he was assigned as observer on the staff of Mao Tse-tung. Mao sent him with a battalion to Yunnan to see "how the military arm is used as a political and economic instrument." Except for three home furloughs of six months each, Krupitzyn was in China for three years. On his last home furlough he married Nada Kolosoff, a fellow foreign service careerist.

In 1949 he returned to Moscow and held a position in the Asia Section of the USSR Foreign Office.

Both he and his wife sailed on the surveying ship *Gorki* which was employed by the Sarkhanese Government to survey and chart the Southeast Asian waters adjacent to Sarkhan.

They then returned to Moscow, where they attended the Moscow School of Southeast Asian Areas. On the class

roster Louis Krupitzyn was listed as "Ambassador-designate to Sarkhan." This position was defined as a first-class
ambassadorship, not only because Sarkhan was a rich
country with over 20,000,000 people, but also because of
its strategic position. Beside "Sarkhan" the Soviets had
placed the number 30, indicating that they hoped to bring
it within the Communist orbit within 30 months.

At the Moscow School for Asian Areas, both Ambassador-designate and Madame Krupitzyn went through two
years of rigorous studies to prepare them for their new
job. They learned to read and write Sarkhanese. They
learned that the ideal man in Sarkhan is slender, graceful,
and soft-spoken; that he has physical control and outward
tranquility; that he is religious (Buddhism is the prevalent
religion); and that he has an appreciation of the ancient
classical music.

The Ambassador-designate molded himself into this
pattern. He dieted and lost forty pounds; he took ballet
lessons. He read Sarkhanese literature and drama, and
became a fairly skillful player on the nose flute. And he
regularly attended lectures in Buddhist religion and
practices.

Ambassador Louis Krupitzyn arrived in Sarkhan exactly one week after the new American Ambassador,
Louis Sears, had presented his credentials.

Only a few officials were at the airport to meet Ambassador Krupitzyn; and after greeting them courteously
in their own language, he got into his automobile and
drove to the Soviet Embassy. The next morning he presented his credentials to the Prime Minister. In the afternoon he traveled to the great monastery on the outskirts
of the capital, where he called to pay his respects to the
Chief Abbot, who was the leader of all Buddhists in the
area. Krupitzyn's arrival caused confusion because it was
unusual for white men to come to the monastery. The
monks in the outer hall looked at him curiously, some of
them smiling and nodding their heads. One of them scurried away to find a superior who would know how to

handle this strange situation. Finally a young man in a bright robe—apparently a newcomer to the monastery—came hurrying in, walked to the Russian Ambassador, and asked in English, "May I help you, sir?"

He replied in English. "I have come to pay my respects to His Reverence, the Grand Master," he said, and presented his calling card which was printed on one side in Russian and on the other side in Sarkhanese.

The young monk excused himself and left the room. Returning in about ten minutes, he said, "The Master will see you now. But he speaks no foreign languages, so I will accompany you as interpreter."

After winding their way through long, dim corridors, they entered an enormous room which had nothing in it except a large gold chair at the far end in which an elderly monk was sitting. When they were in front of the monk, Louis Krupitzyn bowed very low and said in classical Sarkhanese, "It is very gracious of Your Reverence to accord me this privilege."

"You did not tell my secretary that you spoke our language."

Krupitzyn, still bowing low, replied, "It is traditional, Your Reverence, that one saves his best words for the master."

Krupitzyn sat cross-legged on the floor and the Grand Leader of all the Buddhists of Sarkhan and Louis Krupitzyn, the Russian Ambassador, began to talk. At first it was chit-chat, and then it turned to philosophy. They sat there for the rest of the afternoon until it became dark.

There was some bad fortune that year in Sarkhan. Several typhoons blustered over the land just before the harvesting period, and destroyed most of the crops. Several months later, there was famine in the southern areas. The mobs already had ransacked the granaries of the rich.

At the Russian Embassy they learned from one of their informers who was employed as translator at the American Embassy that the United States was shipping 14,000 tons of rice to the stricken area. Soon after, the Russians learned from another informer—the American Ambassador's chauffeur—that the first of the American grain ships would be arriving in two days.

Krupitzyn acted with initiative and boldness. He bought up several tons of rice at black market prices in the capital, loaded the rice into a truck, and drove 300 miles south to the area where the famine was most intense.

When he arrived at Plutal, the main city of the south, a large crowd was gathered. The Communist newspaper there had come out with a special edition whose headlines announced that Russia, the friend of Sarkhan, would relieve the famine; and that the Russian Ambassador would personally arrive that day with the first token contribution of rice.

And then Krupitzyn himself came.

Speaking over a loudspeaker system and over all available radio stations in the area, Krupitzyn said that Russia was bending every effort to help her friends. The five tons of rice which he had brought along with him were all they could find locally. But be patient, he told them, in excellent Sarkhanese; several Russian grain ships would be arriving in a few days with thousands and thousands of tons of rice which would be distributed free. He then went on to say that Sarkhan and Russia were friends and allies and had to stand by each other because it was obvious that the colonial and capitalistic countries would not assist another nation unless they could profit from it.

The first American grain ship arrived two days later in the harbor of Haidho, the capital of Sarkhan. The USIS was there with cameramen and tape recorders. The Prime Minister was present to accept the relief grain from His Excellency Louis Sears, the American Ambassador to Sarkhan. The sirens blew and there were a few fine speeches. When the speeches were over, the stevedores began unloading the bags of rice, carrying them down the dock, and placing them into the American trucks which were waiting to take the rice to the stricken area.

Half-way down the dock, each stevedore stopped at a weighing station so that his bag of rice could be weighed. It is customary in Sarkhan for stevedores to be paid by how much they carry, not by the hour. As each bag was removed from the scale, the checker came up to it and stencilled a few words in Sarkhanese on each of the white bags.

When the trucks arrived in Plutal, they were met by a crowd of perhaps 10,000 people. A loudspeaker announced that here was the rice which had been promised them a short time ago by the Russian Ambassador; and here was proof that Russia keeps her word.

There were objections from the crowd. "But these are American trucks and they are driven by American drivers."

"We have hired them from the Americans," answered the Sarkhanese Communists. "Didn't the Russian Ambassador warn you that the capitalists would do anything for profit?"

The crowd was still doubtful. They had heard that the ships which brought the rice were flying the American flag; and the rice had been delivered by American trucks. But when the trucks were unloaded and the rice was handed out, then the populace knew that what the Communist propagandists were announcing over the loudspeakers was true. The Russian Ambassador had carried out his promise.

On each bag of rice there was stenciled in Sarkhanese for every citizen to see and read for himself: "This rice is a gift from Russia."

The Americans took pictures of the distribution of the rice and the smiling faces of the now happy people. There were no comments from any of the Americans present. None of them could read or understand Sarkhanese and they did not know what was happening.

About a week later, the American Embassy found out what had happened. Ambassador Louis Sears made a fiery speech; and from Washington came angry rumblings about instant retaliation. Subsequent American grain ships were properly safeguarded, but the people of Sarkhan continued to believe that Russia was their friend and provider.

. About a month after the grain incident Ambassador Louis Krupitzyn made his first report to Moscow. He wrote a long letter telling Moscow that the Communist activities and programs were progressing ahead of schedule in Sarkhan. The report went into details of every activity of the Communists' coordinated effort, discussing the cultural, economic, political, religious, and military aspects of Russia's struggle to acquire power in Sarkhan.

Near the end of his report were two short but interesting comments.

"The American Ambassador is a jewel. He keeps his people tied up with meetings, social events, and greeting and briefing the scores of senators, congressmen, generals, admirals, undersecretaries of State and Defense, and so on, who come pouring through here to 'look for themselves.' He forbids his people to 'go into the hills,' and still annoys the people of Sarkhan with his bad manners.

"I note with concern, however, that the American press has been very critical of Ambassador Sears for his inability to counter the tricks we played on him with the grain ships. If these American press attacks continue, it is possible that in time he will be removed. It is to our advantage to have him remain here. Therefore, during the next week or two I will see to it that editorials in the local newspapers will praise him for being an understanding American and a brave fighter. I also suggest that Pravda attack him bitterly. This combination will be all that is necessary to convince the U. S. State Department and the U. S. public that Ambassador Sears is doing a superb job.

"There is another matter which I view with great concern. An agent's report from Burma describes the activities of an American Catholic priest who works in one of the provinces there. His name is Father Finian. If the report is accurate, this man is an agitator of the most extreme skill, and combines with this the typical Jesuitical command of dialectics. The priest is rumored to speak Burmese, eats native food, and is obviously engaged in some sort of Papist plot. I need not remind you of Lenin's warnings about the skill of the Papacy when its interests are threatened. I should appreciate receiving whatever *dossier* material you might have on this man."

# 3

# Nine Friends

---

FATHER JOHN X. FINIAN, SJ—Born 1910 in Worcester, Mass. Parents, John X. and Marie Finian. Three sisters, three brothers. Graduated A.B., Boston University, 1934. M.A. Catholic College, Rome, 1941. Professor of Apologetics, St. Mary's, 1943-44. Chaplain, United States Navy, 1944-47. D. Phil. Oxford University, 1947-50. Thesis: *The Social Doctrines of St. Thomas Aquinas*. Special Assistant to the Archbishop of Boston, 1950-51.

Publications

Articles: "The Agony of St. Therese: An Essay on the Modernity of Humility"; "The Visions of St. Bernard: The Insights of Modern Psychology"; "The New Deal and Catholic Social Theory"; "Some Thoughts on the Strengths of Godless Communism"; "Is Communism Godless?"; "The Rising Threat of Communism."

Books: *The Medieval Religious Visions: A Social Interpretation; The Challenge of Communism* (1951).

In 1952 Father Finian was ordered to Burma with the positions of Overseer of Catholic Missions and Advocate for the General of the Society of Jesus.

As Father Finian read the document which ordered him from comfortable New England ten thousand miles to Burma, he smiled with satisfaction.

Father Finian was a big man—six foot three inches; perhaps from hunching forward to listen to smaller men, he had developed a stoop. His hands were big; and although they were now smooth, they still looked strong. When he was a boy he had delivered ice, hauled crates at the Railroad Express, picked over tons of coal looking for the grey gleam of slate; when he was at Oxford he had rowed on the Merton crew and was recognized as the best stroke they had ever had.

A man knowing the frailness of all men, Father Finian welcomed the assignment to Burma. Although he enjoyed the scholarship of religion, and knew, calmly and without arrogance, that he was considered a promising intellectual among members of the Society of Jesus, the priest felt that a special task awaited him in Asia. With an intensity that was almost physical, he wanted to grapple with it.

He knew of the terrible trouble there, the political plague which infected people who were susceptible because of hunger, poverty, or political disunity. The memory of his own experience with this political plague was bright in his mind, each detail perfect and precise.

It had happened during the war when he was a Navy chaplain. He had been talking to combat-seasoned Marines who were gathered on a small hill in the Russell Islands. Below them, framed in the coconut palms and the white crescent of sand, were the blue-grey hulks of the LCI's which would take them into battle on New Georgia that night.

One young Marine had listened to the priest with unusual interest. He stood quietly with his lips barely parted and his head turned so as to catch every word. Finian became more enthusiastic than usual. He talked volubly of dedication to God, of the need for humility, and of the assurance of everlasting life if one but had faith.

When he had finished, filled with more emotion than he usually allowed himself, he walked quickly around the group to the attentive Marine. "May God go with you on this invasion."

The boy jerked his head up sharply, almost startled. The priest thought for a moment that he might be a Protestant and was embarrassed at the attentions of a Catholic.

Then the Marine spat, coolly and arrogantly. Finian realized that he had misjudged everything. The boy's eyes were cold and hard; and he spoke from a tight-lipped mouth.

"There isn't any God that's going to watch me or anyone else on that LCI, father. You know it, and so do I."

The Marine flicked his finger against the chaplain's gold cross. "I'm a Communist, father. And I'll go into that god-damned miserable island and chew hell out of those Japs . . . but not for you or those fat-assed Rotarians back in the States, but because Communism is worth it."

"My son, Communism. . . ."

"What you ought to be telling us, father, is why we haven't opened a second front. Tell us why a bunch of greedy capitalists don't want to go into Europe until Soviet Russia is bled white. Don't tell us about a make-believe god. He won't help. We have to help ourselves."

The hard-faced boy looked older, wiser, infinitely tougher than any man Finian had met before; he was ut-terly beyond the appeal of words or logic or sentiment.

Father Finian had never forgotten that incident. He had recognized that the zeal in the boy's eyes and the dedica-tion in his face were what made saints of men. Yet this boy was dedicated to something evil.

After that meeting with the Marine, the priest oriented his energy. He began to read Communist literature. At first he merely read the speeches of Stalin and Bulganin and Zhukov as they were reported in the press, puzzling over their vulgarity, obviousness, and lack of subtlety. Their illogicality pained so well-trained a Jesuit as Father Finian; but apparently to millions of people the logic was flawless, the appeal intense.

Slowly the priest concluded that these Communist speeches were a form of secular ritual. The crude slogans were only symbols which meant much to the converted; the incredible promises of an abundant future were as real to them as the Stations of the Cross to a Catholic. Finian learned that the faith of a Communist was no more shaken by news of a bloody purge of "right-wing deviationists" than is the faith of a Catholic by the news that the Inqui-sition was brutal.

The discovery was decisive. The priest realized that

here was the face of the devil. The Communists had duplicated the ritual, faith, dedication, zeal, and enthusiasm of the Church. There was the same emphasis upon training, the same apostolic energy, the necessity to see beyond facts to a greater truth. The only difference was that the Communists served evil. They served it so well that the priest knew that both faiths could not exist in this world at the same time.

Later he read Lenin's *What is to be Done?* and Stalin's *History of the Communist Party*, Engels' *Anti-Duhring*, and finally, Marx's *Das Kapital*, and much more. Through all the tedious reading through economics and politics, sociology and philosophy, the priest never wavered. Others might think that Communism was a result of class conflict, of long-range economic change or political fanaticism; but Finian *knew* that Communism was the face of the devil, altered slyly and shrewdly, but still the devil's face, put on earth to test again the morality of men. Finian meant to meet the test, even if he had to do it alone.

Finian was a practical, tough-minded, and thoughtful man. When he left for Burma he was well-armed. On his long trip via Manila, Saigon, Bangkok, and finally Rangoon, he crystallized his plan of attack. During his two-week stay in Rangoon and his journey up a thousand miles of the Irrawaddy River by slow launch, he studied the Burmans and reviewed his notes on the culture, the history, and anthropology of the country. There was nothing haphazard about Finian.

Because of the Burmese heat, the windows in the residence of the Archbishop of Mokthu had no glass. Instead they were covered by fine wire screens; at night, bamboo shades were lowered inside to assure privacy. Looking through the screens Finian saw many strange insects pressed against the wire mesh.

Beyond the bodies of the insects, which by some trick of the eye seemed to fill the middle distance, Finian saw the lush green rolling of the Mokthu Valley. At the edge of Mokthu Town the tin shacks, the roads, the tiny streams of sewage ended, and the jungle began, green and thick and threatening. It seemed as if the town balanced at the very edge of survival; and that at any moment the eternal, powerful, lazy jungle might come sweeping over the town and bury it like a soft and tropical Pompeii.

"I should like to get out into the country soon," the priest said, quietly. "I would appreciate whatever help you can give me. A jeep perhaps; a tent, a sleeping hammock, some food."

"You are going to stay out for more than a night?" asked the Archbishop.

"Yes. For a few months."

"Father, we have closed our three missions between here and China. The Communists burned one and threw phosphorous bombs into the other two. It is impossible to stay out there."

"Nevertheless, can you assist me?"

"Yes," the Archbishop said, stiffly. "If that is what you must do."

"With your permission, then, I will leave by the end of the week. For three months." Then, because he could not resist it, he added, "Nothing is really impossible." At once he felt a stab of guilt, for he had said it only to bait the Archbishop.

Finian drove north, bumping and slithering along the narrow cart road through the jungle. He knew he had to do three things very quickly. First, he had to find at least one native Catholic who was courageous. Second, he had to learn the language. Third, he had to learn to eat the food . . . which meant he might have to endure several weeks of agonizing dysentery while his intestinal tract developed an immunity to the bacteria in the native food.

Five weeks later Finian stood under a fir tree in the tropical jungle of the area where the Kachin plateau joins the mountains of Assam. The giant tree flung itself out

of the steam and smell and heat of the jungle floor toward
the clean, infinitely removed, asceptic blue-whiteness of
the sky. He had vastly underestimated the difficulties of
his three basic tasks.

He still had a fever from the dysentery, and he was
forty pounds lighter. His face was white and sweated, as
if his vitality had been leached out of his flesh. His bowels
were tender and painful. When he moved, his viscera
came together with a roughness that was incredibly painful. His tongue was dry from fever, and his teeth felt
chalky. His bones ached, and once, in his delirium, he had
imagined that the marrow had been replaced by gelatin.

But he could eat native food; at that very moment his
over-tender intestines were digesting two handfuls of rice,
half of a mango, and a cup of very impure water. He knew
that he would keep it down. He was immune.

Finian had also learned the language. He had chewed
into it like a cold chisel driven into granite. From the first
day in the up-country he spoke nothing but Burmese. He
asked the name of every object he saw, by pointing at it.
Leaf, tree, water, big, little, walk, hop, jump, down, sideways, lizard, river, sea, cloud, yes, no, fire, food, feet, nose,
mouth . . . he was astonished at how few were the
essential words of a language. Even while he was sick
with dysentery he practiced. The grammar came quite
unconsciously; and in four weeks he was speaking simple
sentences. He made no effort to learn complex or difficult
expressions. He wanted complex needs to be put in simple
sentences and was convinced it could be done. His Burmese was the only way he could search for dependable
associates.

After he had found the first Burmese Catholic, it had
been less difficult to find other good men. He had not required that they be Catholic; only that they be anti-Communist and that they be honest and have courage. "Come
to think of it," Finian said to himself, "that was asking
quite a bit."

He pushed himself away from the fir tree and felt the

pain stab in his intestines. But pain or no pain, it was necessary for him to be standing when his eight new associates arrived. He thought for a moment of the difficulties he had had recruiting them. All his training as a Jesuit, all his alertness, every available trick and wile had been necessary; and he had had to look for them while he was still miserably sick. The main problem had been finding the first one, a Burman who was surely and beyond mistake a dependable man. His name was U Tien.

U Tien was a jeep driver on the staff of the Archbishop, and had been ordered to go with the priest. His home was in the north, in the mountains about fifty miles from the Chinese border. This was the area where the priest had decided to work. U Tien was thirty-nine years old, married, had three children and said that he was a devout Catholic. He said it evenly, without fervor; and Finian felt he was telling the truth. But still he had tested U Tien.

First Finian left his briefcase with U Tien while he went away on a short trip. Later, when he examined the briefcase, the thin almost invisible thread which he had twisted through the clasp was unbroken. So he knew, as a minimum, that U Tien was honest.

Secondly, he had told U Tien that he was thinking of negotiating with the Communists so that they would allow the mission schools to reopen. Finian had told him that they could re-open the schools on the condition that they would not teach anything against the Communists. U Tien's face showed no expression. Finian went on to say that Communism was politics and Catholicism was religion and there was no reason why they should conflict. Good Burmans could be good Communists as well as good Catholics, he said. There had been much misunderstanding; it was possible to be a good patriot and a good Communist and a good Catholic. What, he asked, did U Tien think of this?

Agony showed in U Tien's eyes. Finian knew that most Asians dislike saying anything that is unpleasant. Intuitively they say what they think their listener wants to hear. Finian also knew that a Communist would have hesitated, played for time until he could check with higher authority on what he should say. For what Finian was proposing was a capitulation. U Tien wet his lips.

"I think it would be a mistake," he said, and his voice was low and dejected. "I think it would not be possible to be a good Catholic and a good Communist. Somehow, in some way that I cannot tell you clearly, they are not things that can be mixed." He paused, seeking for the right words. "To say it differently: if one way is right, then the other cannot be. That is the best I can put it. I am sorry."

There had been other tests. Some of them were slight and quick, some more deliberate. Finally Father Finian had done what he knew was a cruel thing, but necessary. Finian had gone to the bazaar in Mokthu and had shopped industriously for a leather pouch. He had asked for such a pouch at four shops, and at each he had said, "It must be stout enough to hold a pistol and fifty rounds of ammunition. I want it for my driver so that he can guard the jeep in these troubled days."

The next day U Tien had been late for work. When he appeared, driving the jeep, his face was covered with a long purple welt that ran across his eye and down to his lower jaw. Blood was crusted in the corners of his mouth. Finian asked him what had happened.

"The Communists came last night and beat me," he said. "They thought I had a pistol and ammunition. They said they knew it for a fact. They almost destroyed my room searching for it." He paused and his eyes were bewildered and angry. "You have not been wise in what you have said, sir. It is not wise to say such things."

At that moment Finian dropped his air of innocence.

"It will not happen again, U Tien," he said, placing his hand on the man's shoulder. "This is the end of a time of testing. Now we know one another. It was necessary because there are spies everywhere. I had to find one man with whom I can trust God's work. Now, find out who the spies are."

Within a week U Tien told him. And he also told him who the dependable men were. Some of the dependable men were not Catholics, but they hated the Communists; and U Tien told him the reasons in each case.

"Now," said the priest," we will start our work."

Four men, U Tien among them, came flitting through the trees, nodded at Finian, and stood quietly in front of him. They waited without talking; and in a few minutes four more men appeared. All nine of them crouched to begin talking.

Now it starts, Finian thought. Now the whole work and training of years comes to a point, as if one had worked endlessly on a nail and now, with a few blows, were trying it on tough wood. He felt calm. His physical weakness was enormous, a pervading and maddening softness. But the weakness was only something of the body, something that would yield before food and sleep and exercise. Otherwise he was strong.

He closed his eyes for a moment, asked for guidance so that his strength would not be misused, and then, opening his eyes, began to talk very slowly to the eight Burmans.

"This thing is hard to say," he began slowly, speaking the words he had distilled down from twelve years of work. "But it must be said." He paused. "In usual times the Church cares not what the State does. Each is concerned with different parts of man: one with his soul and the other with his political life. A great saint once said that as long as the sword of the Church is left free to fight sin, it will do nothing to tarnish the sword of the State."

He hesitated, wondering if St. Augustine would quite approve this way of putting it. "But these are not usual times. The men calling themselves Communists say that the soul and the State are identical. The price of being a Communist is that you must give them your soul and your will. They are trying to make themselves gods on this earth."

They were listening intently. These men had lived long

with the threat of violence and death just at their back. They could not be deceived by soft words. They would recognize the truth, even if it were hard.

"The first thing is that we must decide very surely and exactly what it is we want. Before we make the smallest move we must agree on that," Finian said. And then he asked them, with absolute openness, "What is it that we wish to do?"

There was an electric moment in the clearing, a thin tense shred of silence. About each of the men there was a tautness, an expectation that was almost palpable.

"Tell us what is to be done?" U Piu asked. He did not look up.

Finian knew that this was a critical moment, a point of balance. U Piu, he sensed, was testing him.

"It is not for me to say," Finian said flatly. "It is for all of us. It is your country, your souls, your lives. I will do what we agree upon."

Subtly, so subtly that it was beyond the capacity of the eye to tell what was happening, the line of men seemed to become straighter, more firm. Their backs went straighter, their hands stopped playing with twigs and pieces of dirt; they looked up at Finian. The tiny invisible things that make up a posture of decisiveness, Finian could not detect. He only knew that it had happened.

This was, he was sure, the first time that these men had ever been told by a white man that a big and important decision was entirely their own . . . and would be followed by the white man.

"The big thing? That is what we must name?" one of the men said softly, his mind revolving around the question. "The big thing we want is that all of our people become Catholics."

A few of the Burmans looked at Finian for his reaction, but his face was impassive. His pain had come back, but no expression crossed his face. He was taller and more clumsy than any of the Burmans, and he knew it was important that he crouch as they did.

"No, that is not the final big thing we want," U Tien said. He spoke slowly, reaching carefully for the right words. "I do not care if there are Buddhists or Anamists among us. Or if there are Methodists or Baptists, or even nonbelievers. Before the Communists came there were such people among us and they did not forbid me to worship the way I wanted or to raise my children in my faith. But the Communists have made all worship impossible except the worship of Stalin, Lenin, Mao. In the areas the Communists control everyone must believe in one *single* thing: Communism."

Again there was a moment of silence, as the men thought of what had been said.

"U Tien is right," one of the Burmans said. "I too am a Catholic, but I do not require that all of us be Catholics. What this means, I think, is that the thing we want is a country where any man can worship any god he wishes; where he can live the way his heart says. That, I think, is the final big thing."

There was some more discussion, some of it heated. Once or twice the Burmans looked at Finian, but he merely stared back at them. Finally they came to agreement with U Tien.

"If you wish, I will sum up what you have said," Finian said. "The important thing, the big thing, is a country where any man may worship and live as he wishes." Then he added, humbly, "It is not my right to approve or disapprove, but I agree with you."

The Burmans' faces lighted, and the tiny wet clearing rang with laughter. U Piu, who was more exuberant than most Burmans, smacked his hands together with pleasure. Finian, for the first time in five weeks, was unaware of the sullen pain of dysentery.

"Now, the next step is harder, more difficult to think through," he said quietly. "It calls for great honesty and much information and much thought. It is this: Why do we not now have the freedom to worship or live as we please? Why is this?"

"Because the Communists do not permit it," one of the

men said quickly, almost automatically. "They burn the churches; they beat men who follow the politics of U Nu; they ridicule confession and confirmation. The Communists deny us all freedoms."

"But why do Burmans believe what the Communists say?" Finian asked quietly. "Once the Communists were only a few. Now they are many and they control many areas. They are Burmans like you. It means nothing to say Communists deny us freedom. Why do we allow them to deny us the freedom?"

"Mostly because many of our people believe in what they say," U Piu answered.

"But *why?*" Finian asked stubbornly, and his posture made it clear he would not attempt the answers.

The argument became so heated that Finian could not always follow it. Several times one or more of the men were angry. One man, Toki, who was a withdrawn and silent man, stood up, walked over to a tree, and pulled off a branch in his hands as if the intensity of what he felt could only be dissipated through his fingers. But in all the wild, loud talk Finian could tell that there was a pride and a sharp sense of discovery. Finally the talk quieted. Then men looked at U Tien as if he were their spokesman.

"What we think . . . and the words may offend you, Father . . . is three things," U Tien said slowly. "First, the Communists can deny us freedom because many Burmans have become Communists. Secondly, many Burmans have become Communists because they think that the Communists are against the white man . . . the Westerner. I apologize, Father, for saying this. It is hard, but most of us feel that the white man has not always been just. It is a hard thing, but it is true. Thirdly, many Burmans are for the Communists because they think the Communists will do good things for the people . . . for the peasants and cheap-pay workers. Give us land and more food and maybe automobiles and radios and cheap medicine. That, we agree, is why the Communists are able to deny us freedom to worship."

"That seems to me sound and true," Finian said, as if he

were merely summing up their statement. "First, that what we want is freedom to worship and to live. Secondly, that we will not have that freedom again until many Burmans stop being Communists; and they will only escape when they realize that Communism is evil for all. I am sure in my own mind that the Communists care nothing about white men or brown men or black men, but only for power. But you must not take my word for any of this. Together we will look at the facts and see what we discover." He paused and his teeth came together sharply from the pain.

"Tomorrow, if you wish, we will meet again at the same time and will read together what the Communists say they want and how they go about getting it," Finian said. "We will read and find this from things that the Communists themselves write and from things they themselves do. Then, perhaps, we will have the truth and will know what we must do."

He stood up and the pain was suddenly so great that he felt he would faint. His face paled and the beads of sweat broke out on his face and rolled with a salt taste into his mouth. U Tien made a movement toward him, a quick gesture of support, but Finian shook his head. He slowly shook hands with each of the men and thanked them for coming.

The next afternoon the Burmans were back. This time they were eager to talk, full of enthusiasm and words. They had thought since they left and they were, in a quiet way, desperate to communicate their views.

"Father, before we do anything we must have all the information that it is possible to have about the Communists in this area, I think," one of the Burmans said. "It is right to know what we want in a faraway day, but first we must know the difficulties that lie in the way."

Finian held back a smile of excitement. What the Burmans were proposing was exactly what Finian was going to propose as the third step: the gathering of intelligence.

The rest of the Burmans nodded agreement. Eagerly

and in great detail they began to disclose the extent of local Communist power. They told of merchants who were secret Communists, revealed which students were leaders, and which democrats, who were propaganda carriers, where the arms were cached, the extent of guerilla warfare. They talked steadily for two days. They drew sketches in the ground, pointed out locations on maps. They were astonished at the extent of their knowledge and also somewhat frightened—for no single one among them had realized that the Communists were so powerful. There was no village which did not have a shadow apparatus of Communists, no Western organization which was not spied upon. In some villages the Communists dominated everything with a chilling ferocity. Elsewhere they merely propagandized endlessly on the two themes of the evil of the Western white man and the love of the Communists for the common people.

"Now we know all that we can possibly know of the Communists and we know it equally. Each of us is as informed as the rest," Finian said. "We are not like the Communists who carefully conceal information from their people. Now we must decide what can be done. What shall we do?"

The argument raged every afternoon for two weeks. Ideas, words, enthusiasm, anger, commitment, and excitement boiled in their meetings. And finally, painfully and chaotically, agreement came.

Many months later Finian summed up in his report what they had done. By then it was possible to see things more clearly.

"What we discovered," he wrote, "is that men are persuaded of things by the same process, whether the persuading is done by the Catholic Church, Lutherans, Communists, or democrats. A movement cannot be judged by its methods of persuasion for, short of violence, most successful movements use the same methods. What we discovered in our long discussions in the jungle were these things:

1. We desired a community in which choice of life and religion existed.

2. But this was impossible because many Burmans had been deceived into believing the Communists.

3. Therefore, we had to demonstrate to the people that the Communists had no interest in them, but were interested only in power.

4. This had to be done skillfully, but without force. It had to be by a process of persuasion. Therefore, we had to make ourselves experts in persuasion.

5. We had to persuade in terms of events which are known to Burmans.

6. We had to persuade in words which would be understood by everyone.

7. Complex ideas had to be put dramatically and powerfully.

8. Persuasion had to be done at a time when the audience would be receptive. And it had to be done on all levels.

"Once the eight Burmans had agreed on this, the rest seemed almost easy. The hardest part was the waiting and the planning. We had to wait, for the time was not right; and we had to plan, for we were only nine against three thousand active Communists.

"The first thing my eight associates did was publish a small, cheap, newspaper on the ditto machine I had brought with me. They called it *The Communist Farmer*. This was cunning, because the title could mean anything. Initially the Communists did not know whether to support or oppose the newspaper, which appeared mysteriously and suddenly in marketplaces, stores, doorsteps, village squares, buses, and streets. In each issue there was an article by a famous Communist—Stalin, Marx, Lenin, Mao Tse-tung, Chou En-lai, Plekhanov. One issue had an article by Karl Marx in which he attacked the stupidity and backwardness of the peasants. Another issue offered a speech by Stalin in which he justified his slaughter of 'kulaks' on the grounds that agriculture must be collectivized. The rest of the issue was a simple reporting of facts about farming difficulties in Russia, the agricultural progress in the United States, hints on how to increase farm production, advice on how to use fertilizer.

"The Communist Party was confused for only two issues. Then they attacked the paper savagely in speeches, by radio, and in other papers. They pointed out that *The Communist Farmer* was reporting only part of Communist theory; but they could not effectively deny that what was reported was authoritative. They roared in their own papers that Stalin loved the peasants. But this was oddly unconvincing in the light of his murder of the 'kulaks.' Within a month, the Communist press was printing almost nothing except replies to *The Communist Farmer*.

"Then they made an all-out effort to suppress the paper. But this only made the paper more desirable, and copies became prized. Then they threatened to kill the men who printed and distributed it; but here, for the first time, their espionage failed and they could never discover who we were. The Communists slowly became buffoons in the eyes of the local Burmans. People actually laughed at statements made at Communist rallies. In Burma a party may be feared, respected, efficient, fierce . . . but if it is antic, it is hopeless.

"Communist leaders in the northern province were replaced. Then the new leaders were purged . . . and their replacements were in turn removed. A joke began to circulate that the quickest way to die was to be made a high official of the Communist Party.

"And then the climax came. The man from Moscow arrived in Anthkata, a Russian expert on Burma. He was tall, wiry, hard-faced, a veteran of purges, conspiracies, plots, and counterplots. He had never failed. His name was Vinich.

"Vinich had made elaborate plans before he smuggled himself into Anthkata. He had developed a thorough plan for the extermination of *The Communist Farmer*. And he took steps to assure that his presence in Anthkata would not be known. He had discovered long ago that natives should do their own political work . . . foreigners should come in only as a last resort, and then always as quietly as possible.

"His plan was so good it almost deserved to succeed. There was only one thing wrong. The Communist apparatus had been penetrated by a spy: Toki. Toki was thorough and inconspicuous, and his memory was infallible.

"Three weeks after the arrival of Vinich, *The Communist Farmer* began to appear almost daily in bars, teahouses, offices, public toilets, boats, oxcarts, country villages, courthouses, everywhere. And each day it advertised that on June 10, at 2:00 p.m., there would be a radio broadcast of great importance from Myitkyina with a message of importance even to non-Communists.

"On June 10 there were few people in Anthkata, if any, who were not listening to the radio. Somehow the broadcast had become a critical event . . . everyone felt that it was important.

"Promptly at 2:00 p.m. on June 10 the voice of the announcer stated that the following half-hour had been bought by an organization called the Burmese Educational League. Then a rough country voice, heavy with Anthkata accent, came on.

"'We think that the Burmans of Anthkata have been badly misled by vicious propaganda directed at Soviet Russia and the Communist Party,' said the local voice, speaking slowly. 'We think that this is a bad thing. So today we are allowing the official spokesman for the Soviet Union and the Anthkata Communist Party to speak. You will hear the voice of Vladimir Vinich of Moscow, Soviet Russia, who is living in the village of Ton Mou in secrecy. Last week Mr. Vinich called a meeting of the local Communists to discuss what Communist policy in Anthkata would be. To make sure that Communism is presented fairly, we of the Burmese Educational Society tape-recorded that conversation; and I am now going to play part of it for you. Communists, like everyone else, deserve to be judged by their own words, not by the words of any vicious detractors. Friends, the next voice you will hear is that of Mr. Vladimir Vinich of Moscow, Soviet Russia, speaking on Communism's aims.'

"There was a scratching, the whirring sound of a tape recorder, some static, and then a loud, harsh voice speaking excellent, but Russian-accented, Burmese.

" 'You have been arguing for three hours and I have not spoken during that time,' said Vinich's somewhat tired voice. 'It doesn't matter what's happening here. I'm not asking your advice. I'm telling you the facts . . . and the only conclusions that can be drawn from those facts. First, stop talking about Russian tractors and promising we will send some here. We can't do it. We've got all we can do to supply military hardware to Ho Chi Minh in Vietnam. Second, bear down on the owners of property. Don't talk about "socialist ownership of lands." That only scares the peasants. Peasants are backward types. They want private property, not collective farms. Later they'll see the necessity for common ownership, but not now.'

" 'What about the anti-American propaganda, Comrade?' a voice asked.

" 'You've gone too far on that," Vinich snapped. He was obviously at the edge of losing his temper. 'You push anti-Americanism so far it becomes a form of chauvinism and the Burmese begin to overlook the deficiencies of the Burmese government. Don't blame everything on the Americans, save some blame for the local opposition.'

" 'It is hard to criticize our government right now . . .' a Burmese voice said.

" 'Of course it is,' Vinich cut in. 'But you've got to remember that the worse things are, the better they are. Lenin said that. Which means that the mulberry and rice crops have to fail here. Which means that the road transport scheme has to fail.'

"The whir of the tape-recorder grew louder, then stopped. The local Burman's voice, innocent and almost unctuous, came up strongly.

" 'We are sure you are grateful for hearing about the principles and standards of Communism and the Russians' plans for Anthkata from a high Russian spokesman,' the voice said without sarcasm. 'We hope that you feel armed not to believe in the silly lies which enemies spread about Communism.' "

A day after the broadcast the nine men met in the jungle clearing again. For the first time Toki did not tear at small pieces of twig. He was a fulfilled man and he laughed softly at the joking remarks made by his friends.

"What we must do now is to make the same effort in other provinces in Burma," Toki said firmly. "And beyond Burma also. In Sarkhan, for example, the trouble is beginning. Their language is almost the same as ours. We can show them how to fight the enemy before the enemy is too strong to conquer."

He turned and looked at Father Finian. He wasn't looking at him for approval. Toki and his friends had made their own decision and their own way. The look which Toki gave was one of friendship and equality.

Father Finian felt a flush of pleasure. The pain in his bowels had finally disappeared, and he was already calculating the distance to Sarkhan and hoping that the food was not too much different from that of Burma.

Before leaving Burma, Father Finian added a paragraph to his personal diary. "It is reassuring to learn that what is humane and decent and right for people is also attractive to them," he wrote. "The evil of Communism is that it has masked from native peoples the simple fact that it intends to ruin them. When Americans do what is right and necessary, they are also doing what is effective."

# 4

# Everybody Loves
# Joe Bing

The best authority on Father Finian's Burma trip was Ruth Jyoti, the editor and publisher of the *Setkya Daily Herald*, one of the finest independent papers of Southeast Asia. It was Ruth who first heard and broke the story of Finian's adventure, and who made a month's trip into Northern Burma to document it.

Ruth Jyoti was a most unusual Eurasian. Her fair skin and blonde hair were Anglo-Saxon. Her other features were Asian, and so were her attitudes. She had been raised and educated by her Cambodian mother. This is not to say that she did not know a great deal about Europeans and Americans. Her reputation as an Asian editor brought her into contact with many foreigners. And she was attractive, single, and twenty-eight.

Ruth knew many Americans. The city of Setkya, where she published her paper, was one of the important American foreign aid centers and fairly crawled with ICA technicians, USIS press agents, and cultural attachés. Most of these Americans called upon her frequently for help and advice, so that it was inevitable that the USIS would invite her to America.

In 1952 Ruth accepted an offer of a three months' trip to learn about the press in the United States. Her first contact with America came in Hawaii. She was impressed by its beauty and charm—after she was finally able to see it. She was held up for hours in an Immigration and Customs waiting room for aliens. This room was neither dirty nor shabby; but obviously no one had ever given it much thought. And the officials were cold almost to the point of insult.

Ruth was too experienced a reporter either to waste time or to ignore first impressions. She picked up her notebook.

*They may not believe it, but Americans have poorer facilities for visitors than Communist China,* she wrote in her notebook. *At every factory, village, or sports center—wherever you are—in China, there is a guest house. The house is often crude, but it is always the best one available. And this is very effective propaganda.*

In San Francisco she waited at the airport until her State Department escort arrived. Buying herself copies of the *Chronicle* and the *Examiner,* she sat down in the Pan-American guest room and began to read. She went through both papers rapidly without finding the specific news she was looking for. A frown of disappointment crossed her face, and she reached for her notebook.

*Today, in Setkya,* she wrote, *the chiefs of seven major Asian nations are meeting. This conference may have profound effects upon Asian-American relations; yet there is no mention of the South Asian Bloc meeting in either of the two large San Francisco newspapers.*

*I wonder why the American papers do not report this Asian news? I notice that about 70 per cent of the paper space is taken up with advertising and comics. But I must read more papers in different cities before I begin to generalize.*

*Now, about the average American woman I see here at the airport. A great many of them are wearing slacks and . . .*

"Miss Jyoti?"

"Yes," she said, looking up. A debonair man of about

fifty stood in front of her. Removing his black homburg, he bowed slightly.

"I'm Joseph Rivers of the State Department. Welcome to America. I very much enjoyed reading your articles on Father Finian."

"Thank you, Mr. Rivers. You are too generous."

"Of course, Miss Jyoti, as a private citizen Father Finian had a good deal more freedom of action than a person who works officially for our government."

"Of course. Which might suggest that America should encourage her private citizens to do more of the sort of thing that Father Finian did."

Mr. Rivers looked at her sharply, and Ruth smiled at him. They did not mention Father Finian again.

"Mr. Rivers, could you get me a copy of the *New York Times?*" she asked.

"You bet," Mr. Rivers said, leading her through the busy terminal. "Say, Miss Jyoti, I was in Setkya for a few days not too long ago. You know Joe Bing there?"

When she shook her head, Mr. Rivers was genuinely astonished.

"Why you must know him! He's chief of information for the ICA in Setkya. Everyone knows him. There was an article on him in *Life* a few weeks ago."

"We don't see much of *Life* in Setkya, Mr. Rivers. It's a frightfully expensive magazine out there."

"But you have to know Joe Bing. He's six feet tall, fat, wears Tattersall checked vests. Lots of charm. Absolutely a male Elsa Maxwell. Knows everyone. I can remember him sitting in a café at the Hotel Montaigne. Nodded to everyone who went by . . ."

"Nodded to everyone who was European, Caucasian, western-educated, and decently dressed," Miss Jyoti said coldly. "I know the bastard now. He drives a big red convertible which he slews around corners and over sidewalks. And he's got exactly the kind of loud silly laugh that every Asian is embarrassed to hear."

"Oh, come on now, Miss Jyoti," Mr. Rivers said. "Old Joe is an expert newspaper man. He gives out all the copy on our aid program."

"He mails it out, or sends it by messenger," Miss Jyoti replied firmly. "And he has one hell of a big party every month where he brags that every chunk of food and every drop of liquor comes from the good ole U.S.A. And at wholesale prices right out of the commissary store. There hasn't been an Asian at one of his parties for two years. At his first party he only had liquor, when Buddhists and Moslems drink only fruit juice or water or milk. And the word got around."

"I'm truly sorry that you don't know Joe well enough to understand his good points," Mr. Rivers said lamely. He was somewhat frightened by the intensity with which Miss Jyoti spoke. Also he wondered how she could be a friend of America and still say such things about Old Joe. After all, everybody loves Joe Bing. The Department loves him. The newspaper people love him. They chose him to set up the protocol for Nixon's trip. Where the hell does she get off, saying things like that about Joe?

"You know, I heard about Joe Bing from Father Finian," Ruth said sweetly as they got into the limousine for San Francisco. "Father Finian had written him to see if Joe could send him some American ballpoint pens from the American Commissary in Setkya. Father Finian showed me Joe's reply: 'Commissary privileges are extended to American governmental employees and their dependents only' with the relevant government regulation. That was all."

"Well, you have to draw the line somewhere, or everyone would be piling into the commissaries," Mr. Rivers said.

"Oh, I agree. And after all, Father Finian wanted to use the pens for a private purpose—as prizes to the natives who did the best job of distributing their newspaper. At first it was an underground newspaper; but lately it's become one of the best rural newspapers in Burma."

"We couldn't allow individuals to use commissary items to support private business," Mr. Rivers said earnestly.

"Oh, I agree with you," Ruth said.

Mr. Rivers sat back and began to point out the sights of San Francisco.

The San Francisco press gave Ruth a dinner two nights later at which she was asked to say a few words about Americans stationed in Asia. After a few pleasantries about the good food and American hospitality, she dug into her subject with vigor.

"Generally Americans in Asia are not effective. They are what I call the Intellectual Maginot Line. They feel that if the nice rich respectable people like them, they must be doing a good job. I can understand that. You look at foreign faces, hear strange languages—and you just feel more comfortable at the Press Club or the American Club or at the Officer's Club. Or anywhere where quiet people are wearing collars and ties and talking in English. The Asians who wear collars and ties and speak English are a special class, and most Americans have real difficulty meeting any other sort. And I regret having to say this, most of you don't make the effort. I could stand here all night and tell you stories about one American mistake after another. But perhaps it will be more helpful if I tell you about an American who was effective.

"He was Bob Maile of the USIS. Now I'm not saying that all USIS men are effective. Far from it. But Bob Maile was. He did more to raise American prestige than anyone else over there—the ambassador included.

"Bob was in Setkya for about five months before any of the editors even heard about him. Usually the first thing a new USIS official does is to come barging in on us. They fawn all over us—if we talk English—and start making big plans for our country—without knowing anything about it. It's become such a pain in the neck that almost every editor has orders that no American is to be allowed in his office. And if one forces his way into my office, I just pretend I don't speak English.

"Bob was different. I met him and his wife Dorothy at a party given in his honor by the typesetters. You see, instead of barging in at the top with the air of an ambassador, Bob Maile started off by trying to become familiar with our language and country. He made friends with the typesetters, the reporters, the photographers, the circulation boys. He showed the photographers how to raise the ASA speed of their films so that they could take candid pictures without flash. He helped them get chemicals. He got a fan for the dark room and he made the light trap in his own home.

"He did these things without asking for credit or telling anyone. In return, he wanted tutoring in our language, lessons in our cooking for Dorothy, and help in getting his children into our schools. He was humble about everything, and he made it clear that he thought he was getting more than he was giving.

"Now, not all of this is easy. I know enough about western standards to understand that sending an American child to a native school takes some courage. Asian schools are dirty, rowdy, noisy, and infectious by your standards. But Bob Maile's kids did all right. They caught impetigo once, and got mixed up in a couple of fights—but they also got a good education, and they came to understand a different kind of life.

"Let me tell you a story that as newspaper men you'll appreciate. About a year ago a story broke that an American soldier had raped a girl in a temple. The temple part made it the story of the century. If it had hit the headlines we would have had a religious war against the Americans on our hands. The chief American public information man in Setkya, a man whom many of you probably know, just holed up in his office. He never touched what he called 'native controversies.' That meant he hadn't time to buck it up to Washington for an answer.

"Bob Maile, on the other hand, called on the editors of the biggest papers and news services in Setkya. He didn't threaten anyone, or conceal information, or say that the story would be unfriendly to the United States. He just asked if we had checked it out thoroughly.

"This is the kind of question you take from someone you trust. So we checked it out—and it was wrong. An American had gone to a brothel, refused to pay when he left, on the grounds that are unmentionable here, and got into a brawl. Not worth a paragraph in any paper.

"Bob never brags about what his office does. He doesn't have to. In my country good deeds are publicized all over by the bamboo telegraph. Bob Maile is the best known American in my country.

"I wish the other Americans were all like him. If they were, the Communists couldn't last long in Asia."

# 5

# Confidential
# and Personal

From: Ambassador Louis Sears (Sarkhan)
To: Mr. Dexter S. Peterson, Sarkhan Desk, State Department, Washington, D. C.

Dear Dex,

I'm writing this to you personally (even typing it myself) because I need help and I want to make sure you know what the score is out here in Sarkhan. Honest, Dex, these Sarkhanese are really tricky. Sometimes I think they're all Commies. And to tell you the truth, I'm not so sure about the loyalty of some of the Americans here, either.

I guess that by now the Department's been reading all the press lies about Sarkhan. The stories that reporter for the *Times* wrote are false. My relations with the Sarkhanese couldn't be better, and the enclosed editorial from the *Eastern Star* proves it. And his stories about my neglecting that crackpot Colvin because I was ignorant of the circumstances is pure hogwash. I personally saw Colvin right after he got into trouble. Also enclosed are clippings from the Sarkhanese papers published the day after. Colvin has a lot of drag in Wisconsin and may be raising hell through his senators and congressmen. Just show them the clippings.

We got another crackpot here, too—Father Finian. This priest has to be handled with kid gloves. I don't want to get into a beef with the Roman Catholics. But this Finian has just come from Burma where he started a small revolution; now he's organizing here in Sarkhan way up north, and the local papers are beginning to raise hell. If Cardinal Spellman is for him, I can tolerate him, I suppose. But if the Catholic bigshots are down on him, I'll get him shipped back to the States.

Now Dex, aside from those two things—and despite the newspaper lies—everything is on an even keel out here. The Sarkhan politicians keep squawking that if we don't bail them out the country will go Commie. Don't believe it for a damned minute. I get around at one hell of a lot of social functions, and official dinners out here, and I've never met a native Communist yet. And even though the Russian ambassador screwed us for a little while on the rice deal, I had a hundred thousand handbills distributed saying that it was the gool old USA who supplied the rice.

In general, we're in good shape out here.

But what I need in a hurry for my staff are some people I can trust who have initiative. I'm getting damned sick and tired of having to do everything myself. For one thing, we need a new public affairs office. This girl Maggie Johnson is all right, but she agrees with the native press too much. And she keeps bringing newspapermen —especially Americans—in to see me. They pester hell out of me about problems which are none of their business, and which Miss Johnson should handle on her own.

Dex, do you remember Joe Bing? He made a big impression on me when he appeared before the Senate Committee. He's a sharp cookie with his eye on the ball. See if you can get him assigned out here, will you? He was stationed in Setkya for a while, so he should know the Asian picture. Also a few good looking girls as secretaries. They'd be a good advertisement for America, and would help morale.

You can read between the lines, Dex. I don't want to be

torpedoed by a bunch of crackpot internationalists who don't know which end is up. And I want a staff we can be proud of. Get someone in personnel to do some active recruiting for us. Thanks.

LOU

# 6

# Employment
# Opportunities Abroad

"Employment Opportunities Abroad" was printed in bright red across the top of the placards. Maybe 1500 of the handsome cards appeared throughout Washington on bulletin boards in government offices, university halls, Civil Service offices, boarding houses, and the cheap dormitories in which so many "government girls" live. The placards made it clear that there was a shortage of trained people to work abroad; and that if one worked overseas the pay would be good, advancement was possible, and it would be patriotic—as well as an opportunity to see exotic and interesting parts of the world. The placard also said that a meeting would be held in a conference room at American University which would be addressed by "experienced Foreign Service officers who have themselves lived and worked abroad." There would also be a question period.

The conference room was crowded by the time the meeting began. The main speaker was Mr. Hamilton Bridge Upton who had served as a consul in seven different countries. He looked like Brooks Brothers, Dartmouth, confidence, poise, good cocktail conversation, no dirty jokes, and a representative of the United States . . . all of which was true. Sitting with him behind the table was a very fat, warm, jolly man named Joseph F. Bing.

He looked like a traveling salesman, Northwestern U., a "big man on campus," an inside dopester, a good journalist, and a man who knew his way about . . . all of which was true.

Mr. Hamilton Upton spoke first with skill and dignity. His information was precise, and his audience felt that he was a worthy representative of a great power . . . a man who knew how to handle tough situations and tricky foreigners.

"Each of us would like to stay home, develop his profession, widen his friendships, and rear his family," Mr. Upton began. "But in times of such momentous crises, when our country faces challenges unlike any she has ever faced, we must also realize that we have duties as citizens. And not only as citizens, but as members of the world community. In all lands we are beset by an evil world-wide conspiracy. We need our best people abroad to help contain this clever and malignant conspiracy."

I like the way he doesn't call them Communists, those conspiracy people, Marie MacIntosh thought. She was there with her three girl friends, all of whom worked in the Pentagon stenographic pool; they shared a small apartment close to Rock Creek Park.

Mr. Upton talked for fifteen minutes, giving the impression of a discussion between one superior person and another. Marie felt impressed and involved just by being addressed in such a way.

"And now I would like to introduce Mr. Joe Bing," Mr. Upton said when he had finished. "Mr. Bing is a public information officer and an expert on Asian affairs. He has served for several years in Setkya, and served with distinction. He has requested duty in Sarkhan, and will probably be leaving for that country in the near future. Here is a person who is an expert at meeting natives face to face, as equals."

Mr. Upton sat down and Mr. Joseph Bing pushed back his chair, hefted his body up, and walked around the table. He sat on the edge of the table and at once the entire audience relaxed.

"My name is Bing, but I'm a government public relations man and you can call me Joe," he said. Everyone laughed. A few people in the audience said "Hiya, Joe," and he waved his hand. "I work for men like Mr. Upton, and let me tell you it's a pleasure. Foreign affairs is big business and it's important business. You all know that. Now maybe I can tell you a few things about working abroad for Uncle Sammy that you won't read in the handouts. After all, even when you're doing big work and important work, you still have to relax, and I know you'd like to know about the informal side of living and working abroad."

Joe spent a few minutes describing the simple business of getting to an overseas post. Air or ship, he said, but first class. Nothing but the best. Then he winked and the audience shifted in their seats. Marie MacIntosh inched forward and listened intently.

"Now I know what's on your minds. At least on the minds of some of you," Joe said jovially. "Your social life. O.K., let's talk about it. You'll have to work among foreigners, but we don't expect you to love 'em just because you work among 'em. I don't care where you go to work for Uncle Sammy, you'll be living with a gang of clean-cut Americans. And a lot of 'em are single people, so you won't be lonesome if you're not married."

Mr. Upton very carefully was looking over Joe's head at some distant speck on the wall. But there was the faintest trace of a smile on his face, with which everyone in the audience was pleased. They knew that Mr. Upton enjoyed what Joe was saying as much as they, and it made foreign duty seem like a family affair. Mr. Upton was the proper but protective father; and Joe was the uncle who always shows up at Christmas with whiskey on his breath and gifts in his suitcase.

Joe went on for twenty minutes. He was expert at using the concrete example and answering the practical question. He knew about the price of alligator shoes in Brazil, the cost of Scotch in Japan, the availability of servants in Vietnam, the pension one could expect after twenty years of faithful service. He told about commissaries which stocked wholesome American food for Americans stationed all over the world. "You can buy the same food in Asia that you can in Peoria. Even, say, in Saigon they stock American ice cream, bread, cake, and, well, anything you want," said Joe Bing. "We look out for our people. When you live overseas it's still on the high American standard."

"Sounds good, doesn't it?" Marie MacIntosh whispered.

The other three girls nodded. Marie guessed that they were all thinking about the two-room apartment the four of them shared. Two of them slept on a foldaway couch in the front room, and had to get up early so that the table could be opened for breakfast. Their only luxury was a bottle of whiskey every Friday night which they drank with ginger ale because none of them liked the taste.

Joe Bing finished his informal talk and then announced that he or Mr. Upton would be glad to answer questions. No one asked Mr. Upton a thing; but Joe talked steadily for another half-hour.

"What about learning to speak a foreign language?" a small wiry girl asked. "I understand you have to learn the language of a country before you go there."

"Now, just a minute," Joe said, his voice full of good humor, "someone gave you the wrong dope. Uncle Sammy is not crazy. How many people do you think we could round up in this country who can speak Cambodian or Japanese or even German? Well, not very many. I don't *parlez vous* very well myself, but I've always made out pretty well in foreign countries. Fact is, we don't expect you to know the native language. Translators are a dime a dozen overseas. And besides, it's better to make the Asians learn English. Helps them, too. Most of the foreigners you'll do business with speak perfect English."

"I hear everything's expensive overseas," said another listener. "Can we ever save money?"

Joe Bing laughed. "Look, your housing's all paid for. Your only expenses are food, liquor if you drink, clothes, and servants—and you can buy a whole family of servants for forty dollars a month."

Sixty-seven people put in applications, among them Marie MacIntosh, Homer Atkins, a retired engineer, and a newspaperman named Kohler. The newspaperman was rejected because he had once written some articles criticizing the government. Joe Bing was particularly interested in these three, because they had all indicated that they wanted to go to Asia. In fact, two of them mentioned Sarkhan.

"You know," said Mr. Upton a week later, "there's something wrong with our recruiting system. With the exception of Atkins, that engineer, every applicant will be making more money with the government than he does in the job he has now. Frankly, I think we're getting slobs."

"What about that old engineer?"

"I think maybe he'll turn out to be a screwball. He put down that his present income from investments is $150,000 a year."

# 7

# The Girl Who
# Got Recruited

---

Marie MacIntosh was twenty-eight years old and she had a private cry about once a week. She was drab, and she knew it. Her life was drab, and she knew it. What she needed was a husband, and she knew that too. The one hope she had for a change in her routine life was her application for overseas duty.

Although Marie had interesting bosses and a responsible job, life was dull. She left her apartment at six-thirty in the morning so that she could get a seat on the bus, and also so that she could eat breakfast in the government cafeteria. Usually she stayed in her office until five-thirty, and would have dinner in the government cafeteria.

This routine meant she avoided the crowded buses; and it was much cheaper and easier than eating in the crowded apartment.

Marie's nights were almost all the same. After doing her share of the apartment cleaning and her own laundry, she sat in front of the TV set with her three roommates.

Then Marie received a letter of acceptance to her application for overseas duty. She was to go to Sarkhan. Three months later she landed at Haidho airfield.

A month later she wrote her ex-roommates a letter:

Dear Mary, Joan, and Louise,

The trip to Haidho was wonderful. I flew first class all the way—the real deluxe treatment—all paid for. It was great. (Remember the time we flew tourist class to Chicago and packed our lunches in our handbags, and how we had to stand in line?)

Well, naturally I was scared when I stepped off the plane at Haidho (the capitol of Sarkhan). Everything was new and I didn't know what to expect. Well, girls, there was a chauffeur-driven car waiting for me at the airport along with a reception committee. I didn't have to go through customs or anything. When I asked about my luggage, Mister Preston (the man who came to meet me) said never mind, Tonki will look after it. Tonki is a Sarkhanese who works for the embassy here.

Two of the girls who met me are also secretaries and they said that I should live with them if I wanted to; and I'm staying with them now.

You should see our house (picture enclosed). We each have our own bedroom—and there's an extra for guests. There's a dining room, a living room, and maid's quarters.

And there are built-in servants! Honest. We have three servants to look after us. It's a family of them, father, mother, and a fourteen year old girl. They do the cooking, cleaning, laundry—everything. Oh, how they baby us! When they wake me in the morning, they bring a glass of orange juice and a cup of tea. This is real living.

The Americans here are very friendly. They all give parties and plenty of them; there's at least one cocktail party or dinner every night. It's easy to do, of course, because everyone has help. All I have to do is check with my housemates to see if it's okay, and then call the servant. "Ehibun," I say, "we're having ten for dinner next Tuesday. Can you handle it?"

"Yes, mum," she says, and that's all there is to it. And what a dinner for ten it turns out to be! Just like in the movies.

Liquor over here in the government liquor store is dirt cheap. There's no tax on it—so Johnny Walker Black Label, Old Grand Dad, and Beefeater Gin are all less than two dollars a bottle. And we also have a Commissary and PX.

And speaking of things being cheap, I'm buying a new Hillman. I can get it for much less than the U. S. price. It's duty free, and there's some special arrangement so the government brings it over for me from England for nothing.

There are only about a thousand Americans here, and we stick together. That means that we girls get asked to everything. I've been to the ambassador's parties several times; and to lots of dinners at the MAAG (Military Assistance and Advisory Group) and the USIS and the ECA (Economic Mission).

Well, it's time to go to the office—I see my car is waiting in front. We're driven to work and back in a government car pool. I have to get to the office early today so I can take a long lunch hour, because I have an appointment with my dressmaker.

The best thing about being here is that for the first time in my life I can save money. Of course, my rent is free. My basic salary is $3400, but on top of that I get a $680 increase in pay because of location. You see, this is defined by the Department as a hardship post.

Love to you all,
Marie

# 8

# The Ambassador and
# the Working Press

---

It was a year after Ambassador Sears had arrived in Haidho, and it was the Month of the Boar, the middle of the wet season. All day and all night the tropical rains fell with a steady drone. The only people out were the peasants, who splashed through the muddy streets in straw raincoats and enormous straw hats. The smell of dampness—like the odor of mushrooms—was everywhere. Even the airconditioned rooms of the American Ambassador were not truly dry.

In the wet season foreigners wearing tight western clothes suffered from various skin irritations, mostly a kind of fungus growth. Tempers became raw. In this particular wet season occurred the incident of the Royal Sarkhanese Air Base.

About fifty years before the United States government had purchased a thousand acres on the outskirts of Haidho. What the plans had been for the tract, no one remembers; and the land lay idle until 1947. During the rainy season of that year the Sarkhanese Air Force had requested the use of the property for a training area; it was high, hard, flat ground which could be used all year round. Permission was granted and the Royal Sarkhanese Treasury spent many millions improving the land. It was only natural for fashionable suburbs to spring up around it; and the American tract came to be one of the most valuable pieces of real estate in Sarkhan.

The incident began when a newspaper hostile to America printed a rumor that the Royal Sarkhanese Air Force was to be evicted from the American property, so that American land speculators could sell it for building lots. The next day every other paper in Sarkhan picked the story up. So did the Pan Asia Press, the United Press, the Associated Press, the International News Service. So did Tass, Reuters, and Press France.

The hostile paper kept the story alive in its headlines day after day.

"Our tip must be true," they wrote, "because no one at the American Embassy denies it."

The editor of the English language paper, an American, called up the USIS.

"Look," he said, "this silly story—which I know must be a lie—is hurting the United States. This afternoon I'm going to round up the editors of the four leading dailies and bring them to see the ambassador. I'm going to ask him point blank about the Air Force Training Area. The minute he says it's untrue, the story will die. Also, it will make the Commie press lose a lot of face. Okay for two o'clock?"

Joe Bing, the new public affairs officer, was on a cultural trip to Hong Kong; and his assistant, the press attaché, had to carry the ball. When he told Ambassador Sears that he would be interviewed that afternoon, the ambassador's face got red, and his eyes bulged.

"No, by God!" he shouted, banging the desk, "you're not going to foul me up at this stage of the game. You see this?" he yelled, holding up a letter. "This is from the President. And he says that a federal judgeship will open up in four months and he would be pleased if I took it. And I intend to. And I don't intend to get mixed up with a bunch of skunks between now and then. Tell Joe Bing to handle it!"

"He's in Hong Kong, sir."

"Then you take care of them."

"They want to see you, sir. I've already tried to stall them."

The ambassador flopped back in his chair and a cunning look came into his eyes. "All right," he said. "Let 'em come. You can bring your radical friends here at two. I'll be ready."

At two that afternoon the five editors entered the ambassador's office.

"Sit down, gentlemen. What can I do for you?"

The American editor said, "Mr. Ambassador, there's a story making the rounds that the United States is about to evict the Air Force from land lent them by the United States. This would mean that all their millions of dollars of building would have to go. The property is supposed to be turned over to American real estate salesmen to sell as subdivisions."

"Yes, gentlemen. I've read the story."

"Well, sir, is it true or is it a lie?"

The ambassador hesitated for a moment. He poked the end of a pencil into his ear, then smoothed his gray hair, then looked at the ceiling.

"Gentlemen," he said finally. "I have no comment to make."

The four Asian editors looked at each other in amazement, thanked the ambassador, and left. The American remained behind. When they were gone, he shouted, "For God's sake, you've got to comment. This is the same as saying it's true. Hell, it'll be all over the world. You know that eviction story is a goddam lie."

"Tell you the truth, son," said the ambassador, "I don't know if it's true or not."

"Then cable to Washington and ask them if it's true!"

The ambassador pressed a button on his desk. A moment later the deputy chief of mission came in.

"Yes, sir?"

"Say, Charlie," said the ambassador. "Smith here has a darn good idea. . . ."

◎

On February 13th the following message was received at the U.S. Embassy in Sarkhan.

*Personal for Ambassador from Dexter Peterson X This will be advance notice to you that your judgeship has been approved by the President and will become effective immediately on your return X Believe your replacement will be Gilbert MacWhite X Congratulations*

Once his judgeship was assured Lucky Lou was somewhat saddened at having to leave Sarkhan. Almost at once he felt a warm glow of affection for the place.

His affection was not so intense, however, that he forgot practical political matters. He did the following three things before throwing one of the most liquid parties in in the history of Haidho.

He refused to extend protection to one Father Finian on the grounds that he intended to "participate in the domestic politics of another power."

He again recommended to the Sarkhanese government that they refuse a visa to one John Colvin, who, having recuperated at Johns Hopkins Hospital, now wanted to return to Sarkhan. He did this by phone, as he did not like matters such as this to become a part of the official record. They never did anyone any good.

He wrote a long careful report to the State Department pointing out the gains which had been made in Sarkhan during his tenure in that country. He pointed out that "there are always those who pick away at sound policies or tend to exaggerate normal internal political frictions. Sarkhan is more firmly than ever on the side of America."

◎

# 9

# Everyone Has Ears

---

The Honorable Gilbert MacWhite, Ambassador to Sarkhan, was a fit man. At the age of forty-four he weighed exactly the same as he had when he graduated from Princeton with the class of 1934. He had red hair; his body was hard and muscular. When he was in the States or in England he played squash at least three times a week, and in other countries he always managed to play tennis. He smoked little, and always fine, thin, handrolled Havana cigars. He held his liquor well. He preferred martinis, and only one or two each evening. But he could, if he had to, drink immense quantities of vodka, sake, or Scotch; and his tongue never thickened and his mind seldom dulled.

MacWhite was, from his first day in the State Department, a professional foreign service officer. He needed no breaking in. He was competent, exact, and highly efficient. He also was courageous and outspoken, and he had imagination. During the McCarthy excitement he kept his head and ran his desk smoothly. By 1952 he had served as Consul General in four large foreign cities, as Deputy Chief of Mission in two cities, and was regarded by his superiors as a comer.

In 1954, the Honorable Gilbert MacWhite was made Ambassador to Sarkhan. It was an assignment that pleased him deeply. He knew that the Sarkhan government was new, inexperienced, and shaky, and that the eighteen million Sarkhanese were restless. He knew that the Com-

*New Ambassador a good guy*

munists in Sarkhan were strong, competent, and well organized; he had not the slightest doubt that they would attempt a coup against the government. MacWhite's knowledge of Marxism and Lenism, and the Titoist and Maoist versions of the faith, was enormous. He was a recognized expert on Soviet theory and practice.

Ambassador MacWhite prepared for his new assignment with a thoroughness in the best tradition of missionary faith. He learned the Sarkhanese language in fifteen weeks of incredibly difficult work. He read every book he could find on Sarkhanese history and political life. He talked to anthropologists, sociologists, political scientists, diplomats, and businessmen who had visited Sarkhan in the last several years. He read the reports of his predecessor, Louis Sears.

Haidho is almost unbelievable. The city rests on a high plateau which overlooks the Pacific; although the forest presses in around the buildings with a heavy green persistence, each of the buildings is distinct and intact. The people of Sarkhan did not erect monumental buildings. Most of the public buildings and almost all of the private homes were made of a light yellow volcanic stone, which the tropical climate and the constant jungle rainfall covered with a light green patina. The effect was subtle, subterranean, almost a vision of a city seen under the sea.

Haidho was hot, but neither Gilbert nor his wife Molly were dismayed by this. They were prepared to endure the heat of the tropics, and neither they nor their boys had ever complained of hardships. Indeed, as the Honorable Gilbert MacWhite looked from the upper window of his embassy out over the plateau and the ocean beyond, he was aware of how absorbed he had become in his job. In the six months he had been at Sarkhan he had hardly noticed the climate. In those six months Ambassador MacWhite had drawn his lines of battle against the Communists—shrewdly, patiently, with infinite imagination, after almost endless consultations with native leaders, and, he thought, with a certainty of victory. The planning had

been in absolute secret; in fact, only three members of the
U. S. Embassy staff knew about the swift, ruthless campaign which would soon take place. To ensure maximum
security, MacWhite had had all his secret discussions in
the privacy of his residence.

MacWhite was enthusiastic about the battle. He did not
underestimate the strength of the Communists in Sarkhan,
but neither did he underestimate his own strengths and
capabilities. In fact, Ambassador MacWhite regarded his
anticipated combat with the Communists as the capstone
of his career. He saw it as a battle in which the shrewdness
of the businessman, the tactical ingenuity of the military
man, and the intelligence and persistence of the diplomat
would all be combined to achieve a victory which was,
although Ambassador MacWhite would never have said
it in so arrogant a way, almost a personal victory.

This afternoon he meant to cement another fragment
into the wall of his strategy against the Communists. He
was waiting for the Honorable Li Pang. Mr. Li was a
a representative of Generalissimo Chiang Kai-shek. Ambassador MacWhite had invited Li to come to Sarkhan
to meet with the local Chinese leaders. Most of the local
Chinese had lived in Sarkhan for five generations. They
considered themselves native Sarkhanese and highly patriotic. And in a way which was baffling to the Occidental
mind, they also considered themselves patriotic Chinese,
and saw no conflict in this dual obligation.

Li and MacWhite were old friends. They were both
businessmen; and although they had left business for quite
different reasons, they both left rich. They were both
soldiers. And, by a curious coincidence, they were both
Episcopalians. They understood one another. MacWhite
was sure that Li would help commit the local Chinese to
the battle against the native Communists. When he was
sure of this, MacWhite was ready to move.

As he looked out of the plateglass window of the Embassy Residence, Ambassador MacWhite was aware of
the fact that Donald and Roger were in the room behind

him. Somehow the small pitter-patter noises that they were making were a comfort to him. Donald and Roger were both elderly Chinese. The only English words they knew were the names given them by their American employers and a few necessary household terms. They had been trusted servants of the Embassy since an American ambassador to Sarkhan had hired them in 1939. They worked with an efficiency, dedication, and kindliness that never failed to touch Ambassador MacWhite. They often helped Molly with the boys. They were both excellent cooks and superb butlers. They were, somehow, a symbol of the decent Asian, and they made the entire struggle in which Ambassador MacWhite was engaged meaningful and important. They represented the honor and morality which had been taught by Confucius.

Ambassador MacWhite turned and walked toward the stairs as Mr. Li approached.

"Your Excellency, I have prepared a pitcher of very dry and cold martinis in your honor," MacWhite said, smiling.

"Your Excellency, I am prepared to drink the entire pitcher," Li said and smiled back. "Did I ever tell you, Ambassador MacWhite, the story of the woman who got stuck in the lavatory on the thirty-fourth floor of the Waldorf-Astoria, and who lived on martinis because they were the only things that could be siphoned in through the keyhole?"

Ambassador MacWhite laughed, and poured martinis into extremely large and cold glasses. They drank and talked quietly for ten minutes. In another half-hour Molly would join them and they would have a long and pleasant dinner. Before Molly came down, MacWhite had to talk to Li. When Li had finished a story he was telling, MacWhite leaned toward him.

"Li, I have been frank with you and you have, I think, been frank with me," MacWhite said. "I should like to discuss with you a subject which I think is of the utmost importance."

"If it's anything I can do for you, Gilbert, you may be

sure of it." Li said. MacWhite paused while Donald filled their glasses with martinis; then he spoke.

"The problem is simple, Li. With your military background, you'll understand it quickly," MacWhite said. "It's a matter of strategic intelligence. I should like to know which of the Chinese leaders are sympathetic to the Communists. I have an absolutely flawless plan for getting them out of the country . . ."

Li did not stop smiling; but in some subtle, quick way his entire expression changed. He was still smiling, he was still sipping the martini, he was still poised. But his eyes had gone icy hard, and he was looking over MacWhite's shoulder at Donald and Roger who were standing at the serving table about fifteen feet away. He laughed softly, but MacWhite was aware that there was a warning in the laugh. The entire mood of the conversation had changed. MacWhite, a sensitive person, knew that he was in trouble.

"Now please understand me, Li, I would not use this information to hurt any good Chinese in Sarkhan," Mac-White said. "It would be for my ears only; but I think you can see that it would be critical in the coming struggle against the Communists in this country."

"I am aware of that, Gilbert," Li said. "I can see at once the importance of the question."

"But somehow it disturbs you?"

Li finished his martini in a long slow steady sip, and put the empty glass on the table. Then he lit a cigarette, inhaled deeply, and ground the cigarette out in the ashtray. When he looked up his face was utterly foreign to MacWhite. For the first time in his life MacWhite saw a completely furious Oriental. MacWhite was shaken.

"Gilbert, you are a fool. A great fool," Li said. "I am speaking softly so that only you will hear my voice. But to discuss matters of such importance with servants in the room . . ."

MacWhite interrupted him, "Donald and Roger are old and trusted. They don't understand a word of English.

And they're on the other side of the room behind the pantry screen."

"No one, Gilbert, is to be trusted, whether he is an old servant or not," Li said. "Whether he is next to you or in the basement."

From the white marks around Li's nose and mouth Mac-White knew that he was not joking.

"Let me reassure you, Li," MacWhite said. "Neither Donald nor Roger can understand a word of English. Before I hired them I had their credentials checked with the Sarkhan national police authorities. My predecessor vouched for their integrity and honesty. In 1941, these men buried the Embassy valuables when the Japs came. After the war they came back and returned them. That silver service over there is one of the things they saved."

When Li spoke his voice was still flat and cold and the lines had not vanished from his nose and mouth. "Gilbert, I must say it again, I have just seen you do a foolish thing."

There was nothing that Li could have said that would have been more offensive to MacWhite. Li was accusing MacWhite of being neither tough-minded nor security conscious, things that he prided himself he was. In fact, although he would not tell Li this, MacWhite had laid elaborate traps to see if Donald and Roger spoke only Chinese. He had often called peremptory commands to them in English; when their strides never broke, and their faces never changed expression, he had been satisfied that they knew no English. He was also certain that they could not write. He had never seen either of them with a pen or pencil in his hand, nor had either ever sent a letter from the house.

MacWhite scowled, his face reflecting his thoughts. *These two Chinese are my friends. They have served America for almost twenty years. During the war they risked their lives for us.*

The expression on Li's face did not change in the slightest. He walked up to the bar, picked up the pitcher of martinis, and refilled MacWhite's glass and his own. Then he sat down and faced MacWhite.

"You are a clever man, Gilbert," Li said. "Now, if you wanted information from the American Embassy, where would be the perfect place to have your spy?"

"As the ambassador's secretary."

"And next?"

"As his valet," said MacWhite with reluctance.

"And after that?"

"As his switchboard operator."

"Would your spy be a suspicious character, or someone who would earn his boss's trust and confidence?"

MacWhite looked up sharply. For the first time he felt a flash of doubt, a tiny gnaw of anxiety. All of these positions in his embassy and many more—the translators, the messengers, the chauffeurs, the clerks—all were filled by Asians. And he suddenly realized that in every U. S. Embassy in the world, and in all the USIS offices, the military assistance missions, the economic missions, these vulnerable positions were held by aliens. He began automatically, but with panic, to analyze how he allowed this to happen in his embassy.

"How much time do we have before Molly will join us?" Li asked softly.

"Almost twenty minutes," MacWhite answered.

Li leaned back in his chair and roared a command in Chinese. Almost at once Donald and Roger came trotting forward. Donald looked quickly about the room for the martini pitcher, picked it up, and splashed gin and the barest suggestion of vermouth into it. Then he stood in front of the two men and quietly filled their glasses. Li finished half of the fresh martini, placed it on the coffee-table, and stood up slowly. Something about his posture, some slight menace in his face, caused both Donald and Ambassador MacWhite to watch him closely. And as he stood up, Li changed. The smile fell away from his face, his body tensed as if under some enormous strain. Although he was six inches shorter than Donald, Donald drew back sharply as if he had been threatened. Speaking in Sarkhanese, Li ordered Roger to leave the room. Then, with eyes as black and hard as bits of chilled steel, Li turned to Donald. He spoke in Chinese, slowly, and Mac-White was able to follow the conversation easily.

"The American Ambassador tells me that things are being stolen from this embassy," Li said in a low, hard voice. "A valuable wrist watch is missing. Four bottles of Scotch whiskey are missing. The Ambassador is determined to find the person that stole these things, and we know, you cunning scum, that you are the thief."

Donald protested shrilly. He had never stolen anything, he wailed, and he looked beseechingly at MacWhite. Li stepped forward and slapped Donald across the mouth.

MacWhite was shocked. Li's fingers left four red marks on Donald's cheek. Donald's old and kindly face was twisted in surprise, his jaw open.

Li turned to MacWhite as if nothing had happened. He spoke distinctly to MacWhite in English.

"He denies stealing the whiskey and watch," Li said, "but he is lying. Once we establish that he has stolen them we can ask him about the typewriter and the briefcase. Those are what we really want."

MacWhite nodded, going along with Li's deception, but he was angry. Also, he was startled by the change in Li. Li had always struck him as Anglicized, as open and straightforward. Li knew American jokes, English ballads, Irish dialects. He was as American as a tractor salesman. But now he looked menacing, hooded, tight with cruelty. Every word Li spoke was like a whiplash.

MacWhite had seen interrogations before. During the war he had earned a reputation as a skillful interrogator himself. But he had seen nothing like this. It was not so much an interrogation as the deliberate destruction of a person. What Li did was like a physical assault aimed at destroying Donald. It was all MacWhite could do to keep from interrupting.

With exquisite detail Li was telling Donald what the informal penalties for lying were. He told of a Sarkhanese police sergeant who specialized in battering a single testicle to a pulp, of a police corporal who had maimed a common thief for life. He told these facts as if they were commonplace, ordinary, and well-known; and this gave them an awful authenticity.

"Now, Donald, you know the penalties of lying," Li said, quietly. "I have warned you. So tell me the truth. That's all . . . just the simple truth. When you have done that, you can go." His voice ended soothingly, but then changed into a commanding harsh tenor.

"You say you come from Moukung," Li went on. "That is in Western Szechwan province. Did you ever hear of Peng Teh-huai? Answer quickly, at once."

Donald hesitated and licked his lips.

"Yes, I have heard of him," Donald said.

"Did you march with Peng and his Communists to Shensi in 1934?" Li asked.

"No, I did not."

"Where were you in 1934? You have been to school. You speak with an educated accent. But you are the son of a pig peasant in Szechwan and there is nothing so poor as a pig peasant in that province. How did you get the money to go to school?" Li said, and his voice was heavy with loathing.

Donald flushed with anger.

"Even a pig peasant's son can go to school . . ." Donald began, but Li cut in sharply.

"If he is given money by the Communists to go through school?"

"I did not say that. I was trying to say . . ."

"You were trying to lie. You have told Ambassador MacWhite that you could not write, but already you confess that you went to school in Moukung."

Donald's eyes blinked, a quick involuntary tic of surprise.

Li abruptly changed the questioning and began to interrogate Donald about his family. He never allowed Donald to finish an answer. Whenever Donald hesitated, Li supplied the answer; and each of Li's answers damned Donald. Li insulted Donald and teased him about being a *interrogation*

Communist; then he suggested that any honest Chinese should properly be a Communist, interpreted Donald's silence as agreement, and attacked him on that. He ridiculed Donald's family ancestors, and threatened that Donald's children would be hounded to death by Chiang's agents. Donald's answers became more tense, more confusing, more protective. MacWhite had a first suspicion that part of what Li had concluded might be right.

Then abruptly Li looked terribly tired. He seemed to shrink in size, to become more harmless. His voice became pleading. He seemed to wish the interrogation were over.

"Help us all out, Donald," Li said quietly. "Tell us where the whiskey and wrist watch are. That's all we want. Then you can go."

Donald straightened, seemed to grow in strength as Li weakened. MacWhite felt his courage in Donald return. He felt a flash of admiration for the courage of the old man. Donald was even smiling slightly.

"I know nothing of the wrist watch or the whiskey," he said easily. "But I know that the typewriter and briefcase were not stolen. They are both in Ambassador Mac-White's study. I saw them there."

Li wheeled, as quick and sharp as a mongoose, as terrible as a tiger about to kill.

"Who said anything about a typewriter or briefcase, Donald?" he screamed. "Who? Where did you hear that?"

Donald's face was stricken.

"You heard that because I mentioned it in English to Ambassador MacWhite," Li said, and now he was speaking in English. "You understand English. And for months you have been overhearing what the ambassador says as you serve martinis and pick up trays and clear cigarette butts away." He put his face close to Donald's and his intensity was so awful, his presence so menacing, that Donald went rigid.

"Yes, I lied," Donald said in English. It was not flawless English, but it was English, and his voice held both horror and humiliation. "I did it only because the Communists hold my children in Moukung. They will kill them if I do not supply them with information."

"And you have told the Communists of Ambassador MacWhite's plans to smash them in Sarkhan," Li said, and this time it was not a question.

Donald nodded dumbly.

"You may leave the room, but do not leave the house," Li said. "We will want to talk to you later."

Donald left, and MacWhite watched him go. Mac-White knew that all of his careful work, his spending of millions of dollars, his cunning strategy, were all wasted. He knew that he, the Honorable Gilbert MacWhite, had made a terrible mistake. Somewhere in his carefully trained mind, in his rigorous background, in his missionary zeal, there was a flaw. It hit him very hard. Beneath the humility he had always, consciously, kept on the surface, and which he had always believed in, not only as a requirement of the social human, not only as a prerequisite of the receptive mind, but also as a reality of himself— beneath that humility there had been a rigid core of ego which had permitted him to place a fatal amount of faith in his own, unsupported judgment. He did not know where it was or how it got there or even how to remove it. But he knew that it was there, and he hated Li for showing it to him. But he was too tough-minded and analytical to remain stunned.

He looked up slowly. Li was standing in front of the window looking out over the beautiful countryside of Sarkhan, up at the snow white clouds of the Sarkhanese sky. Li swung around and faced MacWhite.

"I am sorry, Gilbert," he said softly. "It is not an easy thing to be cruel to an old man. Nor is it an easy thing to put doubts into a man as skilled and dedicated as you. But it was necessary. But necessary things are not always nice. This was very, very bad."

They were both standing there quietly, looking out over the landscape, when Molly came down the stairs in a simple, light blue, expensive dress from Saks Fifth Avenue, and gaily called for a martini.

◎

MacWhite had learned long ago that recriminations are a kind of luxury, and he never let himself afford such a pleasure. He knew he had made a mistake, and he knew that it was a mistake both of judgment and of information. For two days he sat quietly in his office, analyzing his errors of omission, the nature of his problem, and the alternatives open to him.

He recognized that he did not know enough about the Asian personality and the way it played politics. There was a strain of coldness, an element of finality, about the whole thing he had never encountered before. Politics in Asia were played for total stakes. He also recognized that he could learn from the experience of others.

The evening of the second day MacWhite sent a cable to the State Department.

*Request permission travel Philippines and Vietnam to study firsthand their handling internal Communist problem X Am convinced my fullest effectiveness hinges on broad knowledge Asian problems X Have already made one serious mistake and wish make no more X George Swift fully competent to serve in my absence X Have checked with Sarkhan Foreign Office and trip has their support X*

Twelve hours later the State Department replied that the proposed trips were approved.

The first person MacWhite saw in the Philippines was Ramon Magsaysay. As the Minister of Defense, Magsaysay had led the long and fatiguing battle against the Communist-dominated Huks in the Philippines. Later he led a unified government that efficiently ruled the huge archipelago.

Magsaysay and MacWhite talked long and earnestly, and MacWhite's notes on the conversation became the substance of a long (and well-ignored) report that was sent to the State Department. But there was one point which Magsaysay made that MacWhite did not have to put in writing, and never forgot.

"The simple fact is, Mr. Ambassador, that average Americans, in their natural state, if you will excuse the phrase, are the best ambassadors a country can have," Magsaysay said. "They are not suspicious, they are eager to share their skills, they are generous. But something happens to most Americans when they go abroad. Many of them are not average . . . they are second-raters. Many of them, against their own judgment, feel that they must live up to their commissaries and big cars and cocktail parties. But get an unaffected American, sir, and you have an asset. And if you get one, treasure him—keep him out of the cocktail circuit, away from bureaucrats, and let him work in his own way."

"Do you know any around?" MacWhite asked wryly. "I could use a few on my own staff."

"I do," Magsaysay said. "The Ragtime Kid—Colonel Hillandale. He can do anything. But I hope you don't steal him from here."

MacWhite noted the name.

"What else would you do if you were I?" MacWhite asked. "I'd go up to Vietnam and take a look at the fighting around Dien Bien Phu," Magsaysay said without hesitating. "I know you're a diplomat and that warfare is not supposed to be your game; but you'll discover soon enough out here that statesmanship, diplomacy, economics, and warfare just can't be separated from one another. And if you keep your eyes and ears open, you'll start to see some of the connections between them. It's not something you can learn from textbooks. It's a feel for the thing."

◎

# The Ragtime Kid

---

In the Air Force there is a man with the improbable name of Edwin B. Hillandale. The "B" stands for Barnum. Colonel Hillandale is one of those happy, uninhibited people who can dance and drink all night and then show up at eight fresh and rested. However, the Colonel seldom dances and drinks *all* night. About two in the morning he usually joins the orchestra in a jam session, playing his harmonica close to the mike, improvising Satchmo himself. When he plays with a good combo, it sounds like a concerto for jazz band and harmonica.

But jazz is not the colonel's only pleasure. He enjoys eating, and he loves to be with people. Any kind of people.

In 1952 Colonel Hillandale was sent to Manila as liaison officer to something or other. In a short time the Philippines fascinated him. He ate his meals in little Filipino restaurants, washing down huge quantities of *adobo* and *pancit* and rice with a brand of Filipino rum which cost two pesos a pint. He embraced everything Filipino—he even attended the University in his spare hours to study Tagalog.

Colonel Hillandale became Manila's own private character. The politicians and the eggheads fondly called him Don Edwin; the taxi drivers and the *balut* vendors and the waiters called him the *Americano Illustrado;* and the musicians referred to him as The Ragtime Kid. The counsellor up at the American Embassy always spoke of him as "that crazy bastard."

But within six months the crazy bastard was eating breakfast with Magsaysay, and he soon became Magsaysay's unofficial advisor.

In the summer of 1953, Magsaysay was campaigning for the presidential election. He barnstormed the Philippine Archipelago, and was greeted with enthusiasm everywhere he went. Everywhere—except in one province north of Manila. Here the Communist propagandists had done too good a job. The Reds had persuaded the populace that the wretched Americans were rich, bloated snobs, and that anyone who associated with them—as did Magsaysay—couldn't possibly understand the problems and the troubles of the Filipino.

The political experts predicted that Magsaysay would lose the province.

One Saturday Magsaysay's friend, Colonel Hillandale, went to this province. When he arrived in the capital about half-past eleven, the people of Cuenco saw something they had never in their lives seen before. A tall, slender U. S. Air Force Colonel with red hair and a big nose drove into Cuenco on a red motorcycle, whose gas tank had painted on it in black "The Ragtime Kid." He chugged up the main street and stopped at the most crowded part. He parked his cycle, and smoothed out his uniform; then he sauntered over near a large pool hall and sat down in the street—on the curb. After waving and smiling at everyone, he took out his harmonica and began to play favorite Filipino tunes in a loud and merry way; he played the first few stanzas in the classical manner, and the last two or three in a jazzed-up style. Within about fifteen minutes a crowd of about two hundred people surrounded the colonel. They enjoyed the music, but they were suspicious of this man who represented the richest of the rich Americans.

Colonel Hillandale began playing *Planting Rice Is Never Fun.* After going through a stanza he stopped, looked around at the crowd, and said in Tagalog, "Come on, join in." In a thin tenor he sang a few words; then, jamming the harmonica up to his mouth, he played as loud and sweet as he could. The crowd began to sing—about three hundred Filipinos standing in a tightly-packed circle singing their heads off, and pushing to get a look at this strange man.

At twelve o'clock the church bells sounded the Angelus. The Ragtime Kid put his harmonica in his pocket and stood up.

"Well, I sure am starving," he said. "I'd sure like some *adobo* and *pancit*."

The Filipinos looked at each other shyly.

The Ragtime Kid in colonel's uniform let his eyes go around the circle. "I'm hoping someone here will invite me to lunch. I'm broke."

"You don't have any money?" said one of the Filipinos.

The colonel put his hands in his pockets, dragged out his wallet, opened it, and showed that it was empty. He thrust his other hand into his side pocket and pulled out some change.

"Sixty centavos."

"But Americans are rich."

"Not me."

"You're fooling."

The colonel was still speaking in Tagalog, "We have poor people in America just like you have in the Philippines."

"But you're a colonel in the American Air Force. I know you get about two thousand pesos a month."

"That's right. And that's a lot of money. But I have big expenses. I have a wife and three children back in America. How much does a bottle of rum cost here?"

"Two pesos."

"In America it costs six pesos."

"Honest?"

"Yes. And how much rent do you pay a month for your house?"

"Forty pesos."

"Mine in America costs two hundred and forty pesos—and it's a very small house. I can't get any for less."

"It seems impossible."

The crowd stood silent. "This is undignified," said the colonel quietly. "Never before have I met Filipinos who would turn down a hungry man."

One of the Filipinos thrust through the crowd. "You will eat at my house!"

"No, come to my house."

"I own a restaurant on the corner; you will come with me."

And that's where the colonel went, with about ten Filipinos. They ate *adobo* and *pancit* and rice, and they washed it down with Filipino rum and San Miguel beer; and they sang many songs to the accompaniment of the Ragtime Kid's harmonica. And when lunch was through, the Filipinos invited him to come up again next Saturday, which he did. And the next Saturday after that. And the next Saturday after that, too.

And so, after a while, no one in the area believed any more that all Americans were rich and bloated snobs. After all, their Ragtime Kid who played sweet music on his mouth organ was one of them, and he was a colonel in the U. S. Air Force.

The Communists in the hills and the barrios objected; but the other Filipinos outshouted them. They said, "Do not tell us lies. We have met and seen and eaten and got drunk and made music with an American. And we like him."

And 95 per cent of the inhabitants of that province voted for President Magsaysay and his pro-American platform in the 1953 elections. Perhaps it wasn't the Ragtime Kid who swung them; but if that's too easy an answer, there is no other.

# 11

# The Iron of War

---

MAJOR JAMES (TEX) WOLCHEK—Born March 12, 1924, in Fort
Worth, Texas. Son of Mr. and Mrs. Solomon Wolchek.
Graduated Sam Houston High School, 1941. Enlisted United
States Army, 1942. PFC to Second Lieutenant in Paratroopers,
1st Division. Thirty-five practice drops at Fort Benning.
Broke left ankle twice. Three drops in combat during Nor-
mandy and Southern France invasions. Awarded Silver Star,
Purple Heart with cluster.
Regular Army after World War II. Assigned to Command
and General Staff College, 1947-50. Ordered to Korea in No-
vember, 1950. Platoon, Company Commander, Battalion Ex-
ecutive Officer. Awarded Purple Heart; Bronze Medal.
Permanent address: 11897 South Lane, Fort Worth, Texas.

"Major James Wolchek, United States Army, reporting
for duty as Observer with the 2d Regiment Amphibie,
Légion Étrangère," Major Wolchek said crisply.

He drew himself up sharply in front of the French officer sitting behind the desk and saluted. Major Monet was
a small man, and he was obviously tired. He looked up
from his desk, and examined Wolchek. Then Major
Monet smiled.

"Major, you look like what I have heard Texans call
'whang leather.' I hope that's not an insult; it's not intended so." Major Monet spoke excellent English.

Major Wolchek smiled. "Thank you, sir. I do happen
to be from Texas."

"And, of course, your nickname is 'Tex,'" Monet said.

Wolchek nodded. They smiled at one another for a brief second and then Monet began to go through a drawer, explaining that he had Wolchek's orders.

Tex stared out the open window while he waited. Monet's office was on the outskirts of Hanoi, and Tex could see the long columns of trucks, jeeps, and half-tracks moving out towards the lowlands where the Battle for the Delta was being fought. On both sides of the road, heading in the opposite direction, were lines of Vietnamese natives. They were fleeing to the city.

Tex smiled as he thought of Monet's use of "whang leather." Tex had heard the phrase applied to himself before, though never by a Frenchman. In a way, he thought, it was ironic that he should look so much like the imaginary Texan. His parents had come to Fort Worth from Lithuania two years before Tex was born; they were short, dark, and small-muscled people.

They had always dreamed of the American frontier; they found the American magic in Texas. Something about the sun and the food and the climate made their children grow tall and muscular, and all six of the Wolchek children were models of what Texans thought Texans looked like. Father Wolchek had invested his savings in Fort Worth real estate and had made a fortune. He no longer worked with a needle. He was openly proud of the fact that his oldest son was an officer and a fighter. And the knowledge of his family's love and support had helped Tex through many almost intolerable situations.

Tex's body held bits of the iron of two wars.

The first time he was hit had been in Normandy. He was one of the paratroopers who were dropped in the early darkness of D-Day behind the Normandy beaches. A German flare burst just over his parachute, and on the way down he caught seven machine gun slugs in his legs. By the time he hit the ground his boots were full of blood and he could no longer walk. But he could crawl; and in the next five hours he crawled three miles.

A disorganized platoon of Germans, retreating down a

small road, came upon a tall American leaning casually against a tree. The American was Tex. He had a confident look on his face and a carbine in his hands. He did not speak to the platoon—merely signaled for them to throw down their arms and put up their hands. The German officer attempted to bolt; but before he had gone three steps, Tex shot him. A half-hour later the German platoon realized that their captor was leaning against a tree because he couldn't use his legs, but by that time it was too late. Doctors later removed six of the slugs from his legs; the seventh they had to leave in because it was embedded in the bone. Tex received a Silver Star for this action.

He got his second wound on Pork Chop Hill in Korea, when he led a reinforced patrol over the parapets and into the misty ground between the American and Chinese lines. It was impossible to see, but Tex heard sounds of fighting. They had gone only 100 yards before he realized that the Chinese were launching a massive attack. He knew that his hilltop redoubt could not stand against so many men. He had no choice but to move ahead with his patrol and disrupt the attack. Tex led his patrol through the Chinese like a haymower through a fresh field. He cut through to the divisional headquarters' bunker of the Chinese lines, put it under a heavy grenade attack, and captured it. They killed every man in the bunker, including one general and two colonels; and they also killed 120 other Chinese. But a haymower cannot run backward, and Tex was unable to return with his patrol. They shattered the Chinese attack; but what was left of his patrol, including Tex, was captured.

Tex had two dozen needle-sharp pieces of grenade steel in his back. He administered morphine to himself, and politely asked permission from the Chinese officer in charge if one of his men could cut out the splinters. The American, who had been a butcher in civilian life, did a very efficient but not too delicate job. Consequently, Tex's back was marked by a fantastic tangle of scars. Several tiny bits of Chinese steel had been left in his flesh by the amateur surgeon. On extremely cold nights they felt like jagged chunks of ice, so that Tex had a frantic desire to scratch them out.

Tex escaped from a Communist aid station and returned to the American lines. His regimental commander had recommended Tex for the job of Observer with the French forces operating outside of Hanoi. Later, when the Korean fighting was still in the skirmish stage, Tex went to Vietnam.

The French major laughed, and Wolchek turned toward him.

"Tex, you must excuse me if I use your nickname from the very start," Monet said, "but this is a pretty informal situation, and we might just as well get used to it. Also, I have some bad news for you. Your orders attach you to my company and call for you to drop into Dien Bien Phu with us."

"What's wrong with that?" Tex asked.

"Although the newspapers don't know it, yesterday Dien Bien Phu was completely encircled. There was some talk of relieving it over land, but this has been abandoned as impossible. My company is going in by air drop the day after tomorrow. Even if our High Command would be willing to have a foreign observer drop with our troops, I'm sure that under the circumstances at Dien Bien Phu, you would prefer to remain here."

"Major," Tex said, "how many jumps have you made?"

Monet was busy with the papers, and he answered without looking up. "About two dozen."

"And how many have you made under enemy fire?"

"None. There has never been an opportunity."

"Major, I've made over a hundred practice jumps and I've jumped five times into enemy fire," Tex said softly. "Maybe you'll need an experienced hand along."

Monet looked up from his desk and his eyes went to Tex's upper left-hand breast pocket looking for the parachuter's insignia. There were no medals of any kind on the shirt. Over Monet's face there came an expression which Tex recognized as a look of humiliation. Monet looked down at his desk.

"I am very sorry," Monet said, his voice just barely under control. "There was no way of knowing. I would be very glad if you would jump with us; and I'll make sure that the notification to headquarters of your jump doesn't leave this office until our plane is in the air."

Tex and Monet spent the next two days together in Hanoi. In almost all ways they were opposites; but they did have an important thing in common—they both saw themselves as soldiers and as fighters. Monet came from a family in which there was always at least one son who was a graduate of St. Cyr; in the last three centuries there had been no war in which France had fought in which a Monet had not been a general. Monet was infinitely sophisticated in the art and literature of war. As the two of them went from bar to bar looking for bottles of Hennessey, and from one munitions dump to another gathering materials for their drop, Monet talked as a connoisseur on the history of war. Tex was enchanted. They argued about theory; and both of them worried about the drop into Dien Bien Phu.

On the second day Monet took Tex to visit his company of Foreign Legionnaires. The men were lined up for inspection. Tex understood at once that this was a professional outfit; and he also became aware that the men had an enormous respect for Monet. Like any good officer, he always saw that his men were fed and housed before he himself ate or slept; but more than that, the men had been through action with Monet and knew he was courageous and decisive.

Monet was the only French legionnaire. Among the men were middle-aged blonde soldiers who had been officers in Hitler's army. There were also Poles, Ukrainians, Russians, Argentinians, and even a few Britons. In the middle of one of the lines stood a tall, skinny Negro; and something about his face at once attracted Tex's attention.

He stopped and looked sharply at the man, then turned to Monet.

"Major Monet, I have the honor to inform you that among your troops is at least one American," Tex said in a sharp voice. "Maybe this man told you he was an African or something like that, but I can tell you right now that he's really an American."

The tall Negro smiled, but kept his lips firmly together. Tex knew at once that he was right.

"I wouldn't know, Major Wolchek," Monet said quickly, speaking formally in front of the men. "All I know is that this man is a very good soldier. There is a tradition in the Legion that we do not make inquiries about a man's background."

"Well, there's a tradition among Americans that they shake hands whenever they meet one another," Tex said.

He stuck his hand out toward the Negro, and for a tense moment the two men stared at one another. Then the Negro smiled, and his hand came out. While the rest of the Legionnaires stood at rigid attention, the two Americans spoke briefly and with enthusiasm. The soldier's name was Jim Davis, and he was from Los Angeles. He had gone to UCLA for three years, and had joined the Legion just to see what the excitement was all about. Tex knew at once that he was a man who, for the same reasons that drove Tex and Monet, wanted to be a soldier. They talked for perhaps two minutes. Then the French major moved, and instantly Davis snapped back to attention, saluted, and his face became immobile.

Tex and Monet continued their walk down the columns. Tex decided that it would be silly to tell Monet how he had recognized Davis was an American—that he had noticed that when Davis had heard Wolchek's Texas accent, the trace of an unfriendly smile had flitted across his face. Tex had stopped to make sure that the next smile would be friendly.

"Davis is a good man, Tex," Monet said when they were back at the CP. "He is superb on patrols. And the Vietnamese natives love him, despite their hate for our French North African troops. We have a couple of Viets permanently assigned to the regiment as guides, and Davis is the only man they'll make a night patrol with. He's never lost a Viet yet, and he always comes back with good intelligence."

The next morning the entire company drove in lorries to the airfield to load aboard the planes that would drop them over Dien Bien Phu. The moment they passed through the guard post, Tex knew that something had gone wrong. The guards were tense, officers were excited, too many planes were lined up on the hardtops, too many men were standing around. Tex said nothing to Monet, but he knew the French officer also sensed trouble.

A half-hour later Monet discovered what was wrong. He came walking back from the headquarters building, accompanied by a man who was wearing khakis, but who was obviously an American and a civilian. His face was ashen. The Legionnaires, who were sprawled under the lorries in the shade, took one look at him, scrambled to their feet, and even came to attention. Monet walked up to his group of men and came to a stiff attention.

"Last night," Monet said flatly, "Dien Bien Phu fell. There is no possibility of relief, and all radio communication has been cut off. It is the judgment of higher command, a judgment in which I concur, that we have completely lost the battle."

Tex felt admiration which was mixed with pity. Monet had guts. Most officers would have sugar-coated the pill. Also, Monet had the intelligence and integrity to identify himself with the melancholy news which had come down from higher command. Tex had learned that officers who dissociate themselves from higher commands are invariably poor officers.

Monet walked over to Tex and introduced the tall man.

"Major Wolchek, this is Gilbert MacWhite, the American Ambassador to Sarkhan," Monet said stiffly. Tex was aware of Monet's personal anguish. "Ambassador Mac-

White is on temporary duty from Sarkhan to see how Communists operate. He had managed to obtain a *laissez passer* from our officials, and was planning to go to Dien Bien Phu. Now he would like our views on why we lost the battle."

Tex looked sharply at the ambassador. He felt a quick flash of anger, and then realized it was groundless . . . there was no way for the man to know.

"Major," Tex said, "why don't you let me talk to the ambassador while you get the troops started back."

Monet flashed Tex a look of gratitude and spun on his heel. He started to bark out commands. The Legionnaires filed back into the lorries. One after another the lorries roared, and then crawled into the line of retreating vehicles.

"Mr. Ambassador, I understand your interest . . ." Tex began.

"Just call me MacWhite," the tall man said. His voice was crisp and assured.

"Okay, MacWhite. I'll tell you the truth. We don't know why the French are losing. Neither do they. But Monet is not the man to talk to. He's dying right on his feet from mortification."

"All right. I'm asking you, not him," MacWhite said. "What are we doing wrong?"

In the next few minutes, Tex discovered that Mac-White understood tactics and fighting. He asked tough questions and expected hard answers. They stood on the side of the road, in the midst of exhaust fumes and dust, talking strategy and tactics.

"There just isn't any simple answer," Tex finally said. "We're fighting a kind of war here that I never read about at Command and Staff College. Conventional weapons just don't work out here. Neither do conventional tactics."

"Well, why don't we start using unconventional tactics?" MacWhite asked. "Apparently, the Communists have some theory behind what they're doing."

"Armies change slowly, MacWhite," Tex said. "All our

tanks and planes and cannons aren't worth a damn out here. We need to fight the way they fight . . . but no one is quite sure how they fight."

From behind them came Monet's voice. "Well, we're going to find out in a hurry. The Communists will keep moving in on Hanoi; and we'll have plenty of chance to see them in operation."

"I'll stick around for a few weeks, then," MacWhite said. "Don't worry, Major Monet, I'll get the proper orders, and you won't have to be concerned about my safety."

'Why do you want to watch all this?" Monet asked.

"Because it may happen next in Sarkhan and I want to be ready for it," MacWhite said, simply.

For a long moment the three men stood quietly in the sea of dust, with the smell of defeat about them.

"All right, let's go," Monet said. "Tex, drive so we can overtake the lorries. We've already got orders to occupy a defensive position for tonight."

In the next few weeks the Communists seemed to come sweeping in from everywhere. The tangled, dirty, pathetic mass of refugees grew in Hanoi. Monet and his company of Legionnaires went slashing into the attack at least two dozen times. They would get a report that the Communists were moving up on a distant village. The company of Legionnaires would swoop into the village and take up a well-planned deployment around it. Tex, who had seen it done a hundred times, had no criticism of their communications, armament, or training. But always the deployment was a failure. And always it was a failure for one of two reasons. Either the Communists knew the defensive deployment made by the Legionnaires perfectly, and would shell them with horrible accuracy, or, even more horribly, would send squads of two or three men, armed only with knives, and hand grenades, into the individual foxholes. Or, the Communists would harass them from the rear with carbine and grenade fire. And the moment the Legionnaires turned to meet this fire, they would be fired on from another position.

The Legionnaires fought with enormous courage, and Monet used them with an incredible skill; but each time they lost. Over a period of several weeks, Tex had the experience of serving with a company of seasoned and experienced fighters under skilled leadership, who lost twenty villages to the enemy. But even more frustrating than constant defeat was the fact that at the end of three weeks of fighting, they had not once seen the enemy. The fire-fights always took place at night and were over by dawn; the enemy always slipped away, taking his dead with him; and the men felt they had participated in phantom engagements. The only thing that made it real were the dead Legionnaires.

Meanwhile, Hanoi had become a sick city. It was full of confusion and hunger and swept by fantastic rumors. The worst thing of all was the feeling of impending defeat which was shared by everyone—Vietnamese, French, and American.

One day, after three weeks of desperate, exhausting patrols and futile defenses, Tex had a long and relaxed afternoon with Monet and MacWhite. The Legionnaires had been given a rest period of two days; by the afternoon of the second day Monet had solved all his problems of supply, and was prepared to rest. Tex was cautiously and carefully beginning to talk to Monet about an idea he had had.

"Monet, have you ever had a nightmare and had the feeling that it was something you'd gone through before?" Tex asked. "When I was a kid I remember having a nightmare about leaving a range fence open and letting ten thousand cattle get loose. In the nightmare I sat stupidly and watched the cattle escape because somehow I had the impression that it had all been planned long before and that I was helpless."

Both Monet and MacWhite turned and looked with a puzzled air at Tex. They were sitting in a tiny bar, and had already finished two bottles of very strong cognac.

"Yes, I've had a sensation like that at times," Monet said. "For example, right now; I feel I'm living in a nightmare, but I don't know what the plan or the key to it is."

Tex was encouraged by Monet's words. "You're right—this has been one long goddam miserable nightmare. It's like trying to fight a mountain of syrup blindfolded. Look, Monet, you handle men well. You know how to deploy them and how to use fire power and how to run a real hot fire-fight. By all the rules of the classic western warfare you ought to be winning; but you're not. And I know why."

Monet was looking at Tex with dawning anger.

"It doesn't have a thing to do with the quality of the French fighting, or with your Legionnaires," Tex said quickly and carefully. "It's just that the Communists are fighting by a different rule book. And, like a damn fool, it's taken me almost a month to remember that I once read it. When I was in Korea, I picked up a book by Mao Tse-tung. Now, Monet, don't kid yourself about this. Mao is one hell of a bright guy. I hate what he stands for, but he does have a kind of genius."

"I've never read Mao's military writings," Monet said wearily. "But everything that can be written on war was already written long before him. Clausewitz and Jomini went over the whole thing. It's impossible to write anything new on war."

"Maybe Tex is right, Monet," MacWhite said slowly. "Mao is a clever man. I've read his political things. He's a Communist to his fingertips, and he's also a shrewd student of men. The kind of fight he made in China may have become the model by which all Asian Communists fight."

"I don't mean to be disrespectful, gentlemen, but I doubt very much that Mao has written anything new about war," Monet said.

Tex sighed. He understood that Monet did not want to be forced to learn a new kind of warfare.

"All right," Tex said, "maybe you're right. I haven't studied military history the way you have. Listen while I run over some of the ideas that Mao had in his book, and then tell me where he found them. First of all, take this thing of always finding some of the enemy in your rear. What Mao said to do is send a couple of agents ahead into any village in which the Communists conceivably might fight. If possible these agents should be men who come from that village. They settle down in the village and live like everyone else, except that they have a few sacks of hand grenades and a few burp guns which they keep hidden. While they're there, they line up the villagers who are sympathetic with them. If no one is sympathetic they put it on the line: fight with us or die. It's as simple and direct as that."

Monet was listening, and nodding occasionally.

"Monet, whenever the Legionnaires go into a village, there are already a half-dozen of the enemy behind them. These enemy don't wear uniforms; they don't even dig their weapons up until the critical moment has arrived. But can you imagine the advantage that just five or six people in their position give you in a fire-fight? Imagine if you could have a half-dozen of your own men, looking exactly like the Communists, operating back of their lines?"

"What else does Mao say?" Monet asked. He took a cigarette from a pack and lit it.

For eight hours and a bottle and a half of cognac, they discussed Mao's military strategy and tactics. Both Tex and MacWhite felt that Monet was several times at the point of admitting that they should try Mao's tactics. But he always stiffened and fell back on arguments about Clausewitz and "centers of defense" and "liquid offensives," even though his tone of voice showed he did not fully believe them. Finally he stared at them, his face pale.

"That's enough, gentlemen," he said in a soft voice. "Even if you're right we don't have time to change our tactics. We're losing too fast." He stared down into the glass of cognac and spoke in a voice that was almost inaudible. "Imagine a nation which produced Napoleon, Foch, and Lyautey being beaten by so primitive an enemy."

"But, Monet, don't be a fool . . ." Tex began.

"He's right, Tex," Mac White said sharply. "We've talked enough."

Tex wheeled on MacWhite, and then paused. MacWhite's face was full of warning. Tex realized MacWhite was right. At that moment, Monet was beyond convincing.

Ten minutes later a runner came in with a message for Monet. The final stage in the defense of Hanoi was beginning. Out in the hill country and plains behind Hanoi thousands of Communists were slipping over paddies, around rocks, down ravines. For Monet and Tex and Mac-White and the Legionnaires the next three weeks were unmitigated hell. Monet tried to send MacWhite back, but he wouldn't go. The Legionnaires lacked munitions, food, and reinforcements; and most of all they lacked sleep. Their eyes were redrimmed and tender, and their tempers were drawn thin. They suffered fifty per cent casualties, and then the survivors again suffered fifty per cent casualties. They fought in the thick brown mud around the paddies; when a man was hit he simply slid under and disappeared forever. Mud-clogged rifles ceased to function, and there was never an adequate base on which to mount a mortar. The least ill of the men had dysentery; it was a shared minimum affliction. Some of the men had fever, some hookworm, and some had huge horny scabs on their arms. There was never enough to eat, and they had long ago given up trying to purify their water. They simply drank whatever water was available, and accepted the agonizing cramps.

Both Monet and Tex were injured. Monet had taken a burp gun bullet in his left elbow; after the bones had been set, he continued to command the company. Tex was hit by hand-grenade fragments in the buttocks; with a sigh he told the French corpsman not to bother taking a probe to him. Tex now had the iron of three wars in his body and in some dim way he knew he had expected to all along.

One day Monet changed his mind about using Com-

munist tactics. He changed his mind because the Viet
Communists played a trick. It was not much of a trick.
Things like it had happened before and would happen
again, and it was, Monet knew, a trick that the French
were not above using. But this was the first time it had
ever happened to Monet's men.

Jim Davis and a Viet the Legionnaires had nicknamed
Apache had been sent out to patrol the area in front of a
small village the Legionnaires were defending. They left
at dusk and were to return at dawn. They carried only
burp guns and a signal flare gun.

They returned at dawn, but without their weapons,
crawling up to the edge of the first CP on their bellies.
MacWhite, Tex, and Monet saw them suddenly stand up
and start to walk into the village. Mud dripped from their
clothes, and there was something about their huddled
posture which indicated that something had happened.
The three men walked out to meet them.

Davis was leading Apache. From fifty yards they could
see that there was a gout of blood on Davis's cheek. At
twenty-five yards they could see the mangled remains of
his left eye, hanging in a cluster of tiny glistening cords
and muscles. The dead eye hung level with Davis's nose,
and seemed to be staring at the ground. His right eye was
firm and brilliant in his black face, and was burning with
rage.

"What happened, Davis?" Monet asked.

"They caught us, Major," Davis said, and his voice was
low and cool. "There has to be a first time for everything
and this time they caught us. They let us go, but first they
had to play a trick. Part of the trick was gouging out my
eye."

"What did they do to you, Apache?" Monet asked
quickly in Vietnamese.

Apache's eyes were glazed and almost shut, narrowed
into slits of purest agony. He opened his mouth, wet his
lips with his tongue, and made a sound which came out a
subhuman, mutilated, horrible twisted moan.

"Shut up, Apache," Davis screamed, and the sound trailed off and stopped.

Davis reached over and pulled Apache's hand away from his throat. Squarely in the center of his throat there was a twisted hole. Far back in the hole the muscles and cords of his neck glistened. Blood welled out of the bottom of the jagged wound.

"They cut away his vocal cords," Monet said. His voice was almost casual. "It's a treatment they save for Viets who help the French."

"They left my right eye so that we could find our way back and show ourselves as a lesson to others," Davis said. His good eye rolled slowly back in his head, and he pitched forward in a faint. Monet caught him, twisted him around, and laid him on his back.

"Tex, send for a corpsman," Monet said softly. "And then you and MacWhite join me in the CP. We're going to fight tonight using Mao's tactics against his own people. I'm convinced."

# 12

# The Lessons of War

The next day MacWhite went back to Hanoi to look for a copy of the booklet on war by Mao Tse-tung, and Monet ordered the Legionnaires to relax. They bivouacked in a dirty little group of tents; the Legionnaires, without taking off their clothes, dropped in the shade of the ragged tents and slept like men who hoped never to awaken again.

Late that afternoon MacWhite returned with the Mao pamphlet. His method of procuring it had been simple: he had stopped at the first newsstand he saw and asked the proprietor to get him a copy. The proprietor, obviously alarmed, said that he knew nothing of works by Mao. MacWhite did not argue with him. He merely said that if the pamphlet were delivered in two hours he would pay the sum of 800 piasters, and no questions asked. Within an hour he had the pamphlet.

The three of them gathered in Monet's tent and Mac-White read aloud for an hour and a half. Neither Mac-White nor Tex looked at Monet during this session. The words in the pamphlet destroyed a way of life and a tradition in which Monet believed deeply. Monet did not stir during the reading. He sat with his hands together in his lap as if by holding himself together physically he could compensate for the destruction of part of his world.

When MacWhite had finished there was a long silence.

"On the whole, Mao is right and we have been wrong," Monet said in a steady voice. "Please, let's not talk any more about our traditions. Let us talk about what part of Mao's writings we can use to our advantage."

"Most of what Mao recommends is too long-range for us to use," MacWhite said. "It's the kind of thing you have to accomplish over years. For example, when he recommends sending political organizers ahead of the army, he is talking in terms of years. These organizers never announce that they're Communists; they just keep putting the views of the Communists before the villagers. Then when the fighting starts they organize resistance behind the enemy lines and disrupt as much as possible."

"That explains why we keep getting fire from both the front and rear whenever we have a night fire-fight," Tex said.

"Also it explains why they always have perfect intelligence on the village which we are attempting to defend," Monet added.

"Forgive me for giving an opinion in your area, gentlemen," MacWhite said. "I suggest we forget everything that's going to take a year to accomplish. We have only a few days. Later and in another country perhaps we can use Mao's strategy. Right now we have to concentrate on his tactics."

For hours they argued over the pamphlet. Night came, they ate a cold meal from packaged rations, crawled under the mosquito nets, and continued their discussion until dawn. From the dozens of ideas which Mao had suggested, they took two.

In rough terrain, Mao said, retreat and disappear until the enemy is strung out in pursuit. Then concentrate on one weak point. Time, space, and retreat are the instruments of combat victors. When fighting an enemy who has superior equipment and numbers, success lies in mobility and the use of darkness.

The second idea involved guerilla warfare. Mao suggested that in a sustained guerilla action, the groups of guerillas can only be successful if they have a rigid and completely centralized command. The central command post directing guerillas in operation should never be further from the actual fighting than a man can trot in a half hour.

Monet said, "It's obvious—even though we've never used it."

MacWhite put down the pamphlet. He grinned at Monet and Tex, and they began to smooth a large detailed map of the Hanoi Plain out on the table.

The village they decided they were looking for was located in the midst of a swamp of paddies; two miles beyond it was a large area of firm ground on which stood a clump of bamboo trees. Both Monet and Tex nodded when they saw it. Any field commander would be insane to choose any spot for a command post other than the bamboo trees. A hardtop road ran like an arrow from the trees directly through the village. And, best of all, just before the village was a small hill behind which the reserve troops could be hidden.

"All right, gentlemen, that village will be it," Monet said decisively. His eyes were excited. "Three days from today we'll try to cure our illness with the hair of the dog that bit us."

It was Tex who suggested the surprise weapon. He had seen it used once in Korea with great success. It was quite simple. The bed of a large truck was covered with a thick layer of sheet iron to which were fastened the barrels of twenty 5-inch rocket launchers arranged so that when the rockets were fired simultaneously they all fell in a circle roughly a hundred yards in diameter. Tex assured the other two men that there was very little chance that anyone would remain alive inside the circle.

On the fourth day they made the move up towards the village. For the first time in weeks the Legionnaires were laughing and joking. Monet left with an advance guard of two lorries of men. A half-hour later MacWhite and Tex set out with the main body of troops. Tex rode on the rocket truck and was in radio communication with Monet. MacWhite was riding in a jeep directly behind the rocket truck.

As dusk fell, the main body moved off the highway on to a road that cut across the paddy fields. Tex called Monet on the radio to make sure he had reached his position. Monet's voice came in clearly.

"We're deployed to the south of the village," he reported. "Two Viets left the village a half-hour after we set up positions. They were walking north, but I'd guess they've circled back and are heading for the bamboo grove. It should be another hour before anything happens."

The main body of lorries proceeded as quietly as possible. Tex deployed them in a long line behind the hummock which separated them from the village, and they sat down to wait.

Almost an hour later they heard thin far-away rifle fire, followed by the chatter of a heavy machine gun. Monet's voice came up on the radio.

"I think they've fallen for the bait. They probably think we're weak, and they're moving the troops directly down the hardtop road from the bamboo grove. Just the first patrols have hit so far. They haven't used machine guns yet, although we've opened up with our 50-calibres. Take a weapons carrier with a quadruple 50-calibre machine gun mount on it, and cut your way through the troops on the road. Then make straight for the command post."

"We're on our way," Tex said, and clicked the receiver off.

Moving fast, Tex ordered the quadruple mount 50-calibre vehicle to the head of the column. Directly behind it was a lorry of riflemen. Third in line was the rocket truck.

"Leave your lights off until the machine gun fires," Tex ordered softly. "Then open up with everything you've got. As soon as the rockets fire, get the quadruple mount turned around for the run back on the road. If we have to leave any vehicle we'll leave the rocket truck, so I don't want any men on it after it fires."

They came around the hill as quietly as a column of vehicles can move. At fifty-yard intervals Monet's men were marking the right-hand shoulder of the road with shielded flashlights. The column did not reduce speed when it reached the village, but ground steadily past the tiny thatched houses.

Suddenly they were out of the village and on the plain. Tex was sitting beside the driver of the quadruple mount vehicle, peering ahead. He saw a blur of frantic motion on the road, leaned back, and calmly ordered the machine gunner to fire straight down the road.

The quadruple mount went off with an enormous racket; four streams of tracer rows poured ahead. At the same moment Tex switched on the carrier's lights. Fifty yards in front of them were a group of about fifty Viet-minh troops. They froze, as if bewildered by the light; then, in a collective rush, they headed for the right-hand side of the road. The machine gun swung with them and the bullets hit. Clots of mud, shreds of uniform, and broken bits of rifles exploded into the air. The bodies of the men pitched off the road into the ditch. Although the vehicle was moving fast, and took no more than seconds to close the gap, the action was like a brilliantly-illuminated nightmare in slow motion. Then the wheels of the vehicle bumped over the bodies of three men who had fallen on the road, and they were past the enemy group. A moment later Tex heard the rifles on the lorry begin to open up.

The machine gun clicked off above his head. Tex left the lights on, and they roared down the narrow road. He had only two things in his mind. First, he was praying that the road would support the weight of the column. Secondly, he was calculating exactly when the rocket truck would be 500 yards from the grove of bamboo trees. The night before he had measured the distance at which head-lights would first pick up bamboo trees in total darkness.

It measured out at 600 yards. If he drove at twenty miles an hour for fifteen seconds after the headlights picked up the bamboo trees, the rocket truck should be 500 yards from the grove. At that moment the headlight touched the white and green stalks of a mass of bamboo trees.

"One, two, three, four five . . ." Tex counted aloud.

At ten, he stood up, and at fifteen gave the signal to the rocket carrier. Two things happened almost instantly. The truck came to a shrieking halt—and while it was still moving slightly, the rockets let go. For a second the entire truck looked as if it were on fire, and the hissing sound was deafening. Then came a cleaner sound from the zip of rockets cutting through the air. Two seconds later they hit. There were flashes of light among the bamboo trees— and then, in one great yellow patch of fire, the grove exploded. For several seconds the cone of flame hung over the grove, and in it the bodies of half-a-dozen men turned like puppets. Then the light disappeared, and there was the vast harsh sound of things returning to earth.

"All right, dammit, let's get this carrier turned around," Tex shouted.

The driver backed and filled in quick, desperate jerks. In less than a minute he was edging around the rocket truck to get back to the road.

"There's no need to abandon the truck," Tex said to the driver of the rocket truck as they passed. "Back it down the road with your lights off. You'll be able to see where you're going from our rear lights. When you get to the village you can swing around and drive out."

They rumbled heavily back down the road. The fire-fight around the village had stopped completely. Later Monet told Tex that when the grove exploded, the Viet Minhs had instantly stopped firing and had scattered.

They paused in the village only long enough to pick up the advance guard; and then the entire group headed back toward Hanoi.

"I never heard such damn nonsense in my entire life," the American major general said harshly to Tex. "First you violate the rules of war by engaging in combat when you're supposed to be a neutral observer. And then you have the gall to come in here and tell a bunch of experienced general officers how to run their war."

Tex, MacWhite, and Monet were seated in three chairs at one end of a large conference table in a room on the third floor of the Citadel in Hanoi. At the other end of the table were two French admirals, four French generals, and the American who had just spoken.

"General, I was not personally engaged in combat," Tex answered quietly. "All I did was ride along in the carrier. I didn't touch a weapon. I didn't fire a shot. What I was doing is permissible under the rules which govern the conduct of neutral observers."

"Now look here, Wolchek, don't try to play cute with me," the general said, his voice rising. "Don't try and tell me that some Frenchman dreamed up that idea of the rocket truck. I've been around here . . ."

The senior French general cut in with a chill voice.

"General, we are not interested in the problem of the neutrality of your observer. What interests us more is this fantastic suggestion made by Major Monet and Ambassador MacWhite that the French army revise its operations in accord with the military writings of a Communist bandit."

"General, as you know I was the one who requested this session," Gilbert MacWhite said calmly. "Since December of 1946 the French have been fighting a war which has been maneuvered by the Communists precisely along the lines which Mao outlined in this pamphlet. You are a military man—you will please excuse my bluntness—but you made every mistake Mao wanted you to. You ignored his every lesson for fighting on this type of terrain. You neglected to get the political and economic cooperation of the Vietnamese, even though Mao proved long ago that Asians will not fight otherwise. Gentlemen, I have one simple—and possibly embarrassing—question. Has any of you ever read the writings of Mao Tse-tung?"

There was a moment of silence. The senior French

general, a man of wisdom and excellent connections, turned slightly red. The other French generals blanched. MacWhite leaned forward in his chair waiting for an answer.

"If you are suggesting, Ambassador MacWhite, that the nation which produced Napoleon now has to go to a primitive Chinese for military instruction, I can tell you that you are not only making a mistake, you're being insulting," the senior French general finally said.

"That's not what I said," MacWhite answered. "I asked if any of you had read Mao?"

"Hell no, they haven't read him," the American shouted. "And neither have I."

And he bit his lips as if he were keeping himself from saying more. MacWhite knew that only his personal fortune and his political connections were keeping the general from ordering him out of Hanoi under armed guard.

MacWhite shrugged. "Apparently you gentlemen refuse to use your own eyes and ears."

Monet pushed back his chair and stood up. He was pale and his hands were trembling.

"Gentlemen, I am entirely responsible for the operation which we have just described to you," Monet said in a steady voice. "It contradicts everything that I was taught at St. Cyr and everything that this American general was taught at West Point. But it worked. I tell you, it worked. If I had the opportunity, I would multiply this operation a thousand times. In the months of fighting in Vietnam, it is the only complete victory I have commanded. Multiplied a thousand times it might give us a total strategic victory rather than an unimportant tactical success. If anyone is to be punished, it should be me. But, I beg of you, do not ask me to change my mind on something that my own eyes and my own experience teach me is what should be done."

After that there was nothing to be said, and a nod from the senior French general dismissed the three of them. MacWhite, Monet, and Wolchek left, and without a word headed for the nearest bar. There they paid an outrageous price for two bottles of superior French cognac, and drank in silence. When they had finished the first bottle, MacWhite picked it up by its long narrow neck and with a single blow smashed it on the edge of the table. Then he grinned.

"I just felt like doing it," he said. "Gentlemen, don't worry about disciplinary action. Nothing is going to happen to you. We have stupid men on our side and we have proud men on our side; but they would never be allowed to punish you for simply saying that it is possible to learn from an enemy."

A short time after the French evacuated Hanoi. After months of battle, the consumption of mountains of supplies, and the loss of far too many lives, the French had finally been forced into an armistice with the Viet Minhs. In the armistice they agreed to turn over the city of Hanoi to the victorious Communist army.

MacWhite, Tex and Monet were there to see it. The French departed as if they were leaving town for a magnificent and colorful parade assembly. Fifes whistled, drums ruffled, and air was cut by sharp and ancient commands. The uniforms of the Legion were neat and well-pressed, their high paratroop boots were beautifully shined. They marched in straight smart lines through the almost empty streets of Hanoi. The inhabitants of Hanoi looked at the magnificent parade with astonishment. So did Monet, MacWhite, and Tex. This was the parade of a victorious army.

Behind the parading troops were lines of huge, fast tanks; then columns of self-propelled guns, countless trucks filled with squads of men carrying the latest type of American rifles. Overhead an almost endless stream of French planes performed a fly-by.

"It's a beautiful sight to see," Tex said with admiration.

"It's beautiful, and it's utterly senseless," Monet said. "No one bothered to tell the tankers that their tanks couldn't operate in endless mud. And those recoilless rifles never found an enemy disposition big enough to warrant shooting at it with them."

When the parade ended, the French tricolor was hauled down from buildings and installations all over the city. The last truck swung around the corner. The square where the three of them stood was silent. No one was in the streets; and both shutters and doors were locked tight.

The Communist vanguard were well-dressed and smart looking troops in Russian trucks. They then saw the first regular Communist soldier arrive—an officer on a wobbling bicycle, wearing a padded suit, tennis shoes, and a tiny forage hat. He had a rifle slung over his shoulder. Trotting behind him came a platoon of men dressed in a mixture of uniforms. Some merely wore breech-cloths and what looked like captured French blouses. Many of them were barefooted. Perhaps half of them had rifles; but almost all of them had a string of crude hand-grenades tied around their waists. Each of them also carried a rice-bag over his shoulder.

"Look carefully, Tex, and tell me if you see what I see," Monet said in astonishment. "Three of those men are carrying guns made from pipes."

It was true. Three of the men were actually carrying nothing but home-made rifles. Tex had the feeling that he was looking at people who were fighting a war that should have taken place three hundred years before. These men traveled on foot and carried their total supplies on their backs. They looked harmless and innocent, indeed they almost looked comical. But these were the men whom he and Monet had been fighting for months, and whom they had defeated only once.

The officer on the bicycle held up his hand. The line of men paused, and then, as fast as the slithering of lizards, they disappeared into doorways and gutters. The street seemed empty except for the officer. Monet shouted to the officer in Vietnamese that they were a rear guard, and were leaving at once. The officer smiled and waved his hand. He shouted something, and at once his men appeared from nowhere and began to move cautiously down the street. Tex was aware that around all of Hanoi a huge, silent, and featureless army of men, each of them no more impressive than these, were oozing into the city which they had conquered. There was no point in staying longer. Far off in the distance they heard the sound of the retreating French Army.

"All right, let's go," Tex said harshly. "It's the end of another round, and we've lost again."

# 13

# What Would You Do
# If You Were President?

U Maung Swe probably is the best known journalist in
Burma, if not in all Southeast Asia. His name is mentioned
wherever the world press is a subject for discussion.

U Maung Swe is a college graduate who has spent considerable time in the United States. He speaks the American idiom. He is a Roman Catholic. During World War
II he was a member of the O. S. S. and fought beside
Americans in Northern Burma and Southern China. He
is an anti-Communist.

In 1954, at a dinner party in Rangoon in honor of Ambassador MacWhite, someone said to U Maung Swe,
"British prestige certainly is low in Southeast Asia. What
about America?"

U Maung Swe said, "Poor America. It took the British
a hundred years to lose their prestige in Asia. America
has managed to lose hers in ten years. And there was no
need for it. In fact, she could get it all back in two years, if
she wanted to." In the discussion which followed, U
Maung Swe answered these questions:

*What in general has caused America's loss of prestige?*
The Americans I knew in the United States were won-
derfully friendly, unassuming, and interested in the world.

122

No one who has ever visited America and come to know the country could fail to trust and respect her people.

For some reason, however, the Americans I meet in my country are not the same as the ones I knew in the United States. A mysterious change seems to come over Americans when they go to a foreign land. They isolate themselves socially. They live pretentiously. They're loud and ostentatious. Perhaps they're frightened and defensive; or maybe they're not properly trained and make mistakes out of ignorance.

I've been to Russia, too. On the whole, I have small regard for the Russians as a people. But individual Russians I meet in Burma make an excellent impression. One does not notice them on the street too often. They have been taught our local sensitivities, and usually manage to avoid abusing them. And they all speak and read our language and have no need for Burmese interpreters, translators, and servants; so no Burman sees their feet of clay.

*Can you be a little more specific on some of the things which Americans do which annoy the Burmans?*

Yes. Frankly, for quite a while before we finally refused any further aid from you, none of us enjoyed the way your economic people in Burma conducted their daily lives. Almost all of them arrived with the apparent impression that they had full ambassadorial rank—all chiefs and no indians, as you say. Even clerks acted as if they were chiefs of mission. The wages of servants, the rentals of houses, rose to fantastic prices; and your privates lived better than our generals, so to speak. That hurt our pride.

All we saw was tinsel. A few years ago we heard a lot of talk about how the United States aid was going to help Burma. Hordes of United States press agents—all on the government payroll—swarmed to Rangoon to shout from the housetops about what a wonderful thing United

States aid was for Burma. Maybe there was lots of aid: but the people never saw it; and a few of the things in which the press agents rubbed our noses didn't pan out well.

*Can you remember any examples?*

I remember a few years ago there was a lot of fanfare over a three-quarter of a million dollar dredge the United States was bringing to Burma. This mobile floating dredge, the press agents shouted, would be a great boon for Burma. It was going to dredge rivers so that transportation and trade could flourish in inland areas which had never been within reach of markets before.

This was something the country really needed, and we were delighted at the prospect. Middle-class farmers upstream hoped to have an outlet for their produce; boat builders were instructed to draw plans for deeper-draught boats which could carry greater loads.

Finally the day came when the dredge was to be delivered. The Prime Minister himself was persuaded by the Americans to come to see its arrival. The local press sent reporters and photographers. USIS came down with tape recorders so that the event could be broadcast on the radio.

Well, when the dredge was towed into the harbor it turned out to be a 25-year-old, reconditioned British dredge which had been rusting in Japan. It was a stationary dredge, which needed land connections. This was disappointment enough; but to cap it all off, the American experts who came with the dredge were unable to get it to work. They even flew some Japanese experts in, but they couldn't get it to run either. Everyone involved lost face. Experiences like this made many Burmans doubt the effectiveness of U. S. aid.

*In 1953 Burma was in critical need of money and technical assistance. Yet you terminated all United States aid. Why did you do this?*

In the first place we were offended by the superior airs and what even Americans called the "razzle-dazzle" of the Americans in Burma. Secondly, there were several incidents like that of the dredge; and although American money was flowing into Burma, we couldn't see that it was helping us very much. And, third, we became very angry over the KMT incident. It all added up to more than Burma was willing to swallow just to get dollars.

*What was the KMT incident?*

When the Chinese Reds defeated the Nationalists in 1947, about 10,000 of Chiang Kai-shek's troops fled from China into Burma, and remained in the northwest part of our country. We were a new nation then, and had so many troubles that we were unable to do much about these alien troops in our territory. The Chinese Nationalist troops were living off the land; and troops who live off the land in a foreign country have to get money one way or another. These men started trading in opium, and sometimes turned to banditry. In 1952 Chiang Kai-shek began supplying them by air. I can understand his point of view—he was trying to harass the Chinese Communists. Nonetheless, his troops had no right to be in our country. Then we learned that they were wearing United States uniforms and using United States equipment. I know that the United States was not supplying them; Chiang Kai-shek was.

Burma wanted to bring the matter up before the United Nations, and America agreed—provided that the troops were not identified as Chinese Nationalists and that no mention was made of the American uniforms. And yet, everybody in Southeast Asia knew about it. Everybody knew about it except the American people. They were never told.

When we said that we didn't see why the countries involved shouldn't be named, it was hinted that if they were named, perhaps U. S. aid would be cut off.

That was all we had to hear. Even though we were

desperate for economic and technical assistance, we told the Americans to take their aid and go away. It was a matter of pride—face, as we Asians call it. Face, incidentally, is an element of our life superbly well understood by the Russians.

*Would you welcome United States economic and technical assistance now?*

Yes. I suggest that technical aid be administered the way the Ford Foundation did it in Indonesia. The Ford people noticed that when they brought their own automobiles to Indonesia, they always had to go to a Dutch garage to have them overhauled. The Indonesians didn't know how to repair cars. When the Ford Foundation later brought a group of Indonesians to the United States, instead of telling the Indonesians what they should study or what kind of equipment they ought to spend their money on, they told the Indonesians to look around and pick out what they felt they needed. The first batch of Indonesians pointed to a garage and said that was what they wanted. A replica of the garage was set up in Indonesia, and American mechanics worked side by side with the Indonesians until the Indonesians were able to operate the equipment and overhaul automobiles by themselves. Then the American technicians went home. That is the kind of help we want.

*If you were the President of the United States what would you do to improve the prestige of the United States in Southeast Asia?*

Let me tell you a story. Some years ago two Americans —a married couple named Martin—came to Burma as short-term advisors. They were quiet people about whom nobody seemed to know much, and they quietly went up north to the Shan States, which are pretty wild. They brought no pamphlets, brochures, movies, or any of the other press-agent devices which are so offensive to most of us and on which most Americans rely. They had no automobile and no servants. They just moved into a small town and settled down in a modest house and began living there.

Since the Martins spoke Burmese—a most unusual accomplishment for Americans in Burma—Burmans began stopping in at their house and talking with them. These visitors to the Martins' house were amazed at two things. One was the tremendous size of the vegetables they were growing in their garden; and the second was the size of the garden itself. They wanted to know what two people were going to do with such an enormous amount of food. Surely they couldn't eat it all—and the rest would spoil.

Mrs. Martin took them into the kitchen and showed them a small home canning outfit. The Burmans had never seen anything like it, and didn't know what it was. They came around day after day to watch fruit and vegetables being canned. And then, as the months passed by, the Burmans saw that when the cans were opened the vegetables were still edible.

These two Americans distributed high-quality seeds to all of the townspeople and helped them organize a community canning plan. The people of the village still do most of the growing individually, and a good deal of the canning is done at home; but now they not only put up things for their own use, but for all of Burma. This village is the canning center of the nation, and processes meat, vegetables, and many favorite Burmese foods.

In this section of the Shan States everyone is pro-American because of the Martins. They came to Burma to help us, not to improve their own standard of living.

You don't need publicity if the results of what you are doing are visible and are valuable to the people. The steam from a pot of good soup is its best advertisement.

You asked me what I would do if I were the President of the United States. This is what I would do: I would send more people like the Martins to Burma. That's all you'd need. You could forget about the hordes of executives, PX's, commissaries, and service forces which are now needed to support the Americans abroad. And then, of course, you could save many of the millions of dollars Americans seem to think essential to any aid program.

*You implied earlier that the Russians who went abroad seemed to operate effectively. Can you explain why this is?*

The Russians are professionals. They keep many of their men in Burma for as long as five years. They all know Burmese. They study quietly and live quietly. They employ no Burmese servants, and hence there is nobody to spread gossip about them. All their servants are Russian.

The Russian Ambassador is their social lion. He's the one who attends the cocktail parties. But that's about all he does. The Russian team always has a professional expert who not only knows the area thoroughly, but also has authority. Here in Burma it was a man named Victor Lassiovsky. He had some minor title—I believe it was second secretary. He always opened the door for the Ambassador and walked behind him. He didn't waste much time at parties. He was the real tactical leader of the Russian task force, and he ran the entire Burmese effort for Russia. Lassiovsky was recently transferred to Thailand. I predict that America will be having trouble there soon.

*Is Russian economic aid better than that of the United States?*

No, it is not. But it is much more obvious, and so more effective as propaganda. For example, our Prime Minister flies in a Russian transport plane—a gift from Stalin. This gift made a deep impression not only on the Burmans, but on all Southeast Asians.

The Russians have promised to build us a sports stadium —you know we're all sports crazy—and also a hospital and a graduate school for engineers and doctors. We don't have them yet. But these are projects which the people understand and would like to have. And even though we are all suspicious of the Russians and the Chinese Communists, still, both the man in the street and the young intellectuals discuss what the Russians are doing.

Also, the Communists are extremely skillful in their cultural projects. The Tenth Anniversary of our independence was a tremendous celebration. You could compare it to Christmas, New Years, Easter, the Fourth of July, and Purim, all rolled into one. We had great parades. All the Communist nations participated in these parades with floats, acrobats, and folk dancers. They carried big banners congratulating us on our independence from colonialism. There were no marchers from the United States.

If any of you Americans ever left Rangoon and went up-country, you would see that there are Russian circuses and Chinese entertainers everywhere. True, you send some stars like Benny Goodman, and some opera singers, and they're very welcome—but they play only in Rangoon and only a few of the élite get to see them. Oh yes, I forgot, you also had a cut glass exhibit. We're a nation fighting for survival, and you send us a cut glass exhibit.

I hope I've answered your questions. I'll finish by saying that what America needs in Asia is good, well-trained, and dedicated Americans. They *must* be well-trained and dedicated. The subordinates can be mediocre, but the leaders must be top-notch, with the ability to make their subordinates fit in with Burmese culture, community habits, and needs.

I've known almost every American ambassador, military leader, top economic advisor, and USIS man sent to Southeast Asia in the last ten years. This includes both career people and amateurs. I can recall only two ambassadors, one USIS leader, and one admiral who were trained and dedicated professionals. Ninety per cent of the Russian executives are professionals—no matter what else they may be. You're bound to lose in competition with them until you learn from them.

And yet, I believe firmly that the Americans could drive the Communists out of Asia in a few years if you really tried and were willing to live out here on our level. And if you had a definite policy. But most important—act like Americans. We love Americans—the kind we meet in America.

When the dinner party was over U Maung Swe and Gilbert MacWhite went for a walk. It was one of those soft nights when every sound carries a great distance and the perfume of flowers comes floating in from the jungle.

"What about Sarkhan, Maung?" MacWhite asked. "What should I do?"

"About what?"

"About anything, big or little."

Maung paused for a moment. The breeze brought the sound of distant gongs.

"Gilbert, I heard once of an American who was working on a powdered milk plant in Sarkhan," Maung said. "He planned to develop a taste for milk in the Sarkhanese, and then bring in dairy cattle and set up the business on a sound, self-supporting basis. No concession for foreigners. The whole thing simple and easy to run."

"I remember reading about him in reports," MacWhite said. "He got caught in a scandal. Rape or drugging girls. Something like that."

"Gilbert, those were lies. I never met the man, but I took the trouble to find out the truth of his story. The Communists framed him. He spoke Sarkhanese, he was dedicated, and the people liked him. His idea was sound. His name is Colvin; I think if you brought him back he would do a job for you."

"I'll do it, if I can get him cleared," MacWhite said.

"They're little things, perhaps, but ideas like Colvin's are basic. When we've licked the basic problems, we can move on to grander projects. But we have to start with the little things which are Sarkhanese."

For three more hours they talked of little things.

# 14

# How to Buy an
# American Junior Grade

THOMAS ELMER KNOX—Born April 1, 1920, Sheldon, Iowa. Son
of Mr. and Mrs. Henry Knox. Unmarried.
Graduated from Sheldon High School, 1937. Attended State
University of Iowa; B. S. in animal husbandry and poultry
husbandry, 1941. Enlisted as private, first class, in U. S. Army.
Rose to staff sergeant by discharge in 1946. Participated in
Allied invasion of Europe; served in a tank company. Dec-
orated with Purple Heart and Bronze Medal.
Described in Sheldon High Year Book as follows: "Dead-
serious, big-footed Tom (hates to be called Elmer) made letters in football and shot-put. Reputed to be antifeminine, but
ask Emily Chester about the Class Picnic! Ha, ha! His heifers
and chickens have won every 4-H contest for last three years,
but Tom says he hates beef and eggs. Ambition: To make a
hen lay 365 eggs in a year. Prediction: He'll do it! Ha, ha."
Managed Knox farm from 1946 until 1952. In 1953 accepted invitation to go to Cambodia as Consultant on Poultry for Economic Cooperation Administration.
Publications: "Influence of Commercial Calcium on Egg Production of Rhode Island Reds," *The Iowa Poultryman*, Sep-
tember, 1955.

There were three interesting things about Tom Knox.
First, he was the only American anyone knew of in Cam-
bodia who had spent all of his salary while he was there.
Secondly, he knew more Cambodians than any other

Westerner in the entire country. Thirdly, his capacity and enthusiasm for Cambodian food was at least three times greater than that of his closest competitor.

By the time Tom had been Cambodia for a year, he was easily the best known American in that country. No village was so small that it had not heard Tom's booming laugh, seen his prodigious appetite in action, and benefited from his knowledge of chickens. Day after day Tom drove his jeep into the countryside. When the road dwindled into a path, he unslung a collapsible bike from the rear of the jeep, and pedaled off. When the path became impassable by bike, he walked.

"Hey there, fellow," Tom would say to the first man he saw in a village. "Who's the Number One man around here? My name is Tom Knox. Sheldon, Iowa." Tom would then stick out his huge hand and vigorously pump the small bird-like hand of the Cambodian.

Ten minutes later everyone who could walk, hobble, or crawl would be gathered around Tom. He spoke a chaotic mixture of Cambodian, French, and farmyard English. But no one failed to understand him, and everyone valued the sincerity of his efforts to communicate.

"Now look here, people, you've got a chicken problem in this village," Tom would say. "You've got a bunch of teeny little scrawny chickens, and I'll bet you don't get fifty eggs a year from each one. Now I'm a chicken raiser from Iowa myself, and we've picked up a few tricks that I'm going to pass along to you. But before we do that, I'd like a little food." As the group moved toward the headman's house to eat, Tom established his credentials, by making sure the villagers knew he was a farm boy.

In one place he watched the Cambodians take boiling syrup distilled from cane sugar and pour it into big pot-shaped sugar forms. He noticed that when they knocked the sugar out of the forms, they invariably lost a good part of it when they broke it loose. Tom sat down and designed a wooden sugar-cake form with hinges on the bottom which could be swung open so the cake could be removed intact. In another town he watched Cambodians putting piglets in little bamboo cages to take them to market. Usually one or two pigs would hang his head through the bars and strangle on the way to market. Tom showed the villagers how to tie a twine harness around the chests of the pigs which made it impossible for the pigs to strangle.

He was no less impressive when the time came to eat. In no time at all he had become a formidable expert on Cambodian food. He could tell the district from which different types of rice came. He knew dozens of different condiments and mixtures to go with rice. Cambodians watched with delight when Tom took over the cooking chores. He cooked with the sure hand of an artist; and whether it were river eel or lake fish, he prepared it expertly. Tom made a point of bringing enough food with him so that despite the enormous quantities that he ate his host was better off after Tom had left.

After the meal, Tom turned to business. He would snatch a squawking chicken from the ground, inspect it carefully—push back its feathers, look in its eyes, pull its claws wide, and feel for internal damage.

"Now, what this little feller needs is a bit more calcium in its diet," Tom would say. "Calcium, you know, it's that white stuff you get from the earth. I saw a vein of it in a hill just off the trail about a mile back. Take five or six pounds of that and mix it with a hundred pounds of chicken feed, and you've got a good diet for a chicken; or at least it would be a good diet for *this* chicken."

When the chickens were diseased, Tom either dusted them with powders that he brought, or gave them injections. And he left pamphlets in Cambodian on how to care for the chickens to keep them well.

Tom's success, although minor by the standards by which military aid or big economic aid were calculated, was impressive. Word spread from village to village, untill finally Tom's appearance in a new village became the sign for a carnival. Villagers began storing up prize pieces of fruit, a pot of superior smoked eel, especially good twigs of cinnamon, or a bag of exceptionally good rice in anticipation of Tom's next visit. And the production of eggs soared rapidly. In fact, Tom got a reputation for working magic with chickens. A scrawny and featherless chicken, at the very edge of death, would revive just from being touched by Tom. Five minutes after he had arrived in a village he could tell almost exactly what was wrong with the food being fed to the chickens; and he was invariably helpful on other things too. He was a walking encyclopedia on Cambodian and American folklore on chickens, and there was very little that he did not know about farming in general.

One night Tom was sitting in front of the home of the headman of a hillside village. He had worked twelve hours that day with the people of the village. He was pleasantly tired, and he watched contentedly as the moon came up and turned the green of the jungle below into a rolling sea of darkness. The broad shaft of silvery moonlight was occasionally broken by a flock of birds like a cloud of motes. The headman came over and squatted silently beside Tom.

"Why does a big strong man like you leave his country?" the headman asked softly and politely. "You are a very good man, but we wonder why you left your country to come help us."

It was said with infinite courtesy, and Tom knew that he did not have to reply. His mind automatically recapitulated the formal lectures delivered to all economic cooperation people abroad on the objectives of foreign aid. He ticked them off in his mind, and then felt disgusted.

"Oh, crap!" he said softly.

"What is that word?" the headman asked just as softly.

"Oh, nothing. It's just an expression of anger," Tom said. "I could give you a lot of formal answers, but the simple fact is that I just like people and chickens, and besides I wanted to get away from the farm for a year or so."

It was inadequate, but it was the truth. For years Tom

had had a dream made up of things so soft and intangible that he had never been able to discuss it. Because of this dream he had never married; and because of this dream he had come to Cambodia. When he was a small boy, Tom had discovered that certain words meant enchantment to him. Words like "cinnamon," or "saffron," or "Malacca Straits," or "Hindu" or "Zamboanga" had magic in them. They suggested strange countries, mysterious reaches of green water, smells that he had never yet smelled, and people he had never yet seen. Later, when he learned what the words meant, he wanted to see the places and things for which the words stood. As he grew older he collected other words and stored them deep in his mind. "Raffles Hotel," "monsoon season," "upland plantations," "mahogany forests," "rice paddies," "Yellow River,"— hundreds of names of places and objects of the Far East. He even learned the meanings of very unusual words like "paryanka," which is one of the sitting positions in the Buddhist faith. In fact, as he talked to the headman, he was sitting in precisely that posture, and he was fully aware that the headman attached great significance to it.

"Look, old man, it's very hard for me to talk of these things," Tom said. "I do not use words very well. But for many years I wanted to see a country like this. So I came and saw it."

"And do you like it?" the headman said.

"Yes, I like it very much," Tom said. He realized that he had almost said he loved it. "I like the people in the villages, but I do not like the officials in Phnom Penh. And I do not like the ways of the Americans that work for my mission or in our embassy."

"I do not know these people; but I think that I and my people like a fellow like you very much," the headman said shyly, but firmly.

Tom had been in Cambodia long enough to know that he had just been paid a tremendous compliment. It was one of the happiest nights that he ever spent in Cambodia, or, for that matter, anywhere else.

Two weeks later Tom appeared in Phnom Penh for the

yearly conference which appraised the results of the American Aid Mission to Cambodia. Tom was not happy. For eighteen months he had been slogging through the jungles and he had formed some definite impressions about what the village people needed. His reports were received by Mission headquarters, but action never seemed to be taken on them. Tom wanted to import a few thousand Rhode Island Reds and other breeds of poultry to improve the Cambodian stock. Tom did not delude himself. He agreed at the staff meetings that the road from Phnom Penh to the new sea town of Konponga Som would be valuable for the country. He also agreed that the massive canal building program would be useful. He had no objections to the ambitious military plans which the Mission supported. But he kept insisting to everyone who would listen that most of the millions of people in Cambodia lived off the land, and anything that would help them to live better—even to the extent of a few more eggs a day—was the thing to do.

The day before the conference began, Tom met with all the American agricultural experts, the Cambodian experts, and four French officials to review the work of the year and decide what recommendations to make to the conference. Tom listened to a proposal for a new canal to cost two and a half million dollars, and to another proposal to replace eighteen square miles of mangrove swamp with a mechanized farm. He listened while an American expert proposed importation of two hundred thousand tons of commercial fertilizer per year for four years. Then the chairman of the conference nodded at Tom.

"My recommendation won't sound like much after the money we've been kicking around this table," Tom said with a grin. "I want to do two little things that won't cost much, but will sure as hell help the chicken and egg production of Cambodia. First, I want to bring in a few thousand American chickens and roosters to improve the native stock. Second, I want a couple thousand dollars to develop a machine which could be used to pulverize and treat sugar cane tops so that they could be used for chicken feed and for cattle . . ."

"Tom, you told us this last year," the chairman said wearily. "What our two governments want is something big, that really helps people right away."

"Now, look. Three million people in Cambodia live in villages and what they eat depends on what they can raise themselves," Tom said, and anger started to rise in his chest. "A big source of protein and meat is chicken and eggs. Oh sure, they can get fish, but not everyone lives near enough . . ."

"Okay, okay, Tom," the chairman said irritably. "We've heard that before, and we've made recommendations. The higher-ups haven't moved on them, and I think we ought to give them up and concentrate on really important things."

Tom's face turned red and his back started to arch like an angry bull's. In his mind he saw clearly the thousands of villagers he had talked to. He remembered their friendliness, their gratitude, their ignorance, their willingness to learn, the pathetic condition of the chickens, the scarcity of their eggs. Suddenly he felt, with a pang of guilt, that he was not representing his people well. Only later did he come to ask himself why they were *his* people. Tom smashed his fists on the table, and the entire group looked up with startled faces.

"Now, listen, goddamn it," he roared. "You people have been sitting on your asses here in Phnom Penh and you never get out to see a real person. I'm telling you right now that if we could increase the egg production of this country two hundred per cent we would do as much to help the average Cambodian as we would by building that damn expensive highway or that canal. Now, I'm not going to ask you chair-borne commandos or the officers here what you think. *They'll* agree with me." Tom turned and pointed an angry finger at the Chief of the Cambodian Aid Committee.

The Cambodian looked at Tom, then glanced quickly

around the table. He looked down into his hands, and for several seconds he did not speak.

"Well, come on, tell us what you think," Tom insisted angrily. "You know how the people in the villages live. You know how damn long it will take anything from those highways or canals to improve their living standards. What about my chickens?"

"I consider chicken and egg production to be very important," the Cambodian said carefully.

Tom swung around in triumph.

"There, I told you!"

"Now don't get excited, Tom. I'd like to know what our friend thinks is most important," the chairman said. "If we have money to develop either the mechanized farms or a chicken program, which would you support?"

Tom knew the question was unfair. The Cambodian government was firmly committed to the mechanized farms, and the expert could not express an honest opinion without violating government policy. When the Cambodian spoke, he did not look up from his hands, and his voice was very low.

"I would have to support the mechanized farms," the Cambodian said.

The chairman turned to Tom and shrugged.

Tom knew that he should keep quiet, but he could not. He felt as if the villagers were his constituents, and if he didn't speak for them now, he would have betrayed their trust.

"I'm going to say something just once, and then I'm through," he said, his voice, unsteady, low, and dangerous. The chairman's head came up sharply. "If we don't get this damn chicken appropriation before the conference, I'm going to resign and go back to Washington, and raise hell. Unless you fellows get out into the sticks, you won't know what the score is. There are a lot of congressmen who know about chickens and farming, and I think I can persuade them you're making a big mistake."

It was a threat, and no one at the table misread it. The

chairman stared at Tom while he quickly calculated how his own superiors might react if they were approached by Tom. He decided that they'd stand firm; and that in any case, they could rally more support among congressmen than Tom. He smiled.

"Okay, Tom, if that's the way you want it. As of this moment, I accept your resignation unless you want to reconsider."

Everyone in the room was silent. The Cambodians were not only silent, but deeply embarrassed. The Americans only watched curiously. They had seen this kind of thing happen before.

Tom got up, looked once more around the table, and left the room.

Two weeks later Tom was ready to fly home. He had already written letters to congressmen from agricultural states and outlined his complaint. He had not yet had replies, but there had not been time for airmail to make the round trip. He firmly intended to fly to Washington and put his case before them personally.

The day before he left Tom had a visitor—a high-ranking French diplomat. The Frenchman explained that he had followed Tom's work carefully and had heard excellent reports from the villages which Tom had visited. He regretted that Tom had had a difference of opinion with the American chief. Tom listened impassively.

"As an indication of our gratitude, would you allow us to route your trip home in such a way that you could visit the rest of the Far Eastern countries, India, the Middle East, and France and England?" the diplomat asked him smoothly. "I understand that you flew here over the Pacific—so you would have traveled around the world by the time you return home. As you know, Cambodia pays for such trips out of counterpart funds. We would be delighted to have you make this trip. We are embarrassed over your dilemma, and it would be gracious of you to accept."

Tom was both bored and suspicious. He wanted only to

return to the United States as quickly as possible, and he had long ago discovered that when diplomats make a concrete proposal they usually have some firm objective in mind. As Tom was trying to make up his mind, the Frenchman showed how well he understood American personality.

"I have always felt, sir, that you have great sympathy for Asian countries and peoples," the diplomat said softly. "The trip I'm suggesting would give you a chance to see the magnificent old temples in Bangkok. You could stop off in Indonesia, and I'm sure our diplomatic people in India could arrange for you to see much of that country. It would be a wonderful opportunity. I can tell you from personal experience that there is no sight more stirring than the Taj Mahal in full moonlight."

For Tom it was irresistible. All the exotic words, the suggestions of exotic scenes welled up in his mind. In another five minutes he had agreed, and arrangements were made for Tom to fly to Paris via Air France.

The trip home started very well. The special Air France plane carried a reduced passenger load, so that they could be given luxury service. The first meal Tom ate aboard the plane consisted of a generous slice of *pâté de foie gras*, a tiny loaf of French bread, a bottle of champagne, and a large pat of fresh butter which had had his name impressed on it—and that was only the beginning. Later he had a huge steak with Béarnaise sauce, with which he was served a half-bottle of a magnificent Chambertin; a spinach soufflé delicately flavored with fresh butter and crushed garlic; and for dessert, Brie and crackers.

At Jakarta in Indonesia, Tom was met by a French Embassy official, and a French merchant. Arrangements had been made for Tom to spend several nights at the embassy residence, and they had outlined an itinerary for him while he was there, of which Tom approved eagerly. That afternoon they took him to a tiny village on the outskirts of Jakarta. Even after the beauty of Cambodia, Tom was staggered. The village was like a jewel. Magnificent flowers in more colors than he had ever seen before poured over fences, hung from trees, and climbed up the walls of the native huts. In the largest of the huts, a troupe of Balinese dancing girls were performing. The girls were tiny, and naked to the waist. Behind their ears they wore large red flowers which were like flames against their jet black hair. The sarong-like wraps they wore emphasized their incredible muscular control. For three hours Tom sat transfixed watching the girls dance. The graceful girls seemed utterly boneless. Their bodies flowed into impossible positions, then dissolved into entirely different stances. They danced to an unearthly music played by a line of Indonesian musicians. Tom was very close to tears when he left. He hadn't thought about Cambodia the entire afternoon; and some of the fine edge of his anger had disappeared.

That night in the Embassy he was served a banquet in nineteenth-century Indonesian style—a *rijsttafel*. There were twelve people present; Tom and the ambassador were the only white men. First an Indonesian boy brought each guest a huge bowl of boiled rice. Then a procession of servants carried in condiments to be put on top of the rice, each of which was more succulent than the last. When it was time to eat Tom faced a mound of rice almost buried under dozens of fragrant preparations. One of the servants kept his glass full of good strong beer. The moment they started to eat, two girls from the dancing troupe came into the room. They did not dance, but played two tiny stringed instruments which made a high, piercing sound. At first this music was almost unbearably shrill, but after a while took on practically heavenly purity and precision. Both the food and the music were like something from another world, and Tom several times had to shake off a sense of unreality. It was, he thought, the closest he had ever come to his boyhood dream.

The rest of his stay in Jakarta was equally fascinating, and when he boarded another luxury Air France plane, he welcomed the chance to get some sleep. He awoke eight hours after they had taken off, and was flattered to discover that the French merchant had put a case of imported beer aboard the plane and instructed the steward to serve Tom a bottle as soon as he awoke. By the time he had consumed five bottles of beer the plane was circling for a landing outside of New Delhi in northern India. Indonesia had been lush and rich and bright. India was dusty, hot, and hard. But Tom enjoyed his stay. Again two Frenchmen met him at the airport and arranged for him to stay at a French rest home. They also had planned an elaborate itinerary. Tom visited magnificent century-old ruins, watched a troupe of Indian dancers recreate ancient ritual dances which had formerly been done with cobras, and attended a funeral burning at the river edge. Months later he could still recall the smell that rose from the pyre, compounded of ancient butter, strange perfumes, and burning flesh.

Tom also ate well while he was in New Delhi. When he left, again on a luxury flight, he was given a collection of intricate Indian silver jewelry, a gift from the French Embassy of India. And during his entire stay various people made flattering remarks about his skill in Cambodia.

On the long flight from New Delhi to Nice, Tom tried several times to write up his criticisms of the American agricultural aid program in Cambodia. Somehow he found it difficult to find the right words with which to express his indignation. In fact, he found that his indignation was very difficult to rekindle. He assured himself that once he had returned to the United States he would be able to write up his complaint accurately and soundly; he resolved to go as quickly as possible to Washington after his return.

When his plane landed in Nice he was again greeted by the inevitable Frenchmen. This time they had arranged for him to stay as long as he wanted to in a hotel just outside of Cap d'Antibes. On the rocks below the hotel were a half-dozen women wearing bathing suits smaller than Tom had ever imagined could be legal.

Tom stayed seven days at the hotel, and when he left he discovered that there was no bill to pay. The management assured him that both they and the French government were delighted to have had as a guest so distinguished an American diplomat. The Frenchmen from Nice gave him a present when he left—a suitcase made of Morocco leather, the finest piece of luggage Tom had ever seen.

In Paris Tom was met by a Cambodian who had large agricultural holdings in Cambodia. He had arranged for Tom to stay at a small hotel. He apologized for the fact that it did not have an international reputation, but assured Tom that the service and food were excellent. This recommendation was something of an understatement. Tom discovered, to his astonishment, that the hotel had no established rates. A guest was simply given whatever he asked for, and was then presented with a single unitemized bill at the end of his stay. When Tom asked for Scotch in the bar, the waiter brought him a full bottle of Johnny Walker Black Label and a few bottles of Perrier water, and left. For so small a hotel the menu was incredible. Tom literally could order whatever he wanted—from fresh Beluga caviar to squid soup.

Meanwhile, the Cambodian land owner kept Tom busy with trips to every art gallery in Paris, an evening at the opera, tastings at famous wine cellars, small cocktail parties, carriage rides through the Bois, and a gift-buying expedition which turned out, in some mysterious way, to involve Tom in no expense whatsoever.

One evening he tried to raise the question of agricultural aid to Cambodia. The Cambodian listened courteously as Tom described his plans for increasing chicken and egg yield in that country, and Tom had the feeling that the Cambodian already knew the details of his plan. The Cambodian could not have been more honest or diplomatic.

"Mr. Knox, I'm afraid that you and I differ on this idea," he finally said with great grace. "There is only a limited amount of aid money; and before the golden goose stops laying, I think it would be wise for Cambodia to get permanent installations like roads and canals and ports. Your idea is important and good; but I do not feel that this is the time for it." Tom started to protest; but somehow to protest to so polite and generous a person seemed unreasonable.

Two days later the Cambodian told Tom that through a lucky fluke they had been able to get him a suite on the *Liberté* sailing for New York. And happily he was able to tell Tom that the suite would cost him nothing, because, for a reason which was never quite clear to Tom, the suite was free to them.

When Tom left his hotel his experience on the Riviera was repeated. The hotel was so pleased to have him as a guest that they could not think of taking payment. The manager pointed out confidentially that other people—businessmen and brokers, for instance—could well afford to pay the cost of the small services that the hotel had given Tom. He intimated that Tom was one of a group of people so valuable and important that they were above paying hotel bills.

The suite on the *Liberté* was luxurious without being ostentatious. Every morning fresh flowers were put in his cabin; there was always a note attached to them which expressed the gratitude of the Cambodian government. Also, there were several visits from a Cambodian diplomat who was traveling to the United States; this gentleman made Tom gifts of French wine and a length of the finest French silk.

When the *Liberté* was two days from New York, Tom sat down to write up his thoughts so that he could present them to congressional committees and to newspaper people in Washington. He discovered, however, that not only had his feeling of anger and outrage been blunted, but that it was very difficult to recreate it at all. To his astonishment Cambodia seemed a long, long time away, and glazed over with wonderful memories. These were not so much memories of the village life, as of the generous and courteous attentions he had been given by so many Cambodians on his trip home. The anger, which in Cambodia had seemed so sure and honest a weapon, in his suite on the *Liberté* seemed somehow almost ridiculous. After working for three hours and covering only a half a page, he resolved to wait until he had landed.

Eight months later, when Tom was back on the Knox farm in Sheldon, Iowa, he again saw the half page of paper. When he read it over, he thought for a moment that it must have been written by another person. The handwriting was his, but not the words. The anger he had felt in Cambodia, so hot and bright and curiously nourishing, now seemed childish. Tom folded the paper, and put it away.

◎

In Haidho Ambassador MacWhite had a caller—a farmer who was head of the Midwest Poultry Association. He was making a world tour with his wife, and he came into the embassy with something on his mind.

"Look, Mister MacWhite," he said, for he had never learned diplomatic protocol, "I'm on to something hot. Listen for a second and don't say I'm crazy."

MacWhite pushed a box of cigars towards the man. He took four, lit one, and stuck the other three in his shirt pocket. He puffed up a white cloud of smoke and then talked through it.

"What this country needs, mister, are some good chickens," he said, his voice explosive with excitement.

"I thought there were plenty around," MacWhite said cautiously. There was no disapproval in his voice, for he had learned not to be either disapproving or surprised.

"Damned right there are, but they're sickly," the visitor said. "I found out they only lay about thirty eggs a year. Why, if we could get their egg production up to 200 eggs per chicken per year, and their weights up just 20 per cent, we could save $2,000,000 on food imports a year. Look, I figured it out."

The excited man pushed a dirty piece of paper over

to the ambassador. It was covered with a sprawl of figures; at the bottom, with a circle around it, was written $2,000,000.

MacWhite had the figures checked by his research staff. They were correct.

He then wrote a letter to the American Aid Mission in Phnom Penh in Cambodia, which had the largest number of American agricultural experts of any mission in the immediate area. He asked if they had a chicken expert they could lend to the Sarkhan government.

The letter he received from Phnom Penh was disappointing and it also led to MacWhite's making his second major mistake—one he never discovered.

Dear Ambassador MacWhite, (wrote the Chief of Mission in Phnom Penh)

I don't know what you're doing down there, but it sounds as if you're trying to make sure of a good eggnog supply for the Christmas holidays.

Whatever your motives, I can't help you. We had an egg expert out here, name of Thomas Elmer Knox. There's something about that profession that seems to make them a bit odd. He just didn't work out. Always out in the countryside, always popping off about things he knew nothing about, always threatening to go to Congress if we didn't import some Rhode Island Reds.

He finally left in a huff, why, I never fully understood. The French and Cambodian officials were a bit perturbed at first because they hate to have Americans go away unhappy; but they seem all right about it now. They don't want any more egg experts though. Neither do you. Give it up.

Cordially
Rowe Hendy

And MacWhite did give it up—which was his second major mistake.

◎

# 15

# The Six-Foot Swami
# from Savannah

---

Playing his harmonica softly, Colonel Edwin B. Hillandale of the U. S. Air Force and Savannah, Georgia, ambled down the Street of the White Crocodile in Haidho. He was trying to learn *Nging Gho Hrignostina*, which is Sarkhan's national anthem. Every few minutes the colonel would stop a Sarkhanese and play a version of *Nging Gho Hrignostina*. Then, with gesticulations, appealing grimaces and laughter, he would persuade the Sarkhanese to hum the anthem.

But learning the national anthem of Sarkhan wasn't the only thing the colonel was doing. He was, as he expressed it, "Seeing what makes this burg tick before MacWhite comes back from his trip." Ambassador MacWhite had gotten him on loan from Manila for two months. The colonel noticed that there were a great many pawnshops, and concluded that the city people were in bad economic straits. He observed the shops which sold betel nuts, tobacco, and native medicines. He had seen a clerk in one of them pass something from under the counter, and had guessed that opium was also being sold. He went by fruit stands piled high with red pomegranates, yellow pomolos, pink-brown bananas, and green apples, and passed walking flower vendors carrying great baskets of sweet fragrance. The thing which the colonel noticed most, however, was the large number of signs advertising palmistry and astrology establishments. These places had a clean, elegant, respectable look which made them resemble the offices of fashionable physicians in America. And the shingles which the astrologists and palmists hung outside their places of business all indicated that these practitioners had doctors' degrees.

Well, thought Colonel Hillandale, at last I've found a place where my hobbies will be welcome. I'm sure glad I brought my Ephemeris and log tables with me. And that slide rule. Oh boy, if I can find my diploma from that Chungking School of Occult Science, I'll really be in business here.

He then played *The Little Whistling Pig* on his harmonica, a tune he reserved only for special occasions such as the day he had put the donkey in the general's suite, or last March the 14th, when he had been promoted to full chicken colonel.

After he had seen enough of Haidho to get the feel of it, he returned to the American Embassy and began to read. He went through biographies of all the Sarkhanese politicians, and many different analyses of the current political situation. He submerged himself in these studies for several days, and probably would have continued for longer except that he was interrupted by the Embassy Protocol Officer.

"Colonel, is your nickname 'The Ragtime Kid'?"

"That's what they call me in Manila."

"Then you're the one. The Philippines Ambassador is giving a dinner tomorrow, and requests that you attend. I've already accepted for you. Ambassador Rodriguez seemed particularly eager . . ."

"So, Don Phillippe wangled himself that job after all, the old buzzard. Sure I'll go. I hope he's brought a couple of cases of *tuba*, a wagonload of San Miguel, and those two good looking maids he kept in Manila . . ."

"Eight o'clock," said the protocol officer hastily. "Black tie. And be a little early. The Prime Minister and the Foreign Minister and several other Sarkhanese dignitaries will be there."

"You have a guest list?"

"I'll get you one."

The Philippine Ambassador's dinner party was fully attended because Don Phillippe had already established his reputation as a good and charming host. It was rumored that he paid his chef thirty thousand pesos a year, and that he had stolen him from the Waldorf. Regardless of how much he was paid, or where he had been stolen from, the chef had made Don Phillippe's table famous throughout the Orient.

After about an hour of cocktails and hors d'oeuvres, a servant came up and whispered something to Don Phillippe. A cloud of disappointment shadowed his face, and his forehead furrowed. Don Phillippe thought a moment, then went over to Colonel Hillandale and beckoned him to one side.

"Kid," he said, "a terrible catastrophe. The first course for this evening is *sole escabeche*. I had the fish caught this afternoon from my own boat. But Henri just told me he doesn't have any ginger, and it'll take a half-hour to get it. So I've got to stall. Do you remember the palm-reading stunt you pulled at my house at Baguio? Do you think . . ."

The melody of *The Whistling Pig* began to drift through The Ragtime Kid's mind.

"Why, Don Phillippe," he said, "I'd love to. I'm in a great palm-reading mood tonight. The humidity is just right and it so happens that Venus is in conjunction with the moon . . ."

"Come on then," said Don Phillippe, looking five years younger. "I don't care what lies you tell these people, just amuse them for a half hour."

"Lies? Don Phillippe, you've hurt my feelings."

The Philippines Ambassador tapped on a glass with a spoon and when he had everyone's attention, introduced Colonel Hillandale.

"Ladies and gentlemen. We have with us this evening a most distinguished palmist and astrologer." He paused. During the pause the Americans present laughed and a few, including George Swift, the chargé d'affaires, said "Fake! Fraud!" The Sarkhanese leaned forward with interest to hear the remainder of the announcement, somewhat embarrassed by the Americans' comments.

Don Phillippe continued. "This distinguished man is my old friend and associate Colonel Edwin Hillandale of the U. S. Air Force. He is the only living Caucasian who is a graduate of the Chungking School of Occult Science. I have seen him perform many times, and the things I have heard him say have been both fantastic and miraculous. I remember the day he read the palm and cast the horoscope of our Secretary of Defense, Ramon Magsaysay. The Ragtime Kid—as we affectionately call the colonel—told Ramon that the sixteenth of the month would be his lucky day, but only if he were in the vicinity of Barang. Out of curiosity Ramon went to Barang, a small town in Ilocos Norte Province. And on that day and in that town Ramon surrounded and captured the leaders of the terrible Huks, in an action which broke the back of the whole Huk movement."

The Sarkhanese Prime Minister and his foreign minister nodded at each other appreciatively. George Swift laughed and slapped his knee.

"I asked the Kid if he would read some of your palms after dinner, but he told me that astrological conditions are perfect right now when Venus is in conjunction with the moon. The next half-hour is the best time to read palms, and my chief says he can hold dinner up for that length of time, so . . . I give you Colonel Hillandale."

"Bravo! Bravo!" said the Prime Minister, clapping his hands.

Swift turned to his wife and whispered, "I wonder why MacWhite shanghaied this amateur performer. Can you imagine, vaudeville tricks at a state dinner!"

Colonel Hillandale stood up, raised his hand. "Now, ladies and gentlemen, frankly, I don't like to do this in public. When I read palms I must tell exactly what I see. Sometimes the information is the kind you don't want others to know. I must tell you this ahead of time."

"Start on me, Colonel," said Swift sarcastically, holding out his hand. "I've got nothing to hide. Come on, I dare you."

They sat down under a light. The colonel spread Swift's hand flat on his knee. Everyone crowded around.

The colonel said, "When were you born?"

"You tell me, Mister Prophet."

The colonel peered closely at Swift's hand and then said gently and without reproach, "I know that you were born on the 28th of April, 1913, in Santa Clara, California. I was hoping to get the exact hour and minute, since it would have helped me. But never mind."

The chargé d'affaires didn't say anything.

"You come from a poor family. Your father ran a saloon; I'm not sure, but there are indications that he went bankrupt and deserted your mother."

Mrs. Swift sucked in her breath.

The colonel continued, "You wanted to be a doctor, but you couldn't pass the entrance exams for medical school. You left college after your third year because . . ." The colonel raised his head and looked at Mrs. Swift, saw the anguish in her face, and skipped to the next subject. "You got a job as the office manager for a real estate company, and held it until 1944 when a client of yours got a big job in Washington. He took you along as his office manager and you did lots of little liaison jobs with Congress. Then you went to the State Department in the same capacity. This is your first assignment overseas. I can see in your hand that you don't read much—not many books, magazines, or newspapers, I mean—but you have a capacity for scanning reports and for putting them in proper order. This is your great talent. You hate being scolded and when you are—according to your hand—you take it out on your wife. I could easily tell you what will happen in your future, but as long as you don't want to tell me the exact time of your birth, well . . ."

Swift started to blurt out when he was born, but Colonel Hillandale had already let go his hand and moved on to the next person.

The Prime Minister said, "I would like to have my palm read. But I would prefer it to be in private."

"Your Excellency," said the Philippine Ambassador, "of course." He put his hand on the Prime Minister's elbow and led him into the study. The Ragtime Kid followed.

The Ragtime Kid and the Prime Minister closed the door of the study and stayed there for half an hour. What went on inside the study none of the other guests knew. But when the door opened, the two men came out arm in arm, and the Prime Minister was gazing up at The Ragtime Kid with obvious awe.

Dinner was announced, and everyone went into the dining room to enjoy Henri's celebrated cooking. The meal was superb, and the conversation was spirited and clever; the general subject was palmistry and astrology. The Philippine Ambassador made a mental note that he was considerably obliged to The Ragtime Kid and some day would do something for him in return.

Three days later Ambassador MacWhite returned to Haidho. He stepped briskly off the plane and saw that his Deputy Chief of Mission was waiting for him. He put his hand on George Swift's shoulder and said, "Everything in good shape, old boy? Where did you get that shiner? What a beautiful mouse! You look as though you did fifteen rounds with Marciano. How'd you get it?"

Swift's face flushed with anger. "That vaudeville colonel of yours from Manila . . ."

"Hillandale?"

"Yes, sir. I have an official letter of reprimand ready for your signature . . ."

"Tell me about it."

And Swift did.

The first thing MacWhite did when he got back to the embassy was to send for Colonel Hillandale. When the colonel arrived, MacWhite was very severe and formal with him, and demanded his version of the fight with the Deputy Chief of Mission.

"It started like this, sir," said the colonel. "May I have your permission to sit down and smoke?"

"Yes. But let me tell you right now, I have a feeling you're in serious trouble."

The following explanation of George Swift's black eye was offered by Colonel Edwin Hillandale to Ambassador MacWhite.

"Well, sir," said Colonel Hillandale, "first I have to give you some background. Every person and every nation has a key which will open their hearts. If you use the right key, you can maneuver any person or any nation any way you want.

"The key to Sarkhan—and to several other nations in Southeast Asia—is palmistry and astrology. All you have to do to learn this is to walk along the streets and look at the occult establishments. The men who operate them are called doctors, and they're respected. There are chairs of palmistry and astrology in every Sarkhanese University, and the Prime Minister himself has a Ph.D. in Occult Science.

"There are many things which we don't know much about in the United States which are held in high regard by the Asians, and in which they have developed a genuine skill. Palmistry and astrology are among these.

"The Sarkhanese officials wouldn't make a major decision without consulting a doctor of the occult. Shortly after I arrived a well-known astrologer announced that on the eighteenth a 'big man' would die in Sarkhan. Well, sir, on the seventeenth almost every important official in Sarkhan flew to Rangoon so as to be out of the country on that fateful day. Even the King and the Prime Minister went away. They make no bones about it—they believe.

"It so happens that palmistry and astrology are hobbies of mine; I studied them when I was in China. It was immediately clear to me that I had knowledge which would be helpful in furthering U. S. interests out here.

"When I was asked to read palms at the Philippine Ambassador's dinner, it was a God-given opportunity. All of the Sarkhanese brass except the King were present. And then that knucklehead of an assistant of yours, instead of helping me, started laughing at me and trying to make a fool out of me. If he had an ounce of brains, he would have noticed how serious the Sarkhanese were. And if those fools in the State Department had briefed him properly, he would have known all about palmistry and astrology before he even came here."

"But," interrupted Ambassador MacWhite, "George Swift told me that you insulted him . . ."

"He dared me to read what was in his palm, and I read it. The things I told him were true, and he knows it.

"Mister Ambassador, when I go to a place I make a point of finding out about everyone with whom I have to deal. I ask questions, read their dossiers, and do a thorough investigation. For example, I know that when you were in college you fell in love with and wanted to marry a burlesque girl. Your father threatened to disown you."

"Never mind about me," said Ambassador MacWhite. "Go on with your explanation of the Deputy's black eye."

"Well, the Prime Minister asked me to read his palm. Naturally I was familiar with his background, and I described it to him. Everyone is always amazed if you can tell him intimate details about his youth.

"Then I told His Excellency that he was planning a

six-months' trip around the world, and he damned near jumped out of his underwear.

"Of course you haven't heard about it, sir. No one in your embassy knows what the score is until it explodes in his face—if you'll pardon me for being frank. But about a week ago I was passing the Prime Minister's residence and I saw the servants airing the furniture in the back and putting cotton covers on it. All it took was a little discreet questioning to find out that His Excellency was making a trip around the world. Then I found out from the airline when he was going and who would accompany him. This was a closely-guarded secret."

"What did His Excellency say when you told him he was making a trip?"

"He was surprised, and then he asked me why he was making the trip. Well, I know what the political situation is here; and I told him that two men, both old friends of his, were fighting for power under him, and he didn't know which one to pick. So he was delaying the decision by making a trip around the world."

"Then what did he say?"

"He walked up and down the room for a few minutes, sweating like a Westerner, and then he asked me what the men's names were. I told him I couldn't tell that from his hand, and that I was too new here in Sarkhan to be familiar with officials' names. But I could describe the men from looking at his palm. And I did. I told him one was small, emaciated, and had liver trouble. The other was big and red-faced.

"He paced and sweat some more; then he sat down with a groan and asked me which of the two he should have killed."

Ambassador MacWhite jumped up. "My God, you were speaking of General Saugh and General Bhakal."

"Yes, sir."

"What did you tell him?"

"I didn't know what our policy was, so I advised him that it would be a mistake to kill either; and that a man who was as devout a Buddhist as he is shouldn't even have asked the question. I further suggested that a smarter thing to do would be to send *them* out of the country for about six months instead of his going."

"You did! My God, they announced not an hour ago that Saugh is going to America as Special Ambassador Plenipotentiary, and that Bhakal is going to Russia with the same title. They're leaving next week."

"Well," Colonel Hillandale continued, "before the dinner party broke up the Prime Minister and the Foreign Minister came up and asked me if I would read the King's palm and cast his horoscope. I told them that it would be the greatest honor of my life, and so on, and I would show up day or night at His Majesty's pleasure.

"You see, sir," said Colonel Hillandale, beginning to get somewhat excited, "the Chinese Communist Armies have been mobilizing near the northern border. I knew that if I could once get to the King, I could tell him that the stars ordered that he send the Royal Sarkhanese Army up north for maneuvers. If this were done the Communists would interpret the move as a clear indication that Sarkhan was definitely pro-American and anti-Communist. It would have been a defeat for the Commies and would have been a great propaganda victory for us throughout all Asia. And, sir, I am positive that the King would have done what the stars ordered him to."

"What happened?" MacWhite asked.

"As we were leaving the Philippine Embassy Residence, the Prime Minister called George Swift over. 'Mister Ambassador,' he said, 'my friend here is going to read the palm of His Majesty the King. But in Sarkhan we do these things with very strict protocol. It must be on a government to government level. You, Mister Ambassador, must personally telephone the Sarkhanese Minister of Protocol, that's Prince Moyang here, and tell him that Colonel Hillandale accepts the honor of His Majesty's invitation to cast his horoscope and read his palm.'

" 'I understand. I understand these things perfectly, sir,' George answered.

" 'Now,' said the Prime Minister, 'when you have rung Prince Moyang, he will tell you exactly the time and the place, and the costume, and all of the details which the Colonel should know before going to the Royal Palace.'

" 'I understand completely,' George said. 'I will personally telephone Prince Moyang at nine o'clock tomorrow morning, if that's a time which is convenient for him.'

" 'That will be fine for me,' said Prince Moyang, 'I'll be expecting your call at nine o'clock.'

"This was the climax of the party. It broke up just after that.

"As we were leaving, Swift turned to me and said, 'Now look, you stay in your room tomorrow morning. The minute I make that call, I'll let you know. I want to discuss it with the staff before I let you have the details of it. So you wait in your room, and I'll ring you a little after nine o'clock.'

" 'Yes, sir,' I said, and shoved off.

"I went home feeling fine. I thought I really had the situation under control. I had of course prepared horoscopes of all the big shots in Sarkhan ahead of time—the King's included. And I visualized the whole thing while I undressed and turned in.

"I knew I might have to go to the Palace and work the old boy over two or three different times. In the first reading I planned to tell him about his past personal life. I knew a great story about how he had tried to seduce the niece of the King of Siam in 1928 and had damn near started a war. I got it from the caretaker. The first session would give me an opportunity to know the king and estimate his personality and reactions. It's very important for a palmist or an astrologer to know his man inside out.

"Later, I planned to get gradually into the military and political situation, and to bring it up in such a way that the king would ask me what should be done about this critical situation; or, at least, what the stars say should be done? If everything went really smoothly, I felt I might be able to polish off this job on the first visit to the palace.

"Well, next morning I was up early because I was excited and wanted to be entirely ready. I had all kinds of clothes laid out, just in case I had to rush to the palace about ten minutes after nine. I didn't even go to breakfast because I was scared I might miss Swift's phone call. All I had was two bottles of warm beer and a tin of salami from my emergency rations. I went nuts waiting for the phone to ring. But at ten minutes after nine nobody called me. By ten o'clock nobody had called. So I had two more bottles of beer. By eleven o'clock nobody had called, so I knew damned well that something had gotten fouled up. I couldn't stand it any longer, and I borrowed the dispatcher's motorcycle and went over to the embassy to George Swift's office.

"He wasn't in, but his secretary, a popeyed girl named MacIntosh, looked at me, and said, 'Oh, Colonel Hillandale, we've been looking all over for you for the past hour.'

"I told her I'd been in my room, exactly as instructed, all morning, biting my fingernails up to the elbow.

"'Gracious,' said Miss Popeyes. 'And I've rung every place in town except your room.'

"'Did Mr. Swift get the call through to Prince Moyang?'

"'Oh,' said Popeyes, 'Mr. Swift had to go to the commissary with Mrs. Swift because the Undersecretary of State is expected here at noontime and they had run out of liquor and they're giving this party for him tonight and Mr. Swift felt that he personally ought to go down to help with the shopping because the liquor store normally isn't open today.'

"'He didn't ring Prince Moyang at nine?'

"'No sir; but he telephoned me from the commissary and told me to call Prince Moyang.'

"'Did you call him?'

"'Yes sir, I called him about ten minutes after ten.'

" 'What did the Prince say?'

" 'Well, it was a little confusing, sir. You see, I didn't quite understand from Mr. Swift what this was all about, so when I got Prince Moyang on the telephone I told him that you, Colonel Hillandale, would be delighted to attend His Majesty's reception for the Undersecretary.'

" 'What did Prince Moyang say?'

" 'Well, he asked me, who is it that's speaking.'

" 'And?'

" 'And I told him I was Mr. Swift's secretary.'

" 'And then what did the prince say?'

" 'Oh,' said Popeyes, 'he acted so strange, he didn't say anything, he just hung up on me.'

"Well, I knew that we had insulted the Sarkhanese pretty badly. Not only had we not used our key—but we'd thrown a barricade over the front door. I thought maybe I could fix things up, so I rushed over to Prince Moyang's office to call on him personally to apologize. But the Prince's secretary politely informed me that Prince Moyang was out of town.

"That afternoon I met George Swift and before I could start to blow my stack he apologized for having neglected to call Prince Moyang at nine. 'You know how it is,' he said. 'The Undersecretary of State is arriving and after all he's really here to inspect us. I had to make sure we were ready for him.'

" 'Oh,' he added, 'by the way, we're really lucky that I went down there,' he said. 'You know I've just gotten phone calls from the Prime Minister and the Foreign Minister and Prince Moyang and they all ate something that didn't agree with them and they're all indisposed. None of them will be able to come to the party for the Undersecretary. So, Colonel, you can see how it would have looked with none of them there, and no gin either, so don't stay mad at me.'

" 'But, my God,' I said, 'I told you last night about my plan to get the king to move his troops up north for maneuvers.'

" 'Oh come on, Colonel,' Swift said. 'Those little vaude-ville tricks are okay to liven up a dull dinner party, but when you get into big time diplomacy . . .'

"And it was at that moment," said the colonel, "that I busted the chargé in the eye."

◎

When Colonel Hillandale had left his office, Gilbert MacWhite sat quietly for a moment. He felt something between laughter and anger, but the longer he thought of it the more the anger prevailed. When he finally pushed the button and asked for George Swift to come in, his mouth was drawn thin.

"Yes, sir," the Deputy Chief of Mission said, as he came in the door, anticipation in his face.

"George, have you ever been in downtown Haidho?"

"Yes, sir."

"Have you ever noticed the number of palmistry shops and practicing astrologers?"

"Well, look, sir, we have lots of pawnshops in the U. S., but we don't run our foreign policy by what the pawn-brokers say."

"Have you ever had your palm read? No, of course not. Do you know the kind of people that do?"

"Look, sir, this kind of stuff is a fake. A vaudeville stunt."

"George, nothing is a fake if people believe in it. Your business is not to judge whether or not things are fakes, but who believes them and why and what it means."

George Swift could not believe his ears, and a flush started to crawl up his cheeks. In some incredible way *he* was getting the chew . . . not that chicken colonel.

"George, I'm going to cable the Department and ask for your transfer," MacWhite said wearily.

"On the grounds that I didn't cooperate with a palm-reader?" George asked; and for the first time MacWhite was aware of the animal ability to survive which was responsible for George's rise.

"No; I'll probably tell them that two years here is long enough for anyone, and that you deserve a change."

George's eyes narrowed. He knew he could not change the ambassador's mind. But he also knew that the last word was not in.

◎

# 16

# Captain Boning, USN

---

Solomon Asch sat at the head of the conference table. He was calm and relaxed. Now was not the time for toughness. He knew from long experience that strangers around a table always do some initial sparring before getting down to business. Outside, the noises of Hong Kong rose in the air; Asch had been in the Crown colony only a few weeks; and he found the sounds fascinating.

Asch knew he was both tough and competent. He had a veneer of manners and politeness, but it was very thin. Just beneath it was the knowing Jew who had survived youth on the East Side of New York City. He worked as a union negotiator; and his toughness and honesty had carried him to the top of his profession. He had been pleased when the President of the United States had asked him to serve in the government for six months as head of the American Delegation to the Special Armament section of the Asia Conference.

Asch swung around in his chair and looked over the group of Americans who would make up his staff. He considered those he could count on and those he could ignore. MacWhite, the Ambassador from Sarkhan, was all right. Anderson, the Special Political Officer for Southeastern Pacific Affairs, was not worth a damn. Asch had once asked him how many Communists there were in the Hong Kong trade unions, and the stupid jerk didn't know. Dooling was useful in spots only. He was a career ambassador, afraid to send tough reports to Washington, very solicitous of superior officers; but he had information. Asch would use the information, but he would not allow Dooling to do any hard bargaining.

The rest of the Americans in the room were just average. Asch hadn't had a chance really to size up the Navy Captain. Boning was a small man, and Asch had noted that he wore shoes with elevated heels which increased his height. Sometimes, Asch thought to himself, a good little man can be effective.

"All right, gentlemen, the meeting will please come to order," Asch said. "You all know why we're here. We make up the American Delegation to the conference which will determine what kind of weapons if any the United States will distribute among its allies in Asia. I don't need to tell you the importance of this matter. Nor do I need to tell you the difficulties we are going to have. The Indian, Burmese, and Thai representatives to this meeting are probably going to oppose any installation of special weapons on their soil. Maybe they're right; but our government doesn't think so. Right now we don't have the legislation in Congress to allow us to share our information with our friends; but I'd guess we'll have it awfully damn soon."

Asch grinned. They knew what he meant. Recent developments had made America realize that she had to share knowledge and armaments with her allies.

"Now, gentlemen, you have already read in classified documents the official United States position," Asch went on briskly. "I won't take much more of your time this morning. What I want you to understand clearly is how I run a meeting. First, keep in mind that I am the leader of this delegation. If you have any doubts about statements that I make, raise them with me in private, but not in meetings. I never say anything without a reason. Sometimes it may sound crazy, but don't call me on it. Secondly, gentlemen, take a look at the program brochure of this meeting."

The men around the table all picked up the heavily embossed brochures which covered the three-week program of the meetings, and thumbed through them idly.

"Please note that every afternoon there are two or three cocktail parties, and every night there is a formal dinner," Asch said. His face tightened into a wry grin. "I want none of you to go to any of the cocktail parties. And I want you to go to only two formal dinners a week. I will write blanket notes of regret. We will all go to the last dinner, because then the work will be over."

"Mr. Asch, I wonder if that would be wise," Ambassador Dooling said. His voice was anxious. "Asians are awfully sensitive about such things. They might feel snubbed."

"Also, Mr. Asch, I don't think we should overlook the possibility of picking up stray bits of intelligence at such functions," Anderson, the political officer, said.

"Nuts," Asch replied firmly. "Let's keep our mind on what comes first here. The Asians will respect us if we drive a hard and fair bargain with them at the conference table. That will call for every ounce of energy we have. Success at a conference table is always a delicately balanced affair. If a couple of you have hangovers, or someone misses a cue, we can lose a little part of our deal. If it happens several times, we can lose the whole deal. And let me tell you frankly, Mr. Dooling, that although I'm new out here I think the prestige of Americans might go up if they stayed away from a few more cocktail parties."

Asch swung his head slightly to look at Anderson. Anderson had already slumped back in his chair. He had never heard a diplomat use such direct language, and he was offended.

"Now, Mr. Anderson, about that intelligence at cocktail parties," Asch said. "Let's not try to play Mata Hari on any conference I'm running. I've been to a hell of a lot of meetings in my day, and I've never yet seen a foreigner give away a valuable piece of information at a cocktail party."

Asch looked around the table and nodded his head as a

signal that the meeting was over. He knew precisely how his words had affected each man. Ambassador MacWhite and Captain Boning were the only ones who approved completely. The rest were offended in varying degrees. Dooling would write a sly and acid report to Washington, but Asch was not bothered about that.

As the men got up to leave the room, Asch called in a sharp voice, "Captain Boning, I'd like to see you for a moment."

Captain Boning turned around and came back. Asch noticed that he had a lean compact body, and guessed that he was a man to whom physical fitness was important.

"Yes, sir?" Captain Boning said.

"Boning, I might just as well tell you right now that you're going to be an important man in these negotiations. You're the only one here who really understands the technical use of special weapons, and the rest of us will have to depend on your knowledge. When I call on you to comment, answer exactly the question that I put to you. Nothing more and nothing less, understand?"

"Yes, sir. What if the information you want is classified?"

"Good point. Just say it's classified; but give whatever part of it you can that's been declassified. And don't apologize for the classification. Got it?"

"Yes, sir," Captain Boning said. Knowing that Asch was through, he wheeled and left the room.

The general meetings began the next morning in a huge ornate room which had been built when England's power was at its height in Hong Kong. Over a hundred men sat down. Large, old-fashioned fans turned slowly above them. In a room next to the conference room a battery of translators spoke into microphones. Each delegate had an earphone with a small dial which allowed him to listen to the speech translated into French, English or his native Asian language. The fact that every representative could listen to the speaker in his own native language had been

Asch's idea. He had insisted to the secretariat of the meeting that there was no reason why Asians had to hear everything in French and English, and said the United States would be willing to pay for extra interpreters and translators so that every delegate could hear every speech in his own language.

The meeting opened slowly with a long reading of the minutes of previous meetings, then came the inevitable debate over these meetings, and a complicated and delicate discussion on where the next meeting should be held. Asch wanted the meeting held in India, for the simple reason that the Indian representatives were the most hesitant about using the new weapons. Asch felt further that if the next meeting were held in India it would force the Indians to face the problem of the use of atomic weapons squarely. He also knew that the Indians would resist playing host to a conference on a ground which they would never make public. Asch had heard, via the bamboo telegraph, that they were reluctant to appropriate money for it.

When the debate on the location of the next conference had gone on for six hours and seemed no closer to a solution, Asch made his move. He scribbled a note to the chief Indian representative indicating that the American government would be willing, on a confidential basis, to supply the funds necessary to host the next meeting adequately. After that the problem was quickly solved.

The next day they got down to business, and Asch was satisfied. They moved slowly, but they moved steadily. Asch directed almost all political questions to Ambassador MacWhite, and tossed all the technical military questions to Captain Boning. They both handled them well. They answered firmly and directly, and without any air of condescension.

Asch knew that this irritated both the French and English representatives. They had never gotten used to the idea of talking frankly about arms and military strategy to Asians. And they were also somewhat condescending to the elaborately uniformed admirals and generals of the Asian countries. That evening both representatives called on Asch at his hotel.

"Mr. Asch," the English chief said, "my colleague and I are somewhat disturbed at the direction the meetings are taking." He was a small bird-like man, who had an enormous historical knowledge of Asia which would have been useful in the nineteenth century, but was now almost valueless. "These people have just recently acquired national status, and they're not used to talking about such intricate problems as armament except as it concerns them locally. We feel that the best strategy to take would be for the United States to place a minimum demand before the group; our two nations would then support it, and we would get their reactions."

"Gentlemen," said Asch, "I will concede that you have been at this type of thing longer than we. You also have much more experience with Asians." The two gentlemen nodded modestly. "And you've managed to bitch the whole thing up for the last couple of generations. No one from my delegation is going to lay down minimum standards. If these people take atomic weapons, they may have to suffer the consequences some day. They're big boys now, and they should know what they're getting into. And don't kid yourself, gentlemen; unless you *feel* they're equals and act on that feeling, they'll never respond. I've seen it happen too many times. Make someone feel inferior in a negotiating situation, and he'll be the toughest guy around the table. Gentlemen, that is where I stand, and that is the way I will run my delegation."

The two diplomats left without pursuing the subject further. Just two more reports sent to Washington giving me hell, Asch thought to himself. The hell with it. We're making good headway.

Then, in the middle of the second week, things began to bog down. Asch, sensitive to the moods of meetings, realized that in some way the Asian delegates were being irritated, and they were balking. It was not till the end of the second week that Asch put his finger on the trouble.

It was Boning. His mistakes were only two, and they were small. First, he occasionally dozed at the conference table after lunch. Secondly, he was apt to hesitate a moment before answering questions; giving the impression that he was holding back information or rephrasing it. These were small things, and few men at the conference would have been able to spot them. But they were offensive to the participants. As the Friday afternoon meeting ended, and they adjourned for the weekend, Asch walked out beside Boning. He looked straight ahead as he spoke, but his voice was unequivocal.

"Boning, you'd better get more sleep. You're dozing a bit after lunch. Also, I want you to speak right up when I give you the questions. This hesitating puts people's teeth on edge."

"Mr. Asch, a lot of these technical questions on armament are difficult," Captain Boning answered. "It's not easy to remember all the material and separate out what's classified and what's public."

"Well, if you can't do it, we'll get someone else out here who can," Asch said. "You did all right the first week and your memory seemed okay. What the hell happened this week?"

"Nothing. It's just that I want to be perfectly accurate in what I say," Captain Boning said.

"You sure you're not living it up at night?" Asch asked. He had seen it happen dozens of times before. A man would start fresh and sharp; but then he'd try to ease the tension by drinking and helling around at night, and his performance would get worse and worse.

"No, sir. I am not living it up," Captain Boning said, and his voice was sharp and reproving.

Captain Boning's answer was not entirely true. It was true that he was not drinking, nor was he living a fast life. But, in a special sense, he *was* "living it up."

It had all started with Anderson, the political expert from the State Department. Anderson knew almost everyone in

Hong Kong who had a high position in diplomacy or politics. One day he had introduced Boning to a Chinese woman, Doctor Ruby Tsung. She was a professor at Hong Kong University, and had been educated in the United States. Anderson did not know that Doctor Tsung had also been educated at a special school located in the outskirts of Moscow.

Anderson had suggested that Doctor Tsung might guide Boning around Hong Kong and help him purchase gifts to take back to the States. Also, he added, Doctor Tsung could fill him in on local background and color. Remembering Asch's warning, Boning had been somewhat hesitant; but the moment he met Doctor Tsung his doubts vanished.

Doctor Tsung looked like an oriental miniature of an English country squire's wife. She wore rough English tweeds made up into extremely conservative suits. She wore heavy lisle stockings and hand-made English shoes with low heels designed for nothing but walking. Her thick, gold-framed glasses gave her the look of a scholar. Her language was crisp, efficient, and direct. She was the kind of woman a man could spend time with and not feel disloyal to his job or his family.

The first week of the conferences it had been relaxing for Boning to tour the city with Doctor Tsung. They had visited the Tiger Balm factory, where Boning was intrigued with the ways medicinal herbs and drugs were used by Asians. Later she took him to a street which was lined with shops which sold nothing but dried foods: shark fins, birds' nests, mushrooms that looked a thousand years old, and were as solid and hard as rocks. One shop sold the dried intestines of various sea animals, including the complete reproductive organs of a porpoise. Another shop specialized in spices: bags of saffron, and bottles of soy sauce made by so exclusive and expensive a formula that ounce for ounce the sauce was literally worth more than silver.

On another afternoon she took him to a long, low building where Ming Dynasty replicas were reproduced so expertly that no one had yet been able to disprove their authenticity.

Boning had the impression that Doctor Tsung also enjoyed their outings as a relaxation from her routine scholarly work at the University. He also had the feeling that if she dressed in feminine clothes and put on makeup, she would be an attractive woman. He did not give much thought to this, but it remained in the back of his mind.

At the end of the Friday meeting of the first week Captain Boning took Doctor Tsung to dinner at the Parisian Grill. He intended to spend that evening and Saturday and Sunday reviewing his notes, which had been locked up in the safe of the American Consul. But as he said goodbye to Doctor Tsung on the steps of the hotel, he unaccountably and suddenly became acutely aware that she was an extremely small woman; and this was extraordinarily pleasing.

At the same moment he thought of his wife, Laura. Laura was the only daughter of a wealthy Baltimore family, and her personal fortune had been a great help to Boning in his career, although he prided himself on the fact that he had won every promotion on his own merit. Laura was a tall, stately woman, and Boning had always thought that she looked aristocratic. But standing beside Doctor Tsung, he suddenly wondered whether or not one of the reasons he married Laura might not have been because he himself was short, and she was tall.

"Doctor Tsung, let me drive you to your home in a taxicab," Boning said suddenly. Doctor Tsung looked at him in surprise. On the previous days he had always put her in a cab, paid the driver, and let her go her way alone.

"Why, I would be delighted, Captain," Doctor Tsung said, "but I wouldn't want to interfere with your work."

"It won't take long," Boning said. "I'll just run you out and keep the taxi and come right back. I do have work to do, but I have the whole weekend clear."

The taxi was kept waiting outside of Doctor Tsung's

modest cottage above Victoria for eight hours. When he left in the early morning hours, Boning had come to know her small body well. Not since he had left Annapolis had he felt so physically sure of himself. In the days that followed Ruby Tsung became an obsession with Boning, and he spent most of every night with her.

On the Thursday afternoon of the third week of the conference, everyone sensed that it was reaching a climax. There had been long-drawn-out exchanges of information on manpower, possible naval bases, and the use of atomic weapons by all branches of the armed forces—and endless haggling about the possible control of weapons. During all of this discussion Asch remained relatively quiet. He answered questions when they were asked, but on the whole he let the logic of the situation develop from the statements made by the Asians. Then, on that Thursday afternoon, he gave his first lengthy analysis. At the end of his presentation his voice rose lightly in pitch and became firm.

"I have been frank with you, gentlemen, and I have appreciated your frankness with us," Asch said. "I have told you of the power of our weapons, and you have discussed how they might have usefulness for you. That is your problem, not ours; but I hope that I can take back to our political and military leaders some word on your willingness to have atomic bombs stored in your respective countries."

"There is only one question on which I am still somewhat uncommitted," a tough-faced colonel of the Indian Army said. "The problem of the safety of thermonuclear bombs in time of war. We will have to have a training period; and I am afraid that, given the enormous power of these weapons, we might have an accident that would explode one of them on a training maneuver."

Asch looked quickly from the Indian colonel to Boning. Boning was sitting upright, but his eyes were barely open. Asch was not sure whether he had followed the question or not, but he knew that, if he could assure the Indian colonel on this, he'd be prepared to make a deal. If India made a deal, so would the other countries.

"Sir, that is a good question." He spoke firmly and slowly so that Boning would have the question in mind. "I will ask Captain Boning, to give you a frank answer to the question of how safe thermonuclear weapons are in time of peace."

Boning's eyes snapped open and Asch cursed to himself. The damn fool had missed the entire question. Asch, bargaining for time, decided to put it another way. He looked directly at Boning as he spoke.

"India is a crowded country; so is the United States," Asch said. "We are as worried about the safety of our civilian population as you are of yours. I am certain that Captain Boning can reassure you on this matter."

Boning licked his lips, and cleared his throat. When he spoke his voice was hesitant.

"Well, gentlemen, this is a complicated problem," Boning said tentatively.

"All problems are complicated," a Burmese admiral said in a soft voice heard by Asch and perhaps half of the men in the room. The ripple of laughter added to Boning's confusion. Asch knew that Boning was reaching for an answer, but couldn't give him a moment more.

"In general, one can say that the energy level required to trigger a thermonuclear weapon is so great that normal fires or catastrophes or even the crash of a plane would not achieve it," Boning finally answered.

"Are thermonuclear bombs normally carried in such a way that all the component parts are in a position to be fired instantly?" one of the Indian generals asked.

Boning's face puckered in concentration, and a tiny dew of sweat appeared on his forehead.

The representatives began to stir restlessly at the table. Goddamn the man, Asch said to himself, this is the time when he should have snapped out the answer. They think the son of a bitch is trying to be evasive.

"A simple question, Captain Boning," Asch said crisply. "Give us the simplest answer."

"I think, sir, that substantial parts of that matter are classified and I cannot reveal them," Boning said, but his voice lacked conviction. He looked miserably at Asch.

"This is the way these conferences always end up," said a fat Indian colonel, and his voice was angry. "Just as we are about to tie things up we discover that we are not to have full access to important information. If the Western powers expect us to collaborate on life and death questions, they must treat us as equals. It is clear that Captain Boning's government does not think we are competent to evaluate these issues."

"Gentlemen, I would like to propose that we take a brief recess while Captain Boning and I have a talk," Asch said quietly. He knew the only way to save the conference was to reassure them on the safety of the bomb.

A half-hour later, after reading a sheaf of classified documents, Asch and Boning decided that in fact the answer to the question was declassified, and could be safely given. But when they returned to the meeting, the mood had changed. Obviously there had been excited talk between the Asian representatives. Now, in that maddening way so characteristic of conferences, they were utterly opposed to installation of atomic weapons in their territory.

Asch knew when he was licked. He moved that the meeting be adjourned, and returned to his office. That afternoon, in a long cable which was typically candid and direct, he wired Washington of the failure of his mission. He took full responsibility for the failure.

You can't win every one, Asch thought bitterly to himself when he had finished the report. But this was awfully close. And the margin was so damned slight.

Two days later Asch was on his way back to Washington. And Captain Boning, after buying a bolt of pure silk and a pair of solid silver earrings for Laura, was riding a MATS plane back to Hawaii.

# 17

# The Ugly American

---

"Dammit," said Homer Atkins to himself as he looked around the room at the fashionably dressed men. The princes of bureaucracy were the same all over the world. They sat in their freshly pressed clothes, ran their clean fingers over their smooth cheeks, smiled knowingly at one another, and asked engineers like Atkins silly questions.

What Homer wanted to say was, "Listen, you damn fools, it's a simple problem. Let us engineers solve it and come back with what we've been able to do. Then, if you don't like what we've done, throw me out of the country. But don't bring up these goddamn silly questions about politics and native psychology."

But Atkins didn't say it. He didn't even swear, which was unusual for him. He looked at his hands. This was a trick he had learned long ago. His hands always reminded him that he was an ugly man. Somehow this thought always made him pause, which in turn gave him time to prepare his next step. He had often used the technique during World War II when he was dealing with high government officials, or with corporation executives who wanted the products of his firm. Atkins stared at his hands as if they belonged to a stranger.

His hands were laced with prominent veins and spotted with big, liverish freckles. His fingernails were black with grease. His fingers bore tiny nicks and scars of a lifetime

of practical engineering. The palms of his hands were cal-
loused. Homer Atkins was worth three million dollars,
every dime of which he had earned by his own efforts; but
he was most proud and confident of his ugly strong hands.
Atkins knew that he could always make a living with
them.

Atkins was aware of the fact that he was the only man
in the room not wearing a tie. In fact, he was wearing a
rough khaki shirt, khaki pants, and old Marine field boots.
He still had the smell of the jungle about him; the other
men, Vietnamese, French, or American, all smelled of aft-
ershave lotion. Homer heaved a slow sigh and lifted his
head.

"All right, gentlemen, I'm going to say it once more,"
Atkins said. "The United States asked me to come out
here to give you some advice on building dams and military roads. You know what I am; I'm a heavy construction
man. Earth moving, concrete, road-building, that sort of
thing. Now I've been here for ten months, and I've walked
all over this damn country from Phan Rang to Van Gia
and then back into the hills to Kontum. I've talked to a
thousand people. I've surveyed dam sites and routes for
military hardtop roads and airstrips."

A slender Vietnamese interrupted. He spoke English
with a French accent, and Atkins supposed that he had
been educated at the Sorbonne. Even with the accent his
English was better than Atkins'.

"Mr. Atkins, we are very grateful to you for coming
here to help us," the Vietnamese said gently. "Your government has been generous. You have been generous. Now
we would like your recommendations as to where the
roads and dams should be built."

"I went over all that in the report," Atkins said. "Didn't
you read it?"

"Yes, Mr. Atkins, we all read it," a middle-aged Frenchman said. "But it didn't tell us where the roads and dams
should go."

"Because you don't need dams and roads," Atkins said.

"Maybe later, but right now you need to concentrate on first things—largely things that your own people can manufacture and use. I don't know much about farming or city planning or that kind of thing; but I can tell you that your people need other things besides military roads. You ever hear of a food shortage being solved by someone building a military highway designed to carry tanks and trucks?"

"Mr. Atkins, I think the decision about whether we need dams and highways is a political decision which we must make for ourselves," the Vietnamese said, after whispering rapidly to the Frenchman. "Do I gather that you do not intend to recommend the building of any dams or highways in Vietnam?"

Atkins knew the Vietnamese was trying to scare him, and he felt only a dull anger. He had spent his life making bids involving hundreds of millions of dollars and thousands of men (and his reputation), and it had taught him not to back down.

"Look, mister, I don't know how often you get out of Saigon and into the countryside, but you better go take a look at things," Atkins answered evenly.

Mr. Josiah Gordon, the representative from the American Embassy, was beginning to redden, but Atkins didn't care. "You want big industry," he went on. "You want big factories. You want big T. V. A.'s scattered all over the countryside. That all takes skilled workmen, and mines, and lots of money, and a whole lot of people who are production-minded. Of course you've got good people out there in the boondocks, good hard-working people who are plenty savvy. But they don't want what you want yet. It takes time for that. That's why I recommended in my report that you start small, with little things. And then after you lick them, go on to the bigger things. Hell, we could build dams and roads for you—but you don't have the skill or capacity or need for them now."

"Mr. Atkins, I think that's a political decision which goes beyond your province," Josiah Gordon cut in quickly. Atkins knew Gordon wanted to get the meeting over with. "Let's just let your report stand and we'll discuss it on a higher level."

"Okay, okay. But have any of you birds been *out* in the boondocks?" Atkins asked stubbornly. "Don't give me the statistics, don't tell me about national aspirations. Just answer me: Have you been out in the boondocks?"

The Frenchman, the Vietnamese, the Americans all sat quietly in collective embarrassment. The hint of a sneer showed on the face of the tall Vietnamese, and Atkins was aware again, as he always was when he caught that look on someone's face, of his own personal ugliness.

A tall American stood up in the back. "Mr. Atkins, my name is Gilbert MacWhite and I'm a visitor here, not a participant. But I should like to know what you recommended in your report."

"Ambassador MacWhite, I really don't think we should take the time of these other gentlemen to go over this again," Mr. Gordon said, caught between the antagonism of the French and Vietnamese and his respect for Mac-White.

"It won't take long," Atkins cut in. "I told them the first step was to start things that the Vietnamese can do themselves. Then they can go on to the big things as they pick up skills."

"What kind of things should they start with?" Mac-White asked.

"First, like a brick factory. Cheap to start, easy to run, and it would give them building materials. Second, stone quarries back in the hills. Plenty of good stone there, and it could be used for building."

The Frenchman was red in the face. He spoke quickly to the tall Vietnamese, and then stood up.

"Mr. Atkins," he said in perfect English, "you may not know it, but a French firm has a concession to handle the production of building materials in this country. If everyone started forming brick and quarry companies, it would ruin our relationship."

"That's your problem, not mine," said Atkins. "Third,

someone ought to set up a model canning plant. The country people catch fish and raise vegetables, but they spoil before they can be brought to town. Small, cheap, canning plants in about twenty towns would do plenty to help out. Fourth, the coastal land from Qui Nhom to Phan Rang is acid and it won't grow anything. But right back of it, just over the hills, is a long strip of beautiful rich land. Why not just run little finger-roads back through the jungle so the coastal people can get to the good land? It's cheap and it's easy. Couple of bulldozers could rip out the roads and that would be it."

"Now listen, Mr. Atkins, we didn't bring you out here as an agricultural expert," Josiah Gordon said, his bureaucratic sense of responsibility offended. "We already have lots of agricultural experts here."

"Well, tell 'em to get off their asses and out into the boondocks then," Atkins said, but without anger. He was looking at MacWhite. This was the first man who had listened to him in a long time.

"Ambassador MacWhite, I must insist that we terminate this meeting," Mr. Gordon said. "I am aware of Mr. Atkins' great talents and his personal reputation in the States, but this is most improper—an engineer giving gratuitous advice on farming!"

"And on military requirements!" the Frenchman added.

"Look, Ambassador, I could tell you a lot more little things, but first I have something to say to *him*," and Atkins pointed a finger at the Frenchman. "You've got lots of military experts around here. You've got American planes and tanks and guns. But let me tell you something that you don't know. Do you know that Ho Chi-minh had his Communists build a secret road several feet wide right from the Chinese border, right through the jungle the entire length of Vietnam, almost to Saigon? Damn right you don't know. But that's how he got supplies through to Dien Bien Phu. And the next time he moves he'll be using that road to run supplies down to take Saigon."

The Frenchmen were on their feet, and the Vietnamese were fluttering in the room like frightened birds. Two French colonels were shouting loudly. It was *impossible* to build a road through the jungle, *impossible*.

Atkins stood up, and there was a sudden silence. He said just one word—"Nuts!"—and then he left. No one doubted that he was on his way back to America.

When Atkins was halfway down the hall, he heard footsteps behind him. He kept on walking, then stopped as a hand fell on his shoulder. It was MacWhite.

"Mr. Atkins, I'd like to talk to you for a few minutes," MacWhite said. "I thought that stuff you outlined was good and sound. Let me buy you a drink."

"Then you were the only one in the room who bothered to think about it," Atkins said, and laughed.

Ten minutes later they were sitting in a café drinking beer.

"Was that true about Minh's road down from China to Saigon?" MacWhite asked.

"Damned right it's true. I saw it. It's not a big road, and it's cut so that the overhang of the trees conceals it from the air. But it's big enough so that a couple of thousand Communists can trot a lot of supplies down it. The native that showed it to me said that during the fight for Dien Bien Phu that damned road was solid with two lines of Communists . . . one trotting back for more supplies, the other coming down delivering supplies. That's what surprised the hell out of the French up there."

"Why didn't anyone tell the French?"

"They hate 'em, mister. Even the anti-Communists hate the French."

"Mr. Atkins, if I could get you reassigned to Sarkhan, would you consider coming there?" MacWhite asked. "I know you've had a rough time, and I know you've got plenty to keep you busy back in the States. But I think you could do some valuable things for me. And I'd give you a free hand. You could live in the boondocks if you wanted."

"What kind of problems are you having?" Atkins asked suspiciously.

"Sarkhan is different from Vietnam," MacWhite said. "For example, it's very hilly and they have a hard time getting water from the rivers up to the hillside paddies. They use the old dip lifts which only lift a few hundred gallons a day. Maybe you could work on that."

"Maybe, maybe," Atkins said, and his face puckered in thought. He took a pencil from his pocket and began to sketch on a page of a pocket notebook. Beneath his ugly fingers a pump began to appear. It was a surprisingly beautiful and pleasing sketch. MacWhite said nothing. He knew when to wait. He ordered more beer.

MacWhite sat there for a long time. Atkins said nothing, but the beer was drinkable, and Atkins was a source of constant fascination. He was oblivious of MacWhite, the beer in front of him, and the movements and noises of the café. He worked over the sketch until to Mac-White's eye it appeared to be an incomprehensible, yet obviously meaningful, maze. Finally, Atkins sighed, leaned back in his chair, and took a deep drink of his warm beer.

"Well, maybe that might be interesting," Atkins said after fifteen minutes of silence, as if there had been no lapse of time. "If I did it, would you let me put out a kind of *Popular Mechanics* magazine for distribution throughout the country? If I got a good design I would want it to be used. I've had enough of these damned French. Every time they bring anything into a country there has to be a trade agreement and a patent and a royalty. The result is that no one can afford their things."

"You can have a magazine, and it will be printed in Sarkhanese," MacWhite said.

"Now, not so fast," Atkins said. "I'm not sure I can lick the problem. These things take time." But he was looking back at his sketch, crossing things out and adding new lines. He did not even look up when MacWhite put his card on the table with a note that Atkins' orders would come by cable as soon as it could be arranged.

# 18

# The Ugly American and the Ugly Sarkhanese

Two weeks later Atkins and his wife left by plane for Sarkhan. Emma, a stout woman with freckles across her nose was, in her way, quite as ugly as her husband. She was hopelessly in love with Atkins, but had never been able to tell him why adequately.

She did not blink when Atkins told her they were going to Sarkhan. She told Homer that she'd be pleased to move into a smaller house where she could manage things with her own hands, and where she wouldn't need servants.

Two weeks later the Atkins were living in a small cottage in a suburb of Haidho. They were the only Caucasians in the community. Their house had pressed earth floors, one spigot of cold water, a charcoal fire, two very comfortable hammocks, a horde of small, harmless insects, and a small, dark-eyed Sarkhanese boy about nine years old who apparently came with the house. The boy's name was Ong. He appeared promptly at six each morning and spent the entire day following Emma around.

Emma Atkins enjoyed herself in Sarkhan. She learned enough of the language so that she could discuss with her neighbors the best places to buy chickens, ducks, and fresh vegetables. She learned how to prepare beautifully fluffy rice seasoned with saffron. She liked working in her house, and it was a matter of some pride to her that she was as good a housekeeper as most of her neighbors.

Homer Atkins kept busy with his man-powered water pump. The idea had developed very slowly in his mind. What was needed was some kind of efficient pump to raise the water from one terraced paddy to another. Lifting water in the hilly sections consumed enormous amounts of energy. It was usually done by a pail, or by a cloth sack, attached to the end of a long pole. One man would lower the pail and swing it up to the next terrace where another man would empty it. It was a slow and cumbersome method, but the Sarkhanese had been doing it for generations and saw no reason to change. Atkins had decided that there was no sense in trying to talk them out of an obviously inefficient method unless he could offer them a more efficient method to replace it.

He solved two-thirds of his problem. A simple pump needed three things. First, it needed cheap and readily available piping. He had decided that the pipes could be made out of bamboo, which was abundant. Second, the pump needed a cheap and efficient pump mechanism. This had taken longer to find, but in the end Atkins had succeeded. Outside many Sarkhanese villages were piled the remains of jeeps which had been discarded by the military authorities. Atkins had taken pistons from one of these jeeps and had replaced the rings with bands of cheap felt to make a piston for his pump. He then cut the block of the jeep in two; he used one of the cylinders as a suction chamber, and the other cylinder as a discharge chamber. With a simple mechanical linkage the piston could be agitated up and down, and would suck water as high as thirty feet. The third problem, which Atkins had not yet solved, was the question of what power could be applied to the linkage.

In the end Emma gave him the answer.

"Why don't you just send off to the States for a lot of hand pumps like they use on those little cars men run up and down the railroads?" she asked one day.

"Now, look, dammit, I've explained to you before," Atkins said. "It's got to be something they use out here. It's

no good if I go spending a hundred thousand dollars bringing in something. It has to be something right here, something the natives understand."

"Why, Homer," Emma said, "with all that money
you've got in the bank back at Pittsburgh, why don't you
give some of it to these nice Sarkhanese?"

Atkins looked up sharply, but saw at once that she was
teasing him. He grunted.

"You know why. Whenever you give a man something
for nothing the first person he comes to dislike is you. If
the pump is going to work at all, it has to be their pump,
not mine."

Emma smiled fondly at Homer Atkins. She turned and
looked out the window. A group of Sarkhanese on bicycles, as usual, were moving in toward the market places
at Haidho. She watched them for a few moments, and
then spun around, excitement in her eyes.

"Why don't you use bicycles? There are millions of
them in this country and they must wear out. Maybe you
could use the drive mechanism of an old bicycle to move
the pump."

Atkins looked at Emma and slowly sat up straight. He
slapped his hand against his knee.

"By God, I think you've got it, girl," he said softly.
"We could take the wheels off an old bike, link the chain
of the bike to one large reduction gear, and then drive the
piston up and down with an eccentric."

Atkins began to walk around the room. Emma, a slight
grin on her face, returned to her charcoal fire over which
she had a fragrant pot of chicken cooking. In a few moments she heard the rustle of paper and knew that Atkins
was bent over his drawing board. Two hours later he was
still drawing furiously. An hour after that he went to a
footlocker, took out a half-dozen bottles of beer, and
brought them back to his work table. By dinner time he
had drunk them all and was whistling under his breath.
When Emma tapped him on the shoulder and told him
that dinner was ready, he swung around excitedly.

"Look, baby, I think I've got it," he said, and began to explain it to her rapidly, interrupting himself to make quick calculations on a piece of paper. When she finally got him to sit down, he ate so fast that the chicken gravy ran down his chin. He wiped his chin with his shirt sleeve and made sure none of the gravy got on his precious drawings. Emma Atkins watched her husband fondly. She was proud of him, and she was happy when he was happy. Today she felt very happy, indeed.

"Stop drinking beer, Homer Atkins," Emma said, grinning. "You'll get drunk. And then you'll forget that it was my idea about the bicycle."

"Your idea?' he yelled in astonishment. "Woman, you're crazy. I was thinking about that all along. You just reminded me of it."

But then he went back to the locker, brought back two bottles of beer, and blew suds at her when he filled her glass.

Two days later Atkins had a working model. Not a single item in the crude pump would have to be imported. He had calculated that there was probably enough scrap around the countryside to make a couple of thousand pumps. What he had to do now was to get a couple of pumps actually in operation, to see how they worked. At this point Emma Atkins demonstrated her diplomatic skills.

"Now look, Homer, don't go running off like a wild man," Emma said softly. "You've got a good machine there. I'm proud of you. But don't think that just because it's good the Sarkhanese are going to start using it right away. Remember the awful time that you had getting trade unions in America to accept earth-moving equipment. These people here are no different. You have to let them use the machine themselves and in their own way. If you try to jam it down their throats, they'll never use it."

"All right, Mrs. Foster Dulles, you tell me what to do," Atkins said. He knew she was right and he was grateful to

her. "You tell me how I ought to approach the Sarkhanese."

Emma calmly explained her plan to Homer. He realized
that she had been thinking of this for some time. It was an
intricate, beautiful plan, and he wished that some of the
stuffed-shirts in the American Embassy could hear his
wife talking.

The next day he put into operation Emma Atkins' grand
strategy.

He drove in his used jeep to the tiny village of Chang
'Dong, a community of one hundred souls, living in fifteen
or twenty houses. The village was set precariously on a
steep hill sixty miles outside of Haidho. The soil there was
rich; but the backbreaking, time-consuming process of
lifting water up seven or eight levels—even though the
differentials were small—had always made Chang 'Dong
a poor village.

Atkins politely asked the first person he met in Chang
'Dong where the home of the headman was. He talked to
the headman, a venerable man of seventy-five, without an
interpreter. It was not easy, but he could tell that the headman was pleased that Atkins was making the effort to talk
his language. With infinite courtesy the old man sensed
what words Atkins was searching for, and politely supplied them. The conversation moved along more rapidly
than Homer had expected it would.

Atkins explained that he was an American and that
he was an inventor. He had an idea for a pump to lift
water. He, Atkins, wanted to develop and patent this
pump and sell it at a profit. What Atkins wanted the
headman to find was a Sarkhanese worker with mechanical skill. Atkins said he would pay well for this man's
time and skill; if he was able to help with the pump,
he would become half-owner of the patent. The old man
nodded gravely. They then began a long, complicated,
and delicate negotiation over the matter of how much the
native mechanic should be paid. Atkins understood all
of this quite well—it was just like negotiating with a trade

union organizer in the States. Each man knew that he would eventually have to compromise; and each took pleasure in talking the whole thing out. In the end Atkins got the services of a mechanic for a price which he knew was just slightly higher than the going rate. Both the headman and Atkins were satisfied. They shook hands, and the headman left to bring in the mechanic. Atkins reached in his shirt pocket, took out a cigar, and lit it with pleasure. This would, he thought, be fun.

When the headman returned he brought with him a small, stocky, heavily-muscled man whom he introduced as Jeepo. The headman explained that the name was not a native name. He was called Jeepo because of his reputation as a famous mechanic in the maintenance and repair of jeeps. Atkins didn't listen too closely to what the headman was saying. He was studying Jeepo, and he liked what he saw.

Jeepo looked like a craftsman. His fingernails were as dirty as Atkins', and his hands were also covered with dozens of little scars. Jeepo looked back steadily at Atkins without humility or apology, and Atkins felt that in the mechanic's world of bolts and nuts, pistons and leathers, and good black grease he and Jeepo would understand one another.

And Jeepo was ugly. He was ugly in a rowdy, bruised, carefree way that pleased Atkins. The two men smiled at one another.

"The headman says you are a good mechanic," Atkins said. "He says that you're an expert on repairing jeeps. But I must have a man who is expert at other things as well. Have you ever worked on anything besides jeeps?"

Jeepo smiled.

"I've worked on winches, pumps, Citroëns, American and French tanks, windmills, bicycles, the toilets of wealthy white people, and a few airplanes."

"Did you understand everything that you were working on?" Atkins asked.

"Who understands everything that he works on?" Jeepo said. "I feel that I can work with anything that is mechanical. But that is only my opinion. Try me."

"We'll start this afternoon," Atkins said. "In my jeep outside is a heap of equipment. You and I will unload it and we'll start at once."

By the middle of the afternoon they had assembled most of Atkins' equipment on the edge of a paddy on the second level of the village of Chang 'Dong. Twenty-five feet of bamboo pipe had been fastened together; the bottom of the pipe was put into a backwater of the river that flowed by the village. The top piece of the pipe was fitted by a rubber gasket to the crude pump which Atkins had designed. Above the pump was the frame of a used bicycle with both of its wheels removed. Jeepo had done the assembly entirely by himself. Atkins had made one attempt to help, but Jeepo had gone ahead on his own, and Atkins realized that he wanted to demonstrate his virtuosity. By late afternoon the assembly was ready.

Atkins squatted calmly in the mud waiting for Jeepo to finish. The headman and two or three of the elders of the village were squatting beside him. Although they were externally as passive as Atkins, he was aware that they were very excited. They understood perfectly what the machine was intended for; they were not sure it would work.

"Sir, the mechanism is ready to operate," Jeepo finally said quietly. "I'm not sure we can get suction at so great a height; but I'd be pleased to turn the bicycle pedals for the first few minutes to test it."

Atkins nodded. Jeepo climbed aboard the bicycle and began to pump slowly. The chain-drive of the bicycle turned with increasing speed. The crude pipes made a sucking noise. For several seconds there was no other sound except this gurgle. Then, suddenly, from the outflow end of the pump, a jet of dirty brown water gushed forth. Jeepo did not stop pedaling nor did he smile; but the headman and the other elders could not restrain their excitement about the size of the jet of water that was being lifted to the second rice terrace.

"This is a very clever machine," he headman said to

Atkins. "In a few minutes you have lifted more water than we could lift by our old methods in five hours of work."

Atkins did not respond to the man's delight. He was waiting to see how Jeepo reacted. He sensed that Jeepo was not entirely happy or convinced.

Jeepo continued to pump at the machine. He looked down at the machinery, noted some tiny adjustments that had to be made, and called them out to Atkins. When the small paddy was full of water he stopped, and swung down out of the bicycle seat.

"It is a very clever machine, Mr. Atkins," Jeepo said quietly. "But it will not be a sensible machine for this country."

Atkins looked steadily at Jeepo for a long moment, and then nodded.

"Why not?" he asked.

Jeepo did not respond at once. He moved silently around the mechanism, twisting a bolt here, adjusting a lever there; then he stood up and faced Atkins.

"The machine works very, very well," Jeepo said. "But to make it work a person would have to have a second bicycle. In this country, Mr. Atkins, very few people have enough money to afford two bicycles. Unless you can find another way to drive the pump, or unless your government is prepared to give us thousands of bicycles, your very clever device is a waste of time."

For a moment Atkins felt a flush of anger. It was a hard thing to be criticised so bluntly. For a hot, short moment, Atkins calculated how many bicycles his three million dollars would buy; then, with the memory of Emma's tact in his mind, he put the thought aside. He turned back to Jeepo.

"What happens to old bicycles in this country?" he asked. "Aren't there enough of them to serve as power machines for the pumps?"

"There are no old or discarded bicycles in this country," Jeepo said. "We ride bicycles until they are no good. When a man throws his bicycle away, it's too old to be used for one of these pumps."

For a moment the ugly American faced the ugly Sarkhanese. When he was younger, Atkins would have turned on his heel and walked away. Now he grinned at Jeepo.

"All right, Jeepo, you say you're an expert mechanic. What would you do? Am I simply to give up my idea—or can we find some other way to give power to the pump?"

Jeepo did not answer at once. He squatted in the shallow rice-field, his khaki shorts resting in three inches of mud. He stared fixedly at the improbable machine. For ten minutes he said nothing. Then he stood up and walked slowly to the machine. He turned the pedal and held his finger over the rear-drive sprocket of the wheel as if to test its strength. Then he walked back and squatted again.

The headman looked once at Atkins and then talked in a sharp voice to the elders. The headman was embarrassed at Jeepo's arrogance, and he was saying that the entire village of Chang 'Dong would lose face by this ridiculous performance. Jeepo's ears became slightly red at the criticism, but he did not turn his head or acknowledge that he heard the headman's words.

Atkins felt like laughing. The headman and the elders reminded him very much of the diplomats to whom he had talked for so many months in Phnom Penh. He was quite sure that Jeepo had an answer for these comments, and he was also sure that it was not a political or personal answer, but technical. Atkins squatted down beside Jeepo, and for fifteen minutes the two men sat quietly on their heels studying the machine. Atkins was the first to speak.

"Perhaps we could make the frame of the bicycle out of wood and then we'd only have to buy the sprocket mechanism," Atkins said in a tentative voice.

"But that's the part of the bicycle which is most expensive," Jeepo said.

For perhaps another ten minutes they squatted motionless. Behind him Atkins could hear the shrill voices of the headman and the elders. Although they were attempting to maintain their dignity and manners, it was clear to Atkins that they were trying to find a way to apologize to him and to smooth the whole thing over. It never occurred to Atkins to talk to them. He and Jeepo were hard at work.

Once Atkins walked to the mechanism, turned the pedals rapidly, held his finger on the sprocket gear, and looked at Jeepo. Jeepo shook his head. He understood the mechanical question that Atkins had asked and was giving his answer. Without exchanging a word they demonstrated six or eight alternative ways of making the pump work, and discarded them all. Each shake of the head upset the headman and elders profoundly.

It was dusk before they solved the problem, and it was Jeepo who came up with the solution. He suddenly stood bolt upright, walked over to the bicycle, remounted, and began to pedal furiously. Water gushed out of the outflow of the pump. Jeepo looked back over his shoulder at the lower level of the pump, then started to shout at Atkins in a loud and highly disrespectful voice in which there was the sound of discovery. It took Atkins another five minutes to understand fully what Jeepo was proposing.

It was the height of simplicity. What he proposed was that a treadmill be built which could be turned by the rear wheel of an ordinary bicycle fitted into a light bamboo frame. What this meant was that a family with a single bicycle could put the bicycle in the bamboo rack, mount it, and pedal. The rear wheel would drive the treadmill which in turn would drive the pump with an efficiency almost as great as Atkin's original model. When anyone needed to use the bike, he could simply pick it up from the rack and ride away.

"This man has made a very great discovery," Atkins said solemnly to the headman and the elders. "He has developed a way in which a bicycle can be used to drive the pump and still be used for transportation. Without Jeepo's help my idea would have been useless. What I propose is that we draw up a document giving Jeepo one-half of the profits which might come from this invention."

The headman looked at Jeepo and then at the elders. He commenced talking to the elders in a solemn voice. Atkins grasped that the headman had never heard of a binding legal document between a white man and a Sarkhanese. It became clear to him, also, that the headman was determined to drive a hard bargain. After several minutes of consultation he turned to Atkins.

"Do you propose that you and Jeepo will begin to build such pumps?" the headman asked.

"Yes. I would like to enter into business with Jeepo. We will open a shop to build this kind of a pump, and we will sell it to whoever will buy. If the customer does not have the money, we will agree that he can pay off the cost of the pump over a three-year period. But don't get the idea that Jeepo will be paid by me for doing nothing. He must work as the foreman of the shop, and he will have to work hard. Not any harder than I work, but as hard as I do."

One of the elders broke in excitedly. He pointed out that it was very unlikely that a white man would work as hard as Jeepo. He had never seen a white man work with his hands before, and what guarantee could they have that Atkins would work as hard. Another of the elders agreed, pointing out that this looked like the trick of a white man to get cheap labor from a Sarkhanese artisan. Both of the elders were firmly opposed to Jeepo entering into the partnership.

During all of this discussion, Jeepo did not speak. He tinkered with the pump and bicycle mechanism, tightening gears, checking valves, and tightening the bicycle chain. When the two elders had finished talking, he turned around and came through the mud of the rice paddy to where the group was talking.

"I have listened without speaking to what you foolish old men have been saying," Jeepo said, his voice harsh with anger. "This American is different from other white men. He knows how to work with his hands. He built this machine with his own fingers and his own brain. You people do not understand such things. But men that work with their hands and muscles understand one another. Regardless of what you say, I will enter into business with this man if he will have me."

There was a quick flush of shame on the headman's face. "I think that Jeepo is correct," he said. "This man can be trusted. I will now write up the document which will assure that he and Jeepo share the profits and the work equally."

"And the document should say that neither I nor the American shall license or patent the idea of the pump," Jeepo said. "We will make the idea available to anyone else who can make it. But on the ones we make, we deserve the profit. That is the way of working men."

Jeepo looked at Atkins. Atkins was pleased, and he nodded.

"Also, when we have made some pumps and sold them we will print little books and it will show others how to do it," Atkins said. "We will send it around the whole of Sarkhan, and the village of Chang 'Dong will become famous for its mechanical skills."

Jeepo and Atkins did not wait for the headman to complete their contract before beginning work. Two days later they had rented a large old rice warehouse on the edge of Chang 'Dong. In another day they had hired twelve workers. Jeepo and Atkins drove into Haidho, bought used tools and supplies, and carted them back to the warehouse. In a week the plant was in full operation. Over the entrance to the warehouse a small sign written in Sarkhanese said: "The Jeepo-Atkins Company, Limited." Inside the warehouse was a scene of incredible and frantic effort. Jeepo and Atkins worked eighteen to twenty hours a day. They trained the Sarkhanese; they installed a small forge which glowed red-hot most of the day; they tested materials; they hammered; they swore; and several times a day they lost their tempers and ranted at one another. Their arguments, for some reason, caused the Sarkhanese workmen a great deal of pleasure, and it was not until several months had passed that Atkins realized why—they were the only times that the Sarkhanese had ever seen one of their own kind arguing fairly and honestly, and with a chance of success, against a white man.

Emma Atkins did not stay long in the suburb outside of Haidho. Within a week she had moved their belongings to a small house in Chang 'Dong. She bustled about her home and through the village, buying chickens and vegetables, and making huge casseroles of rice and chicken. Every day at noon she and several of the village women brought two of the casseroles to the warehouse and all of the men ate from them. Emma seemed to find it not at all unusual that her husband should be in a tiny hillside village constructing something as outlandish as bicycle water pumps.

Once a technical advisor from the American Embassy called at the warehouse and watched quietly for several hours. The next day the counsellor of the Embassy called. Taking Atkins to one side, he pointed out to him that for white men to work with their hands, and especially in the countryside, lowered the reputation of all white men. He appealed to Atkins' pride to give up this project. Moreover, he pointed out that the French, most experienced of colonizers, had never allowed natives to handle machinery. Atkins' reply was brief, but it was pointed, and the counsellor drove away in anger. Atkins returned joyfully to his work in the warehouse.

At the end of six weeks they had manufactured twenty-three pumps. When the twenty-fourth pump was finished, Atkins called all of the men together. He and Jeepo then faced the group and between them outlined what now had to be done. Jeepo did most of the talking.

"This is the difficult part," Jeepo started quietly. "You have worked hard and well to build these pumps—now you must sell them. Our friend Atkins here says that in

America one of the best things that can happen to engineers like yourself is to be allowed to sell what they make. So each of you will now take two of these pumps as samples, and go out and take orders for more. For each pump that you sell you will get a ten per cent commission."

One of the men interrupted. He did not understand what a commission was. There was a confused five minutes while Atkins and Jeepo explained, and when they were finished the prospective engineer-salesmen were smiling cheerfully. They had never heard of such a proposal before, but it struck them as both attractive and ingenious. When the discussion was over, twelve contracts were laid out on a table; and each of the Sarkhanese signed a contract between himself and The Jeepo-Atkins Company, Limited.

The next morning twelve oxcarts were lined up outside the warehouse. Two of the pumps were carefully laid out on beds of straw on each of these carts. By noon the twelve salesmen had left for all parts of the province.

Now the waiting began. Jeepo, the headman, the elders, and everyone else in the village realized that everything rested on the persuasiveness of the engineer-salesmen and the performance of the bicycle-powered pump. If no orders were placed, Atkins would have to leave, and the excitement of the factory would disappear. In only a few weeks all of this activity had become very important to the people of Chang 'Dong. The people drifted into the warehouse, and watched Jeepo and Atkins at work, and many of them began to help. The tension grew steadily; and when four days had passed and not one of the salesmen had returned, a blanket of gloom as thick as a morning mist settled over the village.

Then on the morning of the fifth day one of the salesmen returned. He drove at a speed which, for an oxcart, is rare. The ox stumbled and splashed mud in the air, and the salesman beat the animal with gusto and enthusiasm. As the ox labored up the hill, everyone in the village came to the warehouse to learn what would happen. When the cart, covered with mud, drew to a halt, there was a low murmur. They could all see that the cart was empty. The driver got down from the cart slowly, fully aware of his importance. He walked over calmly and stood before his two employers.

"I have the pleasure to inform you, sirs, that I have done wrong," he began, a grin on his face. "You told me that I should bring back the two samples, but I was unable to do it. I have taken orders for eight pumps. But two of my customers insisted that I deliver the pumps at once. Because their paddies were in desperate need of water and the crops might have been ruined, I reluctantly gave them the pumps. I hope I have not made a mistake."

There was a deep sigh from the crowd and everyone turned and looked at Jeepo and Atkins. These two squat, ugly, grease-splattered men stared at one another for a moment, and then let out shouts of joy. Jeepo hugged Atkins. Atkins hugged Jeepo, and then Jeepo hugged Mrs. Atkins. Then everyone in the village hugged everyone else. For several hours an improvised party involved the entire village.

The next morning the village was up early, but not as early as Atkins and Jeepo. As the people went down to the warehouse, they heard the clank of hammers and wrenches. They peered into the dim interior of the warehouse and smiled at one another. Atkins and Jeepo were in the midst of a terrible argument over a modification of the pump. Emma Atkins was laying out a huge breakfast in front of the two men, and they were ignoring it as they continued their argument.

# 19

# The Bent Backs of
# Chang 'Dong

Emma Atkins was a simple and straightforward person. She was not a busybody; but she had learned that when she wanted to know something the best way to find out was to ask a direct question. She had been in Chang 'Dong only two weeks when she asked an unanswerable question.

She was working in her kitchen with two of her Sarkhanese neighbors, trying to make a small guava which grew in the jungle into a jam. The glowing charcoal stove and the sweet aroma of the bubbling fruit gave the kitchen a cozy and homey atmosphere. Emma felt good. She had just finished telling her neighbors about how a kitchen was equipped in America; then through the open window, she saw an old lady of Chang 'Dong hobble by, and the question flashed across her mind. She turned to the two women and spoke slowly, for the Sarkhanese language was new to her.

"Why is it that all the old people of Chang 'Dong are bent over?" Emma asked. "Every older person I have seen is bent over and walks as if his back is hurting."

The two neighbor women shrugged.

"It is just that old people become bent," one of them answered. "That's the natural thing which happens to older people."

Emma was not satisfied, but she did not pursue the problem any further then. Instead, she kept her eyes open. By the time the rainy season was over, she had observed that every person over sixty in the village walked with a perpetual stoop. And from the way they grimaced when they had to hurry, she realized that the stoop was extremely painful. The older people accepted their backaches as their fate, and when Emma asked them why they walked bent over, they only smiled.

Three weeks after the monsoon ended, the older people in the village began to sweep out their own homes, the paths leading from their houses to the road, and finally the road itself. This sweeping was inevitably done by older people. They used a broom made of palm fronds. It had a short handle, maybe two feet long, and naturally they bent over as they swept.

One day, as Emma was watching the wrinkled and stooped woman from the next house sweep the road, things fell into place. She went out to talk to the woman.

"Grandmother, I know why your back is twisted forward," she said. "It's because you do so much sweeping bent over that short broom. Sweeping in that position several hours a day gradually moulds you into a bent position. When people become old their muscles and bones are not as flexible as when they were young."

"Wife of the engineer, I do not think it is so," the old lady answered softly. "The old people of Southern Sarkhan have always had bent backs."

"Yes, and I'll bet that they all got them from sweeping several hours a day with a short-handled broom," Emma said. "Why don't you put a long handle on the broom and see how it works?"

The old woman looked puzzled. Emma realized that in her excitement she had spoken in English. She put the question to the woman in Sarkhanese.

"Brooms are not meant to have long handles," the old lady said matter-of-factly. "It has never been that way. I have never seen a broom with a long handle, and even if the wood were available, I do not think we would waste it on long handles for brooms. Wood is a very scarce thing in Chang 'Dong."

Emma knew when to drop a conversation. She had long ago discovered that people don't stop doing traditional things merely because they're irrational. She also knew that when people are criticised for an action, they stubbornly persist in continuing it. That evening Emma had a talk with Homer.

"Homer, have you noticed the bent backs of the old people in this village?" Emma asked.

"Nope, I haven't," Homer said, washing down a bowl of rice with a bottle of beer. "But if you say they're bent, I'll believe it. What about it?"

"Well, just don't say 'what about it'," Emma said angrily. "I'm getting to the age where when my bones get stiff, it hurts. Imagine the agony those old people go through with their backs perpetually bent. It's worse than lumbago. I've asked them, and they tell me it's excruciating."

"All right, all right, Emma," Atkins said. "What are we going to do about it?"

"Well, the first thing we're going to do is get longer broom handles," Emma said with heat.

However, Emma found that it was difficult to get longer handles. Wood of any kind was scarce in that area, and expensive. The handles the Sarkhanese used for their brooms came from a reed with a short strong stem about two feet long. For centuries this reed had been used; and, centuries ago people had given up looking for anything better. It was traditional for brooms to have short handles, and for the brooms to be used exclusively by people too old to work in the rice fields. But Emma wasn't bound by centuries of tradition, and she began to look for a substitute for the short broom handle.

It would have been simple, of course, to have imported wooden poles, but long ago Homer had taught her that only things that people did for themselves would really change their behavior. With mid-western practicality, Emma set about researching her problem. It was a frustrating task. She tried to join several of the short reeds together to make a long broomstick. This failed. Every kind of local material she used to try to lengthen the broomstick handles failed.

Emma refused to be defeated. She widened the scope of her search, until one day she found what she was after. She was driving the jeep down a steep mountain road about forty miles from Chang 'Dong. Suddenly she jammed on the brakes. Lining one side of the road for perhaps twenty feet was a reed very similar to the short reed that grew in Chang 'Dong—except that this reed had a strong stalk that rose five feet into the air before it thinned out.

"Homer," she ordered her husband, "climb out and dig me up a half-dozen of those reeds. But don't disturb the roots."

When she got back to Chang 'Dong, she planted the reeds beside her house and tended them carefully. Then, one day, when several of her neighbors were in her house she casually cut a tall reed, bound the usual coconut fronds to it, and began to sweep. The women were aware that something was unusual, but for several minutes they could not figure out what was wrong. Then one of the women spoke.

"She sweeps with her back straight," the woman said in surprise. "I have never seen such a thing."

Emma did not say a word. She continued to sweep right past them, out on the front porch, and then down the walk. The dust and debris flew in clouds; and everyone watching was aware of the greater efficiency of being able to sweep while standing up.

Emma, having finished her sweeping, returned to her house and began to prepare tea for her guests. She did not speak to them about the broom, but when they left, it was on the front porch, and all of her guests eyed it carefully as they departed.

The next day when Emma swept off her porch, there were three old grandmothers who watched from a distance. When she was finished Emma leaned her long-handled broom against the clump of reeds which she had brought down from the hills. The lesson was clear.

The next day, perhaps ten older people, including a number of men, watched Emma as she swept. This time when she was finished, an old man, his back bent so that he scurried with a crab-like motion, came over to Emma.

"Wife of the engineer, I would like to know where I might get a broom handle like the one you have," the man said. "I am not sure that our short-handled brooms have bent our backs like this but I am sure that your way of sweeping is a more powerful way."

Emma told him to help himself to one of the reeds growing beside the house. The old man hesitated.

"I will take one and thank you; but if I take one, others may also ask, and soon your reeds will be gone."

"It is nothing to worry about, old man," Emma said. "There are many such reeds in the hills. I found these by the stream at Nanghsa. Your people could walk up there and bring back as many as the village could use in a year on the back of one water buffalo." The old man did not cut one of Emma's reeds. Instead he turned and hurried back to the group of older people. They talked rapidly, and several hours later Emma saw them heading for the hills with a water buffalo in front of them.

Soon after, Homer completed his work in Chang 'Dong, and they moved to Rhotok, a small village about seventy miles to the east. And it was not until four years later, when Emma was back in Pittsburgh, that she learned the final results of her broomhandle project. One day she got a letter in a large handsome yellow-bamboo paper envelope. Inside, written in an exquisite script, was a letter from the headman of Chang 'Dong.

Wife of the engineer:

I am writing you to thank you for a thing that you did for the old people of Chang 'Dong. For many centuries, longer than any man can remember, we have always had old people with bent backs in this village. And in every village that we know of the old people have always had bent backs.

We had always thought this was a part of growing old, and it was one of the reasons that we dreaded old age. But, wife of the engineer, you have changed all that. By the lucky accident of your long-handled broom you showed us a new way to sweep. It is a small thing, but it has changed the lives of our old people. For four years, ever since you have left, we have been using the long reeds for broom handles. You will be happy to know that today there are few bent backs in the village of Chang 'Dong. Today the backs of our old people are straight and firm. No longer are their bodies painful during the months of the monsoon.

This is a small thing, I know, but for our people it is an important thing.

I know you are not of our religion, wife of the engineer, but perhaps you will be pleased to know that on the outskirts of the village we have constructed a small shrine in your memory. It is a simple affair; at the foot of the altar are these words: "In memory of the woman who unbent the backs of our people." And in front of the shrine there is a stack of the old short reeds which we used to use.

Again, wife of the engineer, we thank you and we think of you.

"What does he mean, "lucky accident"?" Emma said to Homer. "Why I looked all over for three months before I found those long reeds. That was no accident."

Homer did not look up at her from the letter. He knew that the indignation in her voice was false. He knew that if he looked now he would see tears glittering in the corners of her eyes. He waited a decent amount of time; when he raised his head she was just pushing her handkerchief back into the pocket of her apron.

# 20

# Senator, Sir . . .

Senator Jonathan Brown had started his political career with two attributes: a craggy face that reminded people of Lincoln's; and a high degree of corruption. As he grew older, his looks did not change much—his hair got gray, and he began to stoop slightly. But somewhere along the line, he completely lost his corruption.

Even his wife never knew about the shadow in his past. In 1924, when Brown was first running for the Senate, he had assumed that every person who went to Washington was either a criminal or a fool. At that point in his life, when he had just shuffled in from one of the most backward counties of his state to become first a State Assemblyman, and later a State Senator, he would much rather have been hung for being a crook than for being a fool. And the device which enabled him to win his Senate race was crude beyond belief. He had simply walked into the office of the president of the state's biggest private electrical company and told the executive that if he, Brown, were elected to the U. S. Senate, he would be prepared to turn over the entire power output of the Elk Heart Dam to the utility company. In exchange he asked only two favors: that the company dissuade anyone else from running; and that they deposit $150,000 in the account of his campaign manager. The president of the utility company, a man of exceptional experience, took one look at Brown, knew that such brashness would surely find its political reward, and promptly agreed to both conditions.

Senator Brown was never quite sure when his corruption passed and his pride in the Senate began. Probably in his second term; but in any case, he suddenly became aware that he was very proud of the way the Senate ran its affairs. He had learned to distinguish between sound speeches and opportunistic speeches, and began to understand and appreciate the beauties of parliamentary procedure. One day he realized that the 96 men in the Senate were, quite literally, the most powerful political group in the world. As he achieved these perceptions, Brown became incorruptible, and his personal conscience became inflexible. Finally, the day came when he stood on the Senate floor and introduced the bill which took the Elk Heart Dam output away from the utility company. He was fully aware of the risk he was taking; and to his great relief when the president of the company came around and shook his hand four months later, he said nothing about the campaign gift.

In 1942, Senator Brown became a member of the Senate Foreign Affairs Committee, and although in his younger days, he had not known whether Cambodia was in Africa or Asia, he now learned carefully and conscientiously every fact he could about foreign affairs. In three years he had become one of the best informed members of the committee. His seniority made it inevitable that he would become chairman of the committee; and when he did, one of his first acts was to make plans for a tour of Asia and the Far East. He intended to take Mrs. Brown along as well as one other Senator, two administrative assistants, and two secretaries.

The itinerary for the trip was long and detailed. Mrs. Brown blanched when she saw it, and reminded the Senator about his heart condition and his arthritic legs. Of both afflictions the Senator was deeply ashamed; he went to great lengths to conceal them, and he never allowed them to interfere with his work. The itinerary included visits to Manila, Tokyo, Formosa, Thailand, Vietnam,

Cambodia, Laos, and Korea. When these inspections were completed, they would return to Washington by way of Europe, stopping briefly in Cairo, Rome, Madrid, and London.

"Now I want no whiskey-drinking, social-butterflying on this trip," the Senator told his staff. "I know these diplomatic boys. They'll try to show us the best side of things to keep their own appropriations up, but we're going to dig into everything. I want to talk to the natives, the low-ranking employees, and technicians in the field, and I don't want to spend too much time with the big boys. Everyone understand that? I'll take my own liquor along. John, you see that there's a case of sour-mash whiskey on that plane, and see that no one drinks it but me."

The cables began to hum as accommodations for the Senator's visit were arranged. Messages went to embassies in all of the countries he would visit; copies went to the Air Force, which would supply the plane. Endless meetings were held to pave the way for the Senator's visit. The Senator was fully aware how much work his trip entailed —but he was determined to get the facts first-hand. Several billion dollars had gone to the Far East, and he was determined to see for himself what effect the money had had.

One of the Americans who received a cable about Senator Brown's visit was the Ambassador to Vietnam, the Honorable Arthur Alexander Gray. He was expecting the cable, for he had already gotten a long informative note from an old Rhodes Scholar friend of his who operated the Japanese Desk at the State Department:

Senator Brown will be hitting Saigon sometime in the next month. I heard it as a rumor on the Hill and checked it out by making a few phone calls. In a few weeks you'll probably have a cable on it. Don't underestimate Brown. He's an old man, and it's true he used to be an isolationist—but when he became aware of world affairs he went into them with a thoroughness I've seldom seen equalled. Behind that whiskey-drinking, hillbilly manner, there's one hell of a tough man, and an honest one. Right now he's convinced that we're facing the final crisis with Russia, and that the next few years will decide whether we're going to win or lose. He's always saying this—in committee meetings, in corridors, and at cocktail parties. And he means it. He'll go to any lengths to get information on which to base legislative recommendations of his committee.

Now all this is well and good, Alex, but there's one thing you have to watch out for. I know that you have nothing to conceal, but you'll have to be careful whom Senator Brown talks to. He has the knack of getting ordinary people to talk to him. He doesn't try to charm them—he looks like one of them, and he talks like one of them, and pretty soon they're spilling their guts to him. Last week I saw him operate with a delegation of natives from Ghana. They knew he was a southern Senator and were suspicious of his attitude toward colored people. My God, Alex, it was a masterpiece. He ambled over to them at a big reception, looking like a combination of Abraham Lincoln and an ape; he handled them beautifully, and there was never any question of his being condescending or prejudiced. He simply swept them off their feet with his information and directness about Ghana—he knew more about it than they did. At the end of the party the entire delegation piled into a taxicab with Brown, and rumor hath it that they spent the night drinking sour mash bourbon. And the rumor also hath it that on the information he got that night Brown is prepared to cut appropriations to Ghana by 30 per cent on the grounds that too much of it is going for administrative overhead and into the big cities.

Need I say more. This guy is honest and tough, and although you have nothing to hide I'm sure there are many ways to tell the same story. I am just writing ahead to tell you to prepare your story and to get it before him forcefully.

Ambassador Gray was not intimidated. He had handled distinguished and tough-minded statesmen before. He hadn't fallen on his face yet, and he wasn't going to this time. He thought for a moment, then turned and pressed a button on his desk.

"Call a full staff meeeting in twenty minutes in the conference room," he said into a small black box on his desk. A half-hour later the ambassador and his staff were well into their plans for the reception, hospitality, and education of Senator Brown.

Sally Vincent started off. "Ambassador, I think I ought to work up a new brochure on the history of Vietnam and the political background for the Senator," she proposed. "I don't mean the ordinary sort of thing, because there's the chance that he may have seen other brochures we've prepared for previous visitors. What I have in mind is a real tough brochure emphasizing the rural problems which this country faces and something of the savagery of the Communists. I could put in some illustrations of typical Vietnamese farms, and mention the rainfall and that sort of thing."

"And something about fertilizer," the ambassador said with an unsmiling face. He had learned long ago that Americans from farm states were unfailingly interested in replenishment of the soil.

"Yes, of course, I'll have a section on fertilizer," Sally answered just as seriously. "In fact, I have some pictures here of that compost project teaching them to use various kinds of wasted vegetation for fertilizer." And she spread some glossy photos on the table for the ambassador to approve.

An agricultural technician officer then outlined an itinerary of a trip which he proposed the Senator take. Everyone was aware that the itinerary was quite artful. It took the ambassador past every agricultural station which the American mission had established; the Senator would never be out of sight of some American aid. That he would not be seeing a typical countryside disturbed none of these realistic people.

An information officer stood up and presented the audiophone devices he would prepare to "capsulize" the whole story. One of these was an hour and a half, specially spliced film which the information officer would put together with his own hands.

"Let me see that, Dick, before you make the final cuts," the ambassador said. "I remember seeing an uncensored French army film of the fighting around Hanoi, and it was a bit unfair. One scene showed a French tank which had been blown up by a homemade native bomb, which gave the impression that tanks aren't useful out here. As we all know, our French colleagues think they're absolutely essential to the kind of warfare we've been fighting out here."

"Yes, sir, I will," Dick replied. "I think you'll agree that the rough-cut film will give a very objective picture of the situation."

The meeting went on for three hours. They discussed what social affairs should be held for Senator Brown, what sort of food should be supplied him at the Embassy (the ambassador struck grits and hominy from the menu as too obvious a device to gain the Senator's approval), Mrs. Brown's interests and temperament, which native leaders the Senator should meet and under what circumstances. Then the Ambassador summed up.

"I think we've got the details under control," he said firmly. "But let's try to get clear on the general atmosphere and mood of this trip. The Senator believes we face a crisis around the world; and I think that none of us would disagree. So what we have to do is show our sense of drive and dedication. I want everyone here in the Embassy early, and I want no one to leave before eight at night. If you have back work to catch up on, this would be a good time to do it and keep the lights burning in the Embassy during the evenings. I want to see no Embassy employee in any French restaurant or café during the Senator's visit. I want no American Embassy employee to drive a car through the streets of Saigon during the Senator's visit. You can take taxis to work, or ride bicycles. In fact, that strikes me as a pretty good idea. Maybe half a dozen of you could rent bikes for the week he'll be here —and have a carpenter whack up a bike parking stand outside the Embassy door."

When the ambassador dismissed his staff, he told two people to remain: Major Ernest Cravath, the military attaché of the Embassy, and Dr. Hans Barre, a naturalized American citizen who had been born in Germany and who was a specialist in Oriental languages. Dr. Barre was on temporary duty at the Embassy and was the only person there who spoke Vietnamese.

"Now, gentlemen," the ambassador said, "I kept the

two of you behind because there are still two things about the Senator's visit that worry me. First, he's going to ask questions about the military situation. As you know, Cravath, this is a difficult problem and there has been much misunderstanding about it in the minds of people not familiar with the situation. American newsmen have been most unfriendly about reporting French military tactics out here. Now you and I know that the French have faced a unique situation with great courage and imagination, but the Senator may be critical. I want you to talk to the French Commissioner-General and tell him the importance of this visit. I think he'll see things our way. The military aid out here runs into millions, and if Senator Brown isn't satisfied that it's being used wisely, it may well slow down to a trickle. Now I also want you to talk to the *Chef de Cabinet* for General Salan and make sure that all the French staff officers are briefed on what to say. This has got to be a good show, or things are going to deteriorate awfully damn fast in this country."

Major Cravath nodded, and left the room. The ambassador turned to Dr. Barre.

"Dr. Barre, this is the first time you have ever suffered through the visit of a politician, and you're going to find it a trying time. Politicians aren't interested in the reality of things; they're only interested in getting votes and occasionally making some Boy Scout points for themselves by proposing a big cut in our foreign aid budget. Brown is a particularly difficult Senator. What I should like you to do is to be at Senator Brown's elbow during his entire visit. He doesn't speak Vietnamese nor does anyone on his staff. What I should like you to do is to translate for him."

"That should not be too difficult, Mr. Ambassador," Dr. Barre said. "As you know, I'm familiar with the language."

"But the Senator is not; and I'm afraid that if he gets literal translations of what strangers say, he may misunderstand," the ambassador answered. He was gazing out the window, his thumb and first finger caressing the Phi Beta Kappa key. "For example, he might stop suddenly and begin to interview a Vietnamese native in a field or along the street." The ambassador swung around, and his face was serious. "Can you imagine, Dr. Barre, the injury that might be done to American foreign policy if the Senator were to take seriously some of the nonsense uttered to him by a native?"

Dr. Barre nodded. His face was tired, and he avoided looking in the ambassador's eyes.

"Now, I don't want you to compromise yourself as a scholar and as an expert, Dr. Barre. What I would like you to do is just to make sense out of what the natives say if the Senator happens to talk to any of them."

Dr. Barre nodded again and stood up. He and the ambassador shook hands.

The reception commmittee that met Senator Brown's party at the Ten-San Airport outside of Saigon was not large. It included only the American Ambassador, the French Commissioner-General, Dr. Barre, and Major Cravath. Ambassador Gray explained that the high-ranking French generals had very much wanted to meet the plane, but urgent military considerations had kept them at work in the field.

"And a damn good thing, too," the Senator grunted as he stepped into the plain Ford sedan which was the ambassador's private property. "That's where generals belong—out in the field and in training camps."

As they drove into Saigon Ambassador Gray asked Senator Brown what he would like to see, and said only that the Embassy staff would aid the Senator in whatever he wanted to do. They had prepared no itinerary, and made no elaborate plans, the ambassador said, for they first wished to know what the Senator's particular interests were.

"Look, son, don't let's kid one another," Senator Brown said truculently. "In the last two and a half years, we've poured a billion a year into this country. I want to see what's been done with it. I also want to talk to the native political leaders, and to a couple of the native precinct leaders or ward bossses or whatever the hell they call them out here. I don't want a lot of fancy receptions and parties at which I only meet other Americans and diplomats. Now if you can't do that for me, just say the word, and I'll go stay in a hotel downtown and arrange my own itinerary."

The Senator sat solidly in his seat, his jaws locked on a cigar.

"Senator, I'll draw up a schedule tonight which will have an absolute minimum of official functions and an absolute maximum of contacts with natives and their leaders. Of course, you'll have to see a bit of the French diplomats and military leaders, but you probably want to do that anyway to get their point of view."

"Damn right," the Senator said.

That night Ambassador and Mrs. Gray and Senator and Mrs. Brown ate quietly in the ambassador's residence. After dinner the information officer appeared with a movie projector and showed a ninety-minute film on the background of politics in all of Indo-China. The information officer was experienced; whenever the Senator asked a question he stopped the film at once and answered it crisply and directly. When he didn't know the answer to a question, he promised to deliver it in writing the next day. Once the Senator asked about the kind of armament which the Communists had, and the information officer said that Major Cravath could supply a fuller answer to that.

"Now, Mr. Information Officer, how much do you estimate it cost you and the United States Government to put that film together?" the Senator asked with a tough grin on his face when the film was over. "That looks like a pretty expensive production."

"Sir, this film cost the United States Government nothing," the information officer answered quickly. "I'm an amateur photographer and movie-maker, and I put this together myself from French and American documentary films. And I might add, sir, on my own time."

Gray flashed the information officer a quick look of approval. After one more drink of sour-mash whiskey and branch water, the Senator went to bed.

The next morning the inspection trip began with a quiet flurry. Major Cravath and Dr. Barre were the only two escorts for the Senator and Mrs. Brown. They traveled in a clean but old weapons-carrier. It was a rough ride; the Senator had no way of knowing that Major Cravath had had the shock absorbers on the weapons-carrier taken up so tight that every bump in the road came through like a blow.

Their first stop was an ammunition depot which they inspected on foot. They then walked to an unloading dock where American military supplies were being unloaded, after which they drove in the weapons-carrier to a French training camp. They were met by a low-ranking French officer who took them off on a half-trot around the camp. They inspected an obstacle course, a tank-training field, a machine-gun range, and a parade field. By 11:30 it was obvious to Major Cravath that the Senator's legs were hurting him; but he did not slacken the pace.

Once Mrs. Brown suggested that they rest, but the Senator shook his head doggedly. She went back to the weapons-carrier, but the rest of the party continued the trip. Senator Brown stopped beside a group of Vietnamese natives who were being given instructions in a recoilless rifle by a French noncom and tapped one of the natives on the shoulder. The native glanced around, and sprang quickly to attention.

"Ask him how many times he's fired that rifle, and against what kind of targets," the Senator said to Dr. Barre. Dr. Barre and the Vietnamese spoke quickly for a few minutes. The native answered that he had never seen the recoilless rifle before this morning, and normally he was a cook. He was bewildered by the sudden change in his assignment, but delighted. The kitchen was hot. Dr. Barre turned slowly to the Senator.

"Senator, he says that he has worked several weeks with the recoilless rifle," Dr. Barre said. "He has not fired at targets because there is an extreme shortage of recoilless shells. He says, however, that he welcomes the chance to practice with the rifle, and would like to use it against the Communists."

"Well, why in the hell don't they ask for more shells?" the Senator asked angrily. "What the hell good is it sending out rifles without shells? Here's a man ready to fight, and we send out a couple billion dollars worth of equipment but not the stuff he needs." The Senator swung his aching body sideways and glared at Major Cravath. Major Cravath and the French officer both answered at once. They both said that the situation was so serious that shells should be fired only at the enemy. Major Cravath pointed out that Indo-China was at the end of a long supply line which stretched across the entire Pacific. The French officer said that they were hoarding all of their ammunition to be used exclusively against the Communists.

The Senator grunted and they moved away. Later Major Cravath and the French officer agreed that it would merely have confused the Senator to point out that the recoilless rifle was an almost useless weapon in Indo-China, since the Communists fought in such a way that there was almost no target worthy of directing a recoilless rifle against. They also agreed hastily that the recoilless rifle would be invaluable if the larger cities of Indo-China ever had to be defended.

They ate a soldier's lunch in the field, and it was authentic. It consisted of French bread, a small tin of canned pork per person, a half-liter of wine, a highly-concentrated chocolate bar, and two huge yellow chunks of candy which tasted somewhat like lemon but which were actually almost pure dextrose. When the lunch was over, Mrs. Brown asked to be excused, and was driven back in a civilian car to the ambassador's residence.

The Senator continued his inspections, which for some reason all had to be made on foot. By four in the afternoon the Senator said he had had enough for the day. He dismissed Major Cravath and Dr. Barre, and said he would ride back to the ambassador's residence by himself. The Major and the translator did not protest. The ambassador had told them not to. Otherwise the Senator might think he was being given a slanted tour. The two men left in a weapons-carriers, and the Senator directed his driver, an American sergeant, to drive slowly back to the town.

"Son, have you ever laid one of these Vietnamese girls?" the Senator asked briskly. "Some of 'em look like pretty nice pieces."

"Sir, we don't fraternize very much with the natives," the sergeant answered.

"Hell, I didn't ask you if you fraternized. I asked you if you ever laid them."

"No, sir. I have my family out here," the sergeant said.

"Have you got a house out here? How many rooms? Any servants? Did you have a car shipped out at government expense?" The Senator's tone was suddenly very firm.

The sergeant had been warned to avoid answering direct questions, but he was being interrogated by one of the world's experts. Long ago Senator Brown had learned precisely how to put questions, and in what order, and with what speed. He also knew, without asking, that the sergeant was a pen-pusher and not a fighting man. The sergeant reluctantly answered "yes," to all of the Senator's questions; then the Senator stopped asking him, for he knew that the sergeant had been briefed. There was no more juice to be squeezed from this particular lemon, so the Senator ignored him and studied the town as they drove slowly through it.

They were halfway through the town when they passed a small outdoor café. Sitting at a round table, and obviously drunk, were two officers. One was a tall, lean American, and the other one was a short, thin French captain. They both wore dirty uniforms and the mud had splashed almost up to their thighs. Their shirts were white where salt crystals of sweat had dried on them. They were not talking to one another; they were merely staring out into the square in front of the café and drinking. Around their table was a circle of broken glasses; a French waiter stood a respectful distance away, obviously trying to ignore the pair.

"Stop the car, sergeant," the Senator said. "It's a helluva thing when we send an American officer over here and he's drunk in the middle of the day."

The Senator left the weapons-carrier and walked over to the table. The two officers looked up at him dully.

"Major, you are dressed in an American officer's uniform," the Senator said harshly. "What the hell are you doing drunk in the middle of the day?"

The American smiled quietly. He motioned for the Senator to leave. When the Senator did not move, the Major kicked a chair around and motioned for the Senator to sit down.

"Buddy, you look and sound like an American," the American said with a Texas accent. "Sit down and have a drink and shut your mouth. My name is Tex Wolchek and this is Major Monet, one-time terror of the French Foreign Legion, and now a hack. We're drunk."

The Senator sat down.

"Major, my name is Senator Brown and I'm here on an inspection trip," the Senator said coldly. "And I asked you a question and I want an answer. What are you doing here in the middle of the day?" ·

The two officers looked at the Senator, smiled, and then filled their glasses again.

"Senator, we are drunk and we are getting drunker," the Frenchman said in perfect English.

"Well, that's no secret," the Senator said. "But it's a damned disgrace. We send American officers over here to help you and then discover them boozing it up in cafés. You men don't seem to realize that we're in a helluva tough spot out here."

Tex Wolchek closed his eyes and smiled faintly.

"Senator, I'll give you five seconds to make a decision," Tex said, with his eyes still shut and his voice very soft. "Either you can have a drink with us and keep your mouth shut, or I'll kick your ass all the way back to that weapons-carrier."

For five stunned seconds the Senator sat still. In his youth he had been a tough man and a competent fighter, and for a moment he thought of accepting the Major's challenge. He was furious that an American officer should be seen drunk in the midst of the kind of crisis America faced in Indo-China. But the Senator was no fool. When Major Wolchek opened his eyes and began to stand, the Senator pushed back his chair and walked over to the weapons-carrier.

The moment he was back at the Embassy, the Senator sent for the ambassador. He described the two officers and gave the ambassador their names. The ambassador called in Major Cravath and they assured the Senator that proper disciplinary action would be taken against the two men. Much later the ambassador remarked to his staff that this episode marked the turning point in the Senator's visit. After it the Senator was much more amiable. And perhaps the extremely long walk he had taken the first day had somewhat diminished the Senator's energies for subsequent trips, because from then on he contented himself with explorations done exclusively in automobiles or weapons-carriers.

One day they took him to one of the outlying bunkers where the French were holding a line against the Communists. The bunker was a model of ingenuity and massive strength, and the Senator wondered how it was possible that such a strongly-defended outpost could be taken by the Communists. Major Cravath and a French general supplied quick answers. It could have been done in only two ways. First, through the use of overwhelming masses of men. "The Communists throw men away as easily as Americans discard cigarette butts," the French general said. "If they want to lose fifteen hundred men in a frontal attack on such a bunker, they can take it. But it is a price that they cannot afford forever.

"The second way in which the Communists could capture a bunker is if the bunker were underequipped with radio equipment, ammunition, guns and supplies." The Senator nodded grimly.

There were, of course, a few other things that the Major and the General did not mention. For one thing, they did not think it relevant that most of the bunkers that had been captured so far had in fact been captured by a single platoon of Communists who infiltrated the bunker position at night and dropped grenades through the slits into the bunker's central room. In theory, the bunker was invulnerable; and important people should not be burdened with exceptions to theories. They also did not tell the Senator that two regiments of French troops were deployed in the jungle in front of the bunker to make sure that no Communist raid was made while the Senator was in this dangerous position.

That night the social pace of the visit picked up slightly. The wife of the assistant to the French Commissioner-General had asked Mrs. Brown to what she called a small French family dinner. It was a small French dinner, but it was not simple. Only the four of them were present; and they took over three hours to eat. Somewhere the assistant to the Commissioner-General had obtained several bottles of Senator Brown's favorite sour-mash whiskey. There were three kinds of wine with the dinner, and they finished up with champagne. Over cigars and cognac the assistant showed Senator Brown a stack of photographs that had been taken during the fighting around Dien Bien Phu. They were black-and-white enlargements, and they had been taken by experts. They were action shots of the battle.

The deeper they went into the pile of photographs, the more savage became the subject matter. There were pictures of Communist soldiers hung up on primitive barricades of bamboo spears, their eyes glassy in death. There were heaps of bodies waiting to be buried after the engagement. There were pictures of natives who had collaborated with the French and had had their hands chopped off by the Communists in revenge. There was an inside shot in a surgical bunker with a tier of six bunks; the photograph was so clear that the Senator could see the blood dripping from one bunk to another.

"What we need, of course, is really modern equipment out here," the assistant said. "Men cannot fight with bare hands alone."

The Senator was almost physically ill. He had never seen such brutality. His admiration for the French mounted steadily.

The next day the Senator asked to be flown into Hanoi where the battle over Dien Bien Phu was reaching a high pitch. They circled over the Delta; Major Cravath and a French paratroop general pointed out where the fighting was taking place. They landed outside of Hanoi, and were driven in black limousines into the city. For the last mile of the trip the road was lined with black North African troops standing at attention. Senator Brown was tired from the food and the exercise and the late hours; but this display brought the cross-examiner's tone back into his voice.

"Now, what the hell, Major Cravath," the Senator said. "All these troops are North Africans and that seems a damn silly piece of business. Why don't the French recruit soldiers from among the natives? This would save the cost of transporting North Africans here, and would give France the advantage of having citizens fighting for their own country."

"Well, sir, the Vietnamese just don't make very good soldiers," Major Cravath said. "Their way of life just doesn't make them susceptible to discipline, and if you give them a burp gun or a carbine they'll sell it or take off with it into the hills."

The Senator's eyes narrowed.

"Well, if the French can't recruit natives, who the hell

are the Communists using as troops?" Brown asked.

It was a question that Major Cravath had thought about once or twice, but had never been able to answer satisfactorily. He turned to the French general, who shrugged.

"Most of the real soldiers in the Communist troops fighting out on the Delta are Chinese," the general said. "They're better fighters than the Vietnamese. Also, the Communists shoot natives if they don't fight well. France, sir, is a civilized country and would not permit herself such barbarity."

"Listen, General, I'd like to talk to some prisoners you've taken," the Senator said. "As soon as we've gone to this damned reception that we're having at Hanoi, I want to go to a prisoners' stockade." He felt sure that if he could talk face to face to a Communist he could find out why the natives would fight for the Communists but not for the French.

Senator Brown never made it to the prisoners' stockade. At the Maison France in Hanoi, where a band and honor guard met them, they at once sat down to a huge lunch and an intensive discussion on the military situation on the Delta. A French major rapidly exhibited maps, blown-up photographs, intelligence summaries, and other information on the situation. The lunch was heavy, and they were served two kinds of wine which their host pointed out proudly was precisely the kind of wine that was issued to the troops in the field. Despite the fact that there was elegant linen on the table and crystal glasses to hold the wine, he observed, perhaps the Senator could sense some of the urgency of the situation. The Senator nodded. When the major showed the last page of his exhibit, it was a graph which illustrated the number of tanks, airplanes, weapons-carriers, and miscellaneous equipment which would allow France to drive the Communists from the Delta.

After lunch they set out for the prisoners' stockade. They drove two miles toward the outskirts of Hanoi; then the French general announced they'd have to walk the rest of the way. They started out on a path that ran between rice paddies, but the path very quickly became pockmarked with mortar-shell holes and finally disappeared almost completely. In a few minutes, to his surprise, the Senator found himself walking in mud high above his ankles, but he was not in the least deterred. His legs did ache a bit, but he said to himself he could stand up as well as the next person. A half-hour later he wasn't so sure. The mud seemed now to have the density of lead, and his legs were painful beyond belief. When the French general suggested a rest, he sat down gratefully on a heap of rocks. Going in the opposite direction was a steady stream of native refugees fleeing toward Hanoi. Dr. Barre had replaced Major Cravath on this venture, and the Senator asked Dr. Barre to interrogate one of the natives.

"Ask that little old lady there with the pile of laundry on her head why she's running away from the Communists," the Senator asked, pointing at a tiny woman who was trotting through the mud.

Dr. Barre talked quickly to the woman. For a few moments she just shook her head; then Dr. Barre gave her a cigarette, and lit it. The woman took a few deep drags on the cigarette and began to talk in a voice heavy with venom. When she had finished talking, and put her bundle back on her head, Dr. Barre watched her trot away and spent a few seconds organizing his thoughts. Then he turned to the Senator.

"Senator, she says it's safer in the city. She says that the French will take care of her while the Communists would probably slaughter her. She says she would rather leave the Delta forever than live there under Communism," Dr. Barre said.

What the woman had actually said was that the French and the Communists were both dogs. The Communists had cruelly slaughtered her eldest son six months before. The French, just as cruelly, had burned down her hut to open a firing lane through her village. Then, she had commented bitterly, the French had abandoned the village without even fighting. She was going to Hanoi because there was food there and there was also the promise of shelter. It was that simple.

The Senator did not insist that they go on to the prisoners' stockade. Instead they walked slowly back toward Hanoi. They were back in the city in time for the Senator to shower and get ready for a large banquet given by the Commissioner-General of Hanoi. Early the next morning they flew back to Saigon.

The next day was crowded with inspections of ammunition dumps, training camps, and diplomatic installations. That night there was a cocktail party and then a banquet. At both of these functions there were French journalists, government officials, military officers, and important businessmen, all of whom spoke frankly and openly to the Senator, and all of whom agreed in what they said. The Senator went to bed exhausted and aware that he had eaten and drunk too much; but in the morning he started again.

A week later the Senator and his party left Saigon. It had been a worthwhile visit, the Senator said to his staff. He now had a clear and first-hand picture of the situation.

Just as the Senator was on the edge of falling asleep in his seat on the plane, one of his political reflexes functioned, and his eyes opened with a start. He had just realized that in all of the time in both Saigon and Hanoi, he had talked to only two natives, and to only three military officers below the rank of general—two of them had been drunk. For a moment he distrusted all his impressions of the visit. But then fatigue and a well-served lunch overtook him, and the Senator fell asleep.

The President of the United States Senate rapped for order, and the commotion on the floor of the Senate subsided.

"The Senator from New Mexico still has the floor, Senator Brown," the President said sternly. "If he wishes to yield, he will have to yield time from his own speech."

Senator Corona was angry, but he was also anxious not to antagonize Senator Brown.

"Mr. President, I shall yield two minutes to Senator Brown when I have talked one more moment," Senator Corona said. "I have one more point to make, and it is this: we have poured four billion dollars into the French Government of Indo-China, and they have succeeded only in losing Dien Bien Phu and the entire Delta. I ask you, gentlemen, how long are we to continue to pour the taxpayers' money down an Asian rathole?"

Senator Corona was no fool. He knew that Senator Brown had some sort of ammunition. Suddenly, and without any firm notion of what he was about, Senator Corona decided to fortify his argument.

"These charges are not idle," he said. "Nor are they based on speculation. They are facts. These facts were given to us by a person who knows the situation well."

"His name, sir?" Senator Brown snapped in a sharp voice, not even asking for formal permission.

Senator Corona answered without thought.

"Ambassador MacWhite, our diplomatic representative in Sarkhan," he said. "We asked Ambassador MacWhite, one of our most experienced diplomats, what he thought of the situation in Vietnam. He was bitterly pessimistic. He was factual . . ."

"Some of his facts, please, Senator," Senator Brown barked.

Senator Corona looked down at his desk, opened a folder. It was clearly marked "Secret-Executive Session," but his reputation was at stake.

"Ambassador MacWhite said the following," Senator Corona said in an angry voice. "He said that the Vietnamese, both Communist and anti-Communist, hated the French. He stated that the French have had to import North African mercenaries, at great expense, to fight for them in Vietnam, and that all of the natives resented this. He stated that the French merchants were more interested in their concessions than in developing the country. He stated that the French were miserably trapped by the Communist military leaders . . . they won no victories, and they suffered continuous defeat. He stated that we were supplying military vehicles that could not even be used in the mud of Vietnam. He stated that the French military forces refused to use guerilla tactics. He stated that the French hoodwinked the American military and diplomats into thinking everything was rosy . . ."

When Senator Corona yielded the floor, Senator Brown rose. "Surely, Mr. President, we have heard enough," he said in a voice that rang with anger and conviction. "The Honorable Senator has cited a number of statements—but they were gathered from an ambassador in another country."

Senator Brown paused. He let the time drag out, and the pause grew tense and became important.

"Gentlemen, all of what the Honorable Senator has said was in error," Senator Brown said slowly, and with obvious regret. The Senate chamber was still and quiet. The newspaper gallery was attentive. The spectators were hushed. The Senator gathered himself, and no person there failed to feel the solemnity and honesty of his words.

"I can tell you this," he said, "from first-hand knowledge because, gentlemen, I was there. . . ."

# 21

# The Sum of
# Tiny Things

Ambassador MacWhite expected the letter long before it arrived. The day Senator Brown had attacked his testimony on the Senate floor, representatives from the AP, UP, and all the foreign news services had descended upon the U.S. Embassy in Haidho. It had been a grim afternoon. MacWhite had assumed that his testimony would be secret because it had been given in an executive session of the Senate Committee; but obviously the newspapers had the complete text. There was nothing to do but defend what he had said about Vietnam, and this MacWhite did to the best of his ability.

Washington was thunderously silent for three weeks. MacWhite knew he would hear something eventually—but when he did, he was surprised. He got a long, handwritten note from the Secretary of State.

Dear Gilbert:
  As you know, Gilbert, I was one of those who persuaded you to join the Foreign Service. I have watched your career with great pride. You are, I have always thought, the kind of American of whom we can be proud. You have always put the security and future of your country ahead of personal benefit. I was pleased when you were given the post at Sarkhan. I had envisaged it as the first of a number of illustrious ambassadorships that you would hold.

I would be less than honest, however, if I did not tell you I have felt grave doubts in the last months. Let me review the record:

(1) In your first report you indicated that you had made a bad mistake. You reported that the embassy staff had been infiltrated by Communist agents, and suggested that we take steps around the world to prevent this. I defended you on the grounds that your report was a courageous act. A lesser man would have said nothing.

(2) You then took a leave of absence. I received complaints from at least two ambassadors in different Asian countries because you had trod on their toes. As you know, Gilbert, I have been trying to dissolve the excessive protocol in the Foreign Service; but your adventures around Dien Bien Phu were really somewhat more extravagant than one would think necessary on a trip to gain orientation and background.

(3) You requested that George Swift, the Deputy Chief of your mission, be relieved because of carelessness. Then it appeared this carelessness was a refusal to allow one of our Air Force Colonels to read the palm of the King of Sarkhan.

(4) And now I have just read your testimony before the Senate Foreign Affairs Committee in Executive Session. As you know, we do not try to control the testimony of our people before such committees; but your comments on affairs in a country to which you were not accredited were most immoderate. Even if true, they were indiscreet.

Let me make myself clear, Gilbert. I am not asking for your resignation. Nor am I suggesting that you leave Sarkhan. But, I must have some assurance that your future behavior will conform to what we expect of foreign service officers. Please, believe me when I tell you that I am using this informal means of communicating with you in an effort to save the Department embarrassment, and to aid your career.

MacWhite put the letter down. MacWhite knew that the Secretary was a deeply religious and profoundly dedicated man. He was a man who traveled endlessly and relentlessly, and he had great courage.

MacWhite thought a long time before he wrote a reply directly to the Secretary. He decided not to answer the four points raised by the Secretary. Each of them, he thought, was part of a larger picture. He would make one last effort to tell the Secretary his thoughts on

American policy, and would let the matter rest there. If the Secretary did not agree, MacWhite would resign.

Dear Mr. Secretary:

I am most grateful for the frankness of your note to me. I should like to respond in the same vein.

As you might have guessed, nothing in my previous experience had prepared me for the silent desperation with which the battle between the Communist world and our world is being fought here. I was not prepared for the fact that in this area politics is, quite literally, a matter of life and death. I had never been really aware that Lenin's remark, "The road to Paris leads through Peking" also meant that the same road runs through Saigon, Tokyo, Bangkok, Djakarta, and even Haidho. But it does.

I do not think that the Russians will ever resort to thermonuclear warfare. They won't have to. They are winning much too easily to run the risk of annihilation by retaliation. Since the end of World War II they have not suffered a major defeat. As you have said often in your public speeches, we will never be the first to launch the bomb. What this means is that the Russians will win the world by their successes in a multitude of tiny battles. Many of these will be fought around conference tables, in the rice fields of Asia, at village meetings, in schools; but mainly they will take place in the minds of men. Only occasionally will the battles be violent; but the sum of these tiny battles will decide whether our way of life is to perish or to persist.

I apologize for this extravagant language; but there is no other way to say what I feel I must: The United States must either prepare itself to win these many tiny conflicts, which are the substance of competitive coexistence; or go down in defeat.

What are we to do? I am not sure I know the whole picture. Perhaps no man does. But a handful of personal experiences have shown me part of the way out of the dreadful dilemma in which we find ourselves. In my tenure here at Haidho perhaps three hundred Americans have passed through the Embassy in one capacity or another. Only five of them were at all valuable in our struggle against Communism. One of them was a Catholic priest, one was an engineer, one an Air Force Colonel, one a Major from Texas, and one a private citizen who manufactures powdered milk. From this tiny handful of effective men I learned some principles. I am not sure that they are applicable in all countries around the world in which the battle is taking place; but I suspect that they are.

The little things we do must be moral acts and they must be done in the real interest of the peoples whose friendship we need—not just in the interest of propaganda. The men I mentioned above, men who have sacrificed and labored here, are not romantic or sentimental. They are tough and they are hard. But they agree with me that to the extent that our foreign policy is humane and reasonable, it will be successful. To the extent that it is imperialistic and grandiose, it will fail.

In any case, I am now prepared to ask you in all humility to allow me to do several things in Sarkhan. If you do not see your way clear to permit these actions, I shall regretfully resign from the Foreign Service. If you are able to grant them, I think there is a better than even chance that I can save Sarkhan from Communism. If I am successful, perhaps my experience will serve as a model.

(1) I request that every American (and his dependents) sent to Sarkhan be required to be able to both read and speak Sarkhanese. I am satisfied that if the motivation is high enough, any person can learn enough of the language in twelve weeks so that he can get along. This should be required of both military and civilian personnel.

(2) I request that no American employee be allowed to bring his dependents to Sarkhan unless he is willing to serve here for at least two years. If he does bring his family, it should be with the understanding they will not be given luxurious quarters, but will live in housing which is normal to the area; their housing should certainly not be more luxurious than they are able to afford in America. They should also subsist on foods available in local stores—which are wholesome and ample.

(3) I request that the American commissary and PX be withdrawn from Sarkhan, and that no American supplies be sold except for toilet articles, baby food, canned milk, coffee, and tobacco.

(4) I request that Americans not be allowed to bring their private automobiles to this country. All of our official transportation should be done in official automobiles. Private transportation should be taxi, pedicab, or bicycle.

(5) I request that all Americans serving in Sarkhan, regardless of their classification, be required to read books by Mao Tse-tung, Lenin, Chou En-lai, Marx, Engels, and leading Asian Communists. This reading should be done before arrival.

(6) I request that in our recruiting program we make all of these conditions clear to any prospective government employee, so that he comes here with no illusions. It has been my experience that superior people are attracted only by challenge. By setting our standards low and making our life soft, we have,

quite automatically and unconsciously, assured ourselves of mediocre people.

I know, sir, that these are unusual demands. In a time of massive armament and in a battle between huge empires they may seem almost comical. But, I repeat, grand patterns are no more than the sum of their tiniest parts, and it is on this basic level that we are losing the struggle. As far as is legal and possible I have already made these demands on personnel new in Sarkhan.

If we cannot get Americans overseas who are trained, self-sacrificing, and dedicated, then we will continue losing in Asia. The Russians will win without firing a shot, and the only choice open to us will be to become the aggressor with thermonuclear weapons.

I look forward to your response.

For three weeks MacWhite heard nothing from Washington, but he was neither worried nor idle. He spent several days at a primitive camp observing Major Wolchek instruct Sarkhanese recruits in guerilla tactics. Next he visited the village of Chang 'Dong to inspect its thriving, although tiny, industrial complex. A Sarkhanese mechanic had designed and was manufacturing a simple machine for the canning of fish. The development of this machine had produced an entirely new industry of fish processing in Sarkhan.

On the way back to Haidho Ambassador MacWhite had lunched at Finian's Station, a small non-denominational college. Here 250 Sarkhanese students, none of whom was over 21, were being given a four-year education. Their curriculum included exposure to the writings of both Communist and Western leaders. Most of the students MacWhite talked to said that after they had graduated they intended to return and work in their own villages.

As the ambassador's car approached Haidho, he saw, in a hilly pasture, fifty reddish brown cattle. These cattle had been imported from America only six months before; but already they were beginning to change the eating habits of some sections of Sarkhan. For the first time in the history of the country, children were drinking fresh milk; and in half a dozen towns, the beginning of a leather industry was springing up.

When a reply finally arrived from Washington, it was a cablegram—and it was brief and to the point.

*Reply negative to all suggestions your handwritten note X Such actions even though they have merit are highly impractical X We would not be able to get Americans to serve overseas under these conditions X Please return continental United States first available transportation X Anticipate substantial replacement your present staff X Please explore with Sarkhanese Government their attitude toward receiving Mr. Joseph Bing as new ambassador X We consider his extensive press and recruiting experience excellent qualification high position X Signed Secretary*

Three weeks later Gilbert MacWhite left Sarkhan.

# 22

# A Factual Epilogue

It is not orthodox to append a factual epilogue to a work of fiction. However, we would not wish any reader to put down our book thinking that what he has read is wholly imaginary. For it is not; it is based on fact. It is our purpose here to give our reasons and our sources.

Although the characters are indeed imaginary and Sarkhan is a fiction, each of the small and sometimes tragic events we have described has happened . . . many times. Too many times. We believe that if such things continue to happen they will multiply into a pattern of disaster.

It is easy in a time of great events—of Sputniks and Explorers and ICBM's and "dirty" and "clean" atomic weapons—to overlook one of the hard facts of history: a nation may lose its power and integrity slowly, in minute particles. We believe that a nuclear cataclysm is unlikely, but that our free life well may be lost in a succession of bits and fragments.

The authors have taken part in the events in Southeast Asia which have inspired this book, and in both the records and in the field we have studied the Communist way to power. As writers, we have sought to dramatize what we have seen of the Americans who represent us in the struggle.

Little documentation will be necessary for some, like Colonel Hillandale, Father Finian, John Colvin, or the Ugly American himself, because they served America well. Suffice it here to record that they were drawn from life. There is an obligation, however, to discuss the validity of less creditable fictions like Louis Sears, George Swift, and Senator Brown.

Ambassador Sears, for example, does not exist. But there have been more than one of him in Asia during recent years. He is portrayed as a political warhorse, comfortably stabled by his party while he awaits a judgeship. It would be out of order to name those diplomats who have demonstrated this system in action (some, luckily, were able, hardworking men), but the roster of our ambassadors throughout the world bears out the fact that too often personal wealth, political loyalty, and the ability to stay out of trouble are qualities which outweigh training in the selection of ambassadors.

Many of Sears's actions are based on real events in which more than one real diplomat took part. The press attack on him in the Sarkhanese press and his inability to read it was part of our fiction. It was inspired, however, by the fact that in the past two years there has been at least one strong anti-American press campaign in every capital city in Southeast Asia, and in most of these capitals the American Ambassador, like Sears, was unable to read the local papers. (One diplomat was sufficiently concerned to send the local newspapers to Washington so that the Library of Congress could translate them for him.)

It would seem a simple fact of life that ambassadors to at least the major nations should speak those languages. Yet in France, Italy, Germany, Belgium, the Netherlands, Norway, and Turkey, our ambassadors cannot speak the native tongue (although our ambassador to Paris can speak German and our ambassador to Berlin can speak French). In the whole of the Arabic world—nine nations—only two ambassadors have language qualifications. In Japan, Korea, Burma, Thailand, Vietnam, Indonesia, and elsewhere, our ambassadors must speak and be spoken to through interpreters. In the entire Communist world, only our ambassador to Moscow can speak the native language.

If the ambassadors were mere figureheads surrounded by experienced, linguistically-trained career diplomats, their inability to speak or read on the job would be little more than an insulting inconvenience to the local officials, as Louis Sears's ignorance was to Prince Ngong of Sarkhan. Unfortunately, ambassadors are more than figureheads; they are in charge, and, like Sears, their misunderstandings can have grave consequences. Moreover, the career men on their staffs are generally not linguistically trained for their jobs. Instead, they are frequently the Joe Bings of our book.

In his masterful analysis of the Foreign Service, John Osborne states that the most important element in a good Foreign Service officer is "the faculty of communication." Yet, as James Reston reported in the *New York Times* of March 18, 1958, "fifty percent of the entire Foreign Service officer corps do not have a speaking knowledge of any foreign language. Seventy percent of the new men coming into the Foreign Service are in the same state." These figures represent those who can speak *no* language other than their own—not even French, Spanish, German, or Italian. The number of Americans in the Foreign Service who can speak any of the more difficult languages is miniscule.

In addition to our Foreign Service staffs, we have more than a million servicemen overseas. Only a handful can speak the language of the country in which they are stationed, and when difficult military and scientific data are involved this handful shrinks to almost zero. So be it, but that our trained representatives in Asia are little better qualified in languages is unacceptable. On the other hand, an estimated nine out of ten Russians speak, read, and write the language before they arrive on station. It is a prior requirement. The entire functioning staff of Russian embassies in Asia is Russian, and all the Russians—the officials, stenographic help, telephone operators, chauffeurs, servants—speak and write the language of the host country.

In the American embassies the servants, the messengers,

and the interpreters are locally hired. The telephone operator in almost every American mission and agency in Asia is an Asian. It is, of course, a maxim of espionage that one of the most useful agents is the planted employee. The story of Gilbert MacWhite and Li Pang is imaginary; but the conditions of the story exist in every American mission in Asia, and models for the two Chinese servants were known personally to one of the authors.

When, in our story, Prince Ngong finally persuades Sears to believe that the press cartoon was favorable, he is demonstrating a fact. Because we must rely on interpreters who are almost always non-Americans, our on-the-spot information is both second-hand and subject to minor censorship and editing without our knowledge. The recent turmoil in Indonesia emphasized this handicap. We had to rely on native translators to interpret the press, the radio, and personal conversation. Following Asian etiquette, by which one avoids telling one's employer of matters which would distress him, the interpreters gave our diplomats rose-tinted reports of local sentiment and events. Only after a dangerous delay did it seep through to our soundproofed representatives that Indonesia was in the grip of political upheaval. In Indochina our military and diplomatic missions could speak only to the French—whose view of the rebellion against them was one-sided, to say the least. One of the authors seeking to hear the Vietnamese side of the question without using either a French or Vietnamese interpreter succeeded only through an American priest who, like the Father Finian of our book, was fluent in the native tongue. Like the Russians, but unlike ourselves, the Church realizes that its work in Asia cannot be done without close communication with Asians.

Blockage of information itself is not the only penalty we pay. Think, for a moment, what it costs us whenever an official American representative demands that the native speak English, or be not heard. The Russians make no such mistake. The sign on the Russian Embassy in Ceylon, for example, identifies it in Sinhalese, Tamil,

English, and Russian. The American Embassy is identified only in English.

John Foster Dulles stated what was in our minds when we wrote the stories of Colonel Hillandale, the Ragtime Kid, and John Colvin, on the one hand, and of Sears and Swift and Joe Bing, on the other. He said, "Interpreters are no substitute. It is not possible to understand what is in the minds of other people without understanding their language, and without understanding their language it is impossible to be sure that they understand what is on our minds."

Mr. Dulles' point is at the heart of our story about "The Six-Foot Swami from Savannah." George Swift could not speak the language and could not understand what was in the minds of the Sarkhanese; and so he offended. His story is fiction, but the protocol blunder actually happened to one of the authors almost exactly as told, although he did not punch anyone.

Americans like Swift, who cannot speak the language, can have no more than an academic understanding of a country's customs, beliefs, religion, and humor. Restricted to communication with only that special, small and usually well-to-do segment of the native population fluent in English, they receive a limited and often misleading picture of the nation about them. A recent American ambassador in Ceylon—an able, extremely popular diplomat—had an experience which pointed up this dilemma. He had become intimate with the leaders of the political party in power, a group relict of colonial days composed largely of the rich and English-educated upper-class. The ambassador apparently got all his information from them because he gave no warning to our State Department before the nationalistic political upheaval occurred which suddenly left his friends with but 8 of 101 seats in the government.

On the other side of the ledger, we have told the story of the ugly engineer and Colonel Hillandale who, speaking the language, were able to go off into the countryside and show the idea of America to the people. These characters are based on actual Americans known to the authors. There are others like them; but by and large they are not beloved of the American officials in the various Asian capitals, and are a wild exception to the rule.

While the few Hillandales and the many Russians roam the barrios and the boondocks, most Americans are restricted both by official tethers and by language barriers, to communion with each other. The kind of ingrown social life portrayed in the story of Marie McIntosh is real, though she is not. The Asians themselves have given it a name. We first heard it one day in Bangkok when we invited a Thai to spend the evening with us. He replied that unfortunately he had to attend an "S.I.G.G." When we asked what he meant, he expressed surprise that we did not know the term.

"We use it," he said, "whenever we are referring to an American cocktail party, dinner, or gathering of any kind. It means 'Social Incest in the Golden Ghetto.' "

Vice President Nixon, in his National Press Club speech on his tour of Latin America, said, "I could have concentrated on a whole round of cocktail parties and white-tie dinners. If we continue to concentrate on that area we can figure we will lose the battle." What our diplomats need to do, he said, is to get out and mingle with students, labor leaders, and opinion makers, who comprise the "wave of the future."

In his report on the U. S. Operations Mission to Vietnam, Leland Barrows stressed the fact that too many of the Americans there were to be found concentrated in the capital cities, while there were almost none out in the countryside. The models for Joe Bing and George Swift are not fiction.

In the story "Everybody Loves Joe Bing," the fictional Ruth Jyoti makes the point that the Red world is far better at public relations than is the free world. Her speech and her interviews are fabrications, but her point is not. For example America brings large numbers of Asian students to America each year. This is a constructive idea; but, unfortunately, America requires that all candidates for these fellowships speak English, since their instructors here will be able to speak nothing else. This means that the Asian students must be drawn from one class—the well-to-do minorities of the bigger Asian cities. And Asia is very largely an agricultural area.

The Communists are not so restricted in their approach. In Yunan Province, China, they have a vast schooling system for students from Southeast Asia. The students, roughly 30,000 strong, come from Indonesia, Burma, Thailand, Laos, Cambodia, and the fringe areas of Vietnam. The term is eighteen months, and lectures are delivered in the native language of the student. Courses include agriculture, tanning, printing, blacksmithing, and other crafts which country people from small towns need. The students live in dormitories with their fellow countrymen, and religious guidance is provided by clergymen of their own faith.

It is not surprising that when the Southeast Asians return home to their farms and villages they are enthusiastic about the Chinese Communist regime.

In the stories of Major Wolchek and Major Monet, "The Iron of War" and "The Lesson of War," we have tried in fiction to describe a condition of avoidable ignorance. For years both we and our allies have put in much expensive effort trying to ferret out in advance the Communist plan for both tactical maneuvers and great conquests. Yet, during the struggle in Indochina the authors could find no American (or French) military or civilian official who had read, or even studied a precis of, the over-all Communist operation plan contained in *The Selected Works of Mao Tse-tung*, published by Lawrence Wishart, Ltd., London and International Publishers in the U. S. A four-volume edition was published in 1954, but the basic material was available in print as early as 1934. (A useful shorter study is *The Organizational Weapon— A Study of Bolshevik Strategy and Tactics*, by Philip Selznick, McGraw-Hill, 1952.)

In his remarkable work Mao, one of the brilliant tacticians of our time, analyzes almost every campaign and battle in which his Red Armies fought. He dissects every defeat (very few) and most victories, and he explains what they taught him. In doing so he lays down a pattern of strategy and tactics which the Communists of Southeast Asia have followed undeviatingly.

The battles which led to Dien Bien Phu were classic examples of the Mao pattern. And yet our military missions advised, and the French went down to defeat, without having studied Mao's writings.

Why our representatives abroad have not learned the languages they need or studied basic sources of information such as Mao's writings is a question which involves the entire American nation. Whatever the reasons, our overseas services attract far too few of our brightest and best qualified college graduates. The system of recruiting overseas employees we have portrayed in the stories "The Girl Who Got Recruited" and "Employment Opportunities Abroad," and Ambassador Sears's report on the kind of staff he thought he needed, represent the sort of recruiting that actually goes on.

The most recent recruiting pamphlet issued by the State Department (*Career Opportunities*, December 1956 Edition) describes salaries, living conditions, perquisites, and benefits. It shows young people boarding a sleek airplane, headed for their first assignment. It shows Americans shopping in the bazaar in Isfahan, Iran. But it does not have a *single* word which indicates the work will be demanding, not a *single* word to indicate that we are locked in a quiet struggle around the world and that recruits will be a part of that struggle. It is a pamphlet designed to attract mediocrities. We believe it is successful.

In extensive interviews with superior graduating seniors, the authors have discovered that the brightest seniors reject foreign service because it is "too dull, too bureaucratic." Many of these students would be attracted to overseas duty if the standards were higher, if contact with natives were possible, if the "good living" were not stressed so much and the challenge stressed more. The lack of challenge appeals to the George Swifts, the Bridge

Uptons, and Joe Bings we have known overseas.

When we do get good men—and of course we get many, but not enough—we have a tendency to misuse them. The fictional Gilbert MacWhite of our book has his counterparts. He is an able, dedicated, intelligent man who puts tremendous energy into his work. In the end, in our story, he is forced to resign, as much by his own sense of failure as by pressure from above. Statistics from our recent diplomatic history to document this sort of thing do not exist, but the resignation of George Kennan is in point.

In "Senator, Sir," we have made the charge that our diplomats overseas spend a great deal of time entertaining highly placed Americans instead of working at their primary jobs. We have seen embassies in Asia which are so active in the entertainment of VIP's that they resemble tourist agencies. The time spent on arrangements, briefings, cocktail parties, protocol visits, and the care and maintenance of wives leaves almost no time for the study of the local situation. Mr. Nixon took notice of this in his statements after his recent trip through Southeast Asia.

In the story of Tom Knox, our fictional chicken expert who was first balked by official disbelief, then softened by sweet words and a rich life until even he forgot what he had been so enthusiastic about, we tried to point out the fact that we spend billions on the wrong aid projects while overlooking the almost costless and far more helpful ones.

Most American technicians abroad are involved in the planning and execution of "big" projects: dams, highways, irrigation systems. The result is that we often develop huge technical complexes which some day may pay dividends but which at this moment in Asian development are neither needed nor wanted except by a few local politicians who see such projects as a means to power and wealth. Technicians who want to work on smaller and more manageable projects are not encouraged. The authors of this book gathered statements from native economists of what projects were "most urgently needed" in various Asian countries. These included improvement of chicken and pig breeding, small pumps which did not need expensive replacement parts, knowledge on commercial fishing, canning of food, improvement of seeds, small village-size papermaking plants (illiteracy in many countries is perpetrated by the fact that no one can afford paper), sanitary use of night-soil, and the development of small industries. These are the projects which would not only make friends, while costing little, but are also prerequisite to industrialization and economic independence for Asia. They must be realized before Communism can lose its appeal. We pay for huge highways through jungles in Asian lands where there is no transport except bicycle and foot. We finance dams where the greatest immediate need is a portable pump. We provide many millions of dollars' worth of military equipment which wins no wars and raises no standard of living. This is what we meant by the story of the ugly engineer, Homer Atkins. He again is a fiction, but the authors knew just such a man working among the back-country people.

American efforts are not always misguided, of course. The Russian, and particularly the local Communist, reaction to our various programs is an interesting guide to the worth of our efforts. The story of Louis Krupitzyn, the Russian Ambassador to Sarkhan, includes a fictional account of an American shipment of rice to a starving Asian nation. In our story the Communists show their appreciation of the effectiveness of this decision by stencilling on the bags, "This rice is a gift from Russia." This, too, is a story based on fact.

Not long ago, while one of the authors was in Pakistan, our economic mission delivered a shipment of American tractors. Within a few days it was commonly accepted throughout the countryside that the tractors had been given to Pakistan by Russia. After considerable argument with a prominent Pakistani newspaper editor, the author persuaded him to inspect the tractors. They turned out to be American, of course; but on every flat surface of each tractor local Communists had stencilled a red hammer and sickle.

The picture as we saw it, then, is of an Asia where we stand relatively mute, locked in the cities, misunderstanding the temper and the needs of the Asians. We saw America spending vast sums where Russia spends far less and achieves far more. The result has been called "an uneasy balance," but actually it is nothing of the sort. We have been losing—not only in Asia, but everywhere.

Without pitting one Soviet soldier against one American soldier, the Soviet has won a staggering series of victories. In the few years since the end of World War II, Russia has added 700,000,000 people to the multitude already under direct rule. Its land empire has been swollen by about 5,000,000 square miles. In Asia alone, Communist arms have won wars in China, Indochina, and Tibet, and gained prestige and a restless stalemate in Korea. In Italy, Egypt, Indonesia, Cambodia, Laos, to name but a few, Communist parties have become strong contenders for power. In a recent poll taken in India, Chou En-Lai, the Chinese Communist leader, was a three-to-one favorite over President Eisenhower. In the Middle East our prestige has rapidly diminished while that of Russia has increased. In South America our Vice President has been spat upon and assaulted in a shameful demonstration of antagonism toward our country.

Even among the nations which have seemed committed to us there is a rising tide of anti-Americanism. We have been attacked by the press in the Philippines, Japan, and the Republic of China, as well as in those less firmly committed lands whose friendship we seek by spending large sums in foreign aid—Laos, Cambodia, India, Indonesia, and Pakistan. The fictional John Colvin's brutal treatment at the hands of his former friend, Deong, can stand for what has happened to America in Asia. The Communists got to Deong; the Americans did not.

We do not need the horde of 1,500,000 Americans—mostly amateurs—who are now working for the United States overseas. What we need is a small force of well-trained, well-chosen, hard-working, and dedicated professionals. They must be willing to risk their comforts and—in some lands—their health. They must go equipped to apply a positive policy promulgated by a clear-thinking government. They must speak the language of the land of their assignment, and they must be more expert in its problems than are the natives.

If the only price we are willing to pay is the dollar price, then we might as well pull out before we're thrown out. If we are not prepared to pay the human price, we had better retreat to our shores, build Fortress America, learn to live without international trade and communications, and accept the mediocrity, the low standard of living, and the loom of world Communism which would accompany such a move.

Actually, the state in which we find ourselves is far from hopeless. We have the material, and above all the human resources, to change our methods and to win. It is not the fault of the government or its leaders or any political party that we have acted as we have. It is the temper of the whole nation. If knowledge of the problem becomes widespread, and if the enthusiasm of the people can be aroused, then we can succeed. As Cordell Hull once said, "The Government of the United States is never far ahead of the American public; nor is it very far behind."

We have been offering the Asian nations the wrong kind of help. We have so lost sight of our own past that we are trying to sell guns and money alone, instead of remembering that it was the quest for the dignity of freedom that was responsible for our own way of life.

All over Asia we have found that the basic American ethic is revered and honored and imitated when possible. We must, while helping Asia toward self-sufficiency, show by example that America is still the America of freedom and hope and knowledge of law. If we succeed, we cannot lose the struggle.